HAPPY ENDINGS

Alice Winters

Cover designed by Cate Ashwood Designs
Edited by Lori Parks

Alice Winters
Visit my website at www.alicewintersauthor.com

Printed in the United States of America

First Printing: Dec 2017

Chapter One

My day's been going pretty smoothly. I haven't had any interruptions, and I just picked up a really good book on the various ways people have failed at summoning demons. It's always fun to laugh at the failures of others.

Or at least it *was* going smoothly until I sense someone heading toward my store who I've never met before. Which probably means that I don't want to meet them. With my finger, I draw the sign of Illusion on my left hand and then on my right, and with just a thought, I throw an illusion on myself. The illusion allows me to disguise my actual features and make me appear to be something different to the viewer. No longer do I look like the twenty-six-year-old man I am with dark brown hair, longer on the top, and dark blue eyes, instead, I now appear to be a person a little more appropriate for screwing with someone.

An eighty-four-year-old woman.

People automatically react to an older woman much differently than they would to a guy in their twenties, so I feel like it's an appropriate illusion.

The door dings as it is pushed open, and two men walk in, instantly looking around. One is a man in his thirties, who appears to be Latino with dark hair that's cut short. His dark brown eyes turn right to me as I watch him. The man next to him is older, with light brown hair and blue eyes and seems much more confident in the way he moves up to the desk. They reek of cop long before they pull their badges out.

"Good morning, ma'am," the older man says. See? Instant respect. "My name is Detective Ian Smith."

"Detective Sam Diaz," the younger one says as they both show me their badges. "We are looking for a man named… what was that name again?"

Ian pulls out a paper. "Milliant Sh… Sha… Shiv… voldeshve?" he asks, completely butchering the name.

"Milliant Shavoldeshve?" I ask, pronouncing it correctly.

"Yes," he says. "Can we speak with him?"

I shake my head and realize that an even *better* idea is being a half-deaf older lady. "Who? Millie's gotta shave?" I ask, pretending that I didn't just correctly pronounce the name a moment ago.

"You just said his name correctly for us."

"Who?"

"Milliant. We're here to show him a message."

"A massage! Oh! Yes!" I say, and realize that I am too bored to not have fun with these guys. "You're here for a massage?"

"No, we need to speak to Milliant Shavoldeshve," Sam says sternly.

I shake my head. "Hmm… no, no. We give massages. We don't give Milliants. Just massages."

"We were told to find him here. Could you tell us who he is?" Ian asks.

"What? Could I tell you about what? About the massage? Normal massage… OH!" I make my eyes super wide. "I know what you young'uns want. Happy endings!" I declare eagerly.

"Is there prostitution going on here?" Sam asks as he looks at me in alarm.

"No! No! No one's getting prosecuted! Just massages! Massages and happy endings," I say.

"Yes, 'happy ending' is an act of prostitution," Sam says. "And it's illegal. So, unless you want us to report you, you'll need to tell us who the man we are looking for is."

"No, of course not! There are no prosthetics!" I wave at my chest where my breasts hang low. "*Alllllll* real!" I say. "Wanna feel?"

"*Prostitution.* A happy ending is…"

Ian then proceeds to mimic someone getting jerked off, and I have to try my hardest not to laugh.

I mimic the motion. "What? You boys and your lingo! I'll cut you a deal. Twenty dollars. Happy ending is forty."

"She claims it's not prostitution but continues to try to sell it to us!" Ian says to Sam. They are both watching me in exasperation, and I'm loving every moment of it. It's not often I get to screw around with people like this.

"Hmm… hold please!" I hold up a finger in front of their faces to emphasize that I want them to wait a moment, then I pull open the door behind me. "Yoko-chan! Yoko-*chan*!"

Yoko walks through the door, looks at me and then at the two men as she raises an eyebrow. She's clearly confused but is smart enough to figure out that the person behind the illusion is me.

"Police officer. Happy ending," I say.

"Me?" she asks pointing at herself. Yoko is a gorgeous Japanese woman in her mid-twenties. To help pay for her schooling as a witch, she has been working for me for two years. Her long black hair falls around her face, her pale skin highlighting her rich brown eyes. She's wearing dark blue skinny jeans and an oversized t-shirt from a band she went to see a week ago. She is supposed to be in uniform while working with the customers, but she seems to think that everything in her wardrobe *is* uniform material.

"Yes," I say.

"No!" the officer says, alarmed.

"He want you," Yoko says, quickly picking up a horrid accent, even though she was born and raised right here.

"No. Silly little lass. Strip," I order with a very stern voice. I roll up a magazine and jab it at her for emphasis.

"For my family!" she cries as she picks up her shirt and starts pulling it off.

"No! Stop! Please. We are just looking for a man named Milliant Shavoldeshve," Sam says, sounding very exasperated.

"Strip, whore, strip!" I say as I begin beating her with the magazine. "She likes it! I promise!"

"Please, no!" Sam says as he looks at Ian in alarm

"Virgin," I say to the detectives who are losing their minds. "Unless you want someone more experienced!" I cup a hand over my mouth and lean into him. "I have *lots* of experience." Sam is trying to calm Yoko, and Ian is trying to get her to put her shirt back on while Yoko cries.

I pull out my phone and snap a picture of him with his hands on her shirt and Yoko wearing just a bra. "Souvenir!"

"Oh god. No. Delete that," Sam says, now flustered.

I pull my phone back before he can grab it.

"Delete that picture," he says.

"No. If you leave, the picture will be deleted. If you come back, the picture will ruin your lives," I threaten.

"We're leaving," Ian says as he hurriedly backs to the door before slipping through it. Sam quickly follows while muttering something about me being crazy.

"Yay! Happy ending!" I say.

Yoko bursts out laughing as she pulls her shirt down. "What the hell was that?"

"That, my sweetheart, is how you get people to leave," I say as I drop the illusion on myself and pick my book back up.

She laughs harder as she shakes her head. "What happens when they come with a warrant for your arrest?"

"And when they walk through and see it's a coffee shop, what are they going to do?"

"That's true," she says. "I better get paid overtime for that."

"Just take it out of all the money you owe me for 'borrowing' supplies and *never* returning them."

"Why do you have such a good memory?"

"A gift, my dear," I say as I pick my book up and continue reading.

***

You have to be kidding. They're coming back? Maybe they're masochists. That could be the only reason, right?

I throw on an illusion of a super busty, blonde female who barely looks legal. The door dings as the two men and Ravera, a competitor in the charms department, walks in.

That bitch sold me out. I should have guessed it was her.

"Happy, happy endings!" I shout as they walk in.

Of course she told them. She'd sell out her own children to get the law on her side so when she does shitty things, they'll look the other way. No wonder why they're sniffing around here. I should've known she was the one behind this.

"Massage?" I ask. "New special! Happy, *happy* ending!"

"You sure this is the place?" Sam asks desperately.

"Yes. Can we talk to Milliant?" she asks.

“Ahh! Yes, yes! One moment, please!” I say.

I walk through the door into the café where people are enjoying their beverages in peace. It is a small café tucked back, out of sight and out of mind, just how I like it. The tables are full enough just by word of mouth.

Right inside the door, a woman is sitting at a table working on a novel she has been writing for years. I just pray she doesn’t force me to read it like the last one she wrote. I had to spell my eyes open just to stay awake. But it’s the cat curled up on the table that I’m more interested in.

“Hey, it’s Miles. Can I borrow your familiar?” I ask since I still have the illusion on.

The witch looks up at me in surprise. “Hey, Miles… um… what for?”

The cat in question opens his eyes and looks at me curiously as I try to think of how to explain the situation. “I would like to scare a rat.”

She looks at me in confusion, but she knows I wouldn’t harm the creature, so she nods slowly. The hesitation probably has to do with me being a mage who could incinerate a rat with just a glance.

I pick him up, and cradling him in my arm, I carry him into the front room and set him on the desk. “Milliant!”

They all stare at the cat as they try to figure out if it’s really the “Milliant” they’re searching for. He stands up, stretches, and then meows rather loudly. I’m sure it is some kind of complaint since his sleep has been interrupted.

The back door opens, and a large man comes in from the café. Seeing an escape, the cat jumps off the counter and slips through the open door. “Hey…” He looks between me and the others, then to the cat disappearing into the café. “Uh…” Baron is easily six foot six and stocky. He doesn’t have an ounce of fat on him, and I swear his muscles have muscles. He looks like he could snap a man in half, but he is easily the nicest person I know. I still can't fathom how he became alpha of a nearby werewolf pack. I can't see him fighting for any position. He probably won it by using the power of kindness.

"These people want you to give them a happy ending," I say.

"Like…" he points to his groin. "Happy ending?"

"Yes. Happy ending."

"No, we don't. We are looking for a man named Milliant," Ian says.

"Who the heck is Milliant?" he asks as he looks at me in confusion. Poor simple Baron. "Is that even a name? Who would name their child that?"

My mother.

"Milliant, this isn't funny. We know he's here. Are you him?" Ravera asks as she eyes Baron skeptically.

"You don't know what he looks like?" Sam asks Ravera.

"He's a mage. He can use an illusion. I'm sure he sensed us coming miles away and put on an illusion, but I'll show you the sure-fire way to find out," Ravera says as she comes over to my side of the table.

She walks up to Baron and looks him in the eye and then walks over to me. I'm not quite sure what she thinks she's doing, since there's no way for anyone to see through my illusion, but she walks up very close and looks at me. Then goes to knee me in the crotch. I jerk back and cup my groin instinctively.

"This is him. No woman is so quick to protect her crotch," she says.

I laugh. "Ravera, Ravera, why?" I ask.

"Because they told me they'd look the other way with my little…project if I sold you out," she says.

"Of course you did," I say.

"Drop that illusion, I don't like being the second prettiest in the room," she says.

"Even if I drop it, you still are," I joke. "We can clearly see that the title goes to Baron."

"Huh?" Baron asks as he looks at me.

I ignore him and turn back to Ravera. "So, what do you guys want so badly?"

"Wait… you were the older lady yesterday?" Ian asks.

"I was," I say as I shift my illusion to her.

"Why couldn't you just help us?" Sam asks.

"Honestly, I want nothing to do with either of you," I admit as I drop all illusions.

They look at me in even more surprise than before. "What?" I ask.

"You're a lot younger than I expected. With all the prestige your name has riding on it, I assumed you were older," Sam says.

"Don't let him fool you, he's older than he lets anyone believe," Ravera says.

"Uh… boss, I had a customer ask for some Vil Greens in their tea," Baron says, remembering that he is supposed to be in the kitchen.

"Who is it?" I ask.

"Terrance."

"Uh… yeah, teaspoon, no more," I say.

"Thanks," he says as he passes through the door.

"So, what's up?" I ask, knowing that I might as well relent and give them what they want so they can be on their way.

"We need a document read, and Ravera believes that only you can read it," Sam says as he hands it to me. It's an old, yellowed letter written in a foreign language. I take it carefully, curious if it would crumble to ashes if I moved it too quickly.

I scan over the paper as everyone watches me. "Oh… oh my god…" My eyes continue to move over it. "Oh... Eh! No! NO!"

“What does it say?” Ian asks eagerly. Everyone leans forward, and Ravera looks down at the document expectantly.

I look up at him. “Are you sure you’re ready for this?” I ask. “I mean… this could change everything.”

“Please, just tell us what it says,” Sam requests.

“I don’t know, I can’t read it,” I admit.

“What? You mean we went through all of this, and you can’t even read it?” Sam asks sounding irritated.

“Correct,” I reply as I pass the paper back to him.

“I’m sure you have a way to decrypt it,” Ravera says stubbornly.

I look at her expectantly. “Why? Things like this are sometimes best left alone. So why should I worry about it? I need a reason.”

The detectives look at each other for a moment and think about it.

“You have no reason not to tell him,” Ravera says. “You can trust him.”

“A man named Ether West was killed two days ago, and this note was left on his chest. The key to figuring out his murder could be written in that document.”

“Ether West was killed nine days ago,” I say as I watch them closely. This may go deeper than I thought or want to deal with.

“What are you talking about? His body was found two days ago, and his autopsy report states that he died that day,” Sam says. “And how do you know about his death? Nothing has been made public.”

I shrug. Clearly, he doesn’t understand my position in this city. “I know everything that goes on in this city. A familiar told me that Ether West was killed nine days ago. The body most likely appears to have died only two days ago to hide the tracks of the killer. A simple spell really, to preserve the dead.”

“And you didn’t tell anyone?”

I shrug. "Why draw suspicion onto myself? He was already dead. I'm not sure if you've noticed, but I kind of like staying under the radar."

"This was not the first murder. There were fifteen deaths in various districts at the same time."

Now, that isn't what I was expecting to hear. Maybe I should stick my nose into this a bit. "Intriguing. You have spiked my interest. Do you have a list of the deceased?"

"I do," Sam says as he pulls the paper out and hands it to me.

"This is completely confidential," Ian informs me before Sam lets go of the paper.

"Understood." I set it on the desk and read through the list of deceased. I recognize all the names, but I don't know them very well. "This is quite interesting."

"You know any of them?" Sam asks.

"I know all of them, though not well," I say. "Just in passing or by name."

"Can you think of anything that connects them? Or think of why they were targeted?"

"Let's figure out what this letter says. Where exactly did it come from? You said you found it on Ether West, but where?"

"It was folded up inside his pocket."

"Interesting," I say. "Alright, come along."

I pull open the door and step into the café that I run. It's mostly open to people with abilities or half-humans. There are some regular humans who show up, but they have to be fine with everyone because in here, no one has to hide who they are. Along the walls are shelves with books, charms, and potions that I also sell. Some of which I made, some that Yoko made. The two detectives look around curiously, and Ravera immediately tries touching a locket that's sitting on a shelf.

"Ravera," I warn. "Hands to yourself."

"Just looking," she says, but Ravera is known to just take what she wants.

"Mine." I pry it from her fingers.

Ravera is a witch, which means that she can do simple spells, but her main focus is potions. I am a mage, which means that I can easily work with magic, illusions, spells, elements, and demons, but I have an affinity for fire. It is the main type of magic that I am able to connect to and can use with ease. I don't need to draw a spell symbol for it and only need to speak its name in order to control it.

We walk into the next room, and I turn on the lights. The room is nearly empty with black walls and a gray floor and ceiling. There are no windows and only one door, to cut down on distractions. I shut and lock the door, which makes the detectives look at each other uneasily.

"You're summoning someone?" Ravera asks, suddenly realizing what this room is used for.

I nod as I walk farther into the room. "I am."

"You're letting us watch?" she asks, thrilled.

"I am. Please stand with your back against the wall and be quiet. Do not talk to the demon unless I give permission, and do not disturb me."

In the corner of the room, I pick up a bowl that is full of powder and a piece of chalk I bought in the kids' aisle at the Dollar General. Using the bright pink, star-shaped chalk, I draw a perfect circle on the floor and then create the symbol for the demon realm in the middle. I pick up a knife, which was lying next to the bowl, and press it against my palm, cutting my skin just enough to allow blood to bubble through. I hold my hand down, and a few drops of blood drip out and splatter onto the floor. Then I kneel on the floor since my skin has to make contact with the summoning circle. I press my hands down onto the circle and feel my magic rumble within me.

"Havoc, I call upon you," I say, skipping out on all the mumbo jumbo I had to spout when I first learned how to summon demons and the like.

Silence.

"Goddammit, Havoc, I know you're there," I snap, knowing he is doing this just to avoid me. Demons are not always known for being the most compliant of beings. And the ones I deal with seem particularly stubborn.

I can feel the magic bubbling under my palm as the circle glows white. Yet I can feel Havoc persisting and fighting against my summoning, which means that this isn't going to go as planned.

"Havoc!" I snap. "You lazy son of a bitch. Get out here."

The ground begins to shake, and the floor breaks away as a hand reaches out from the deep recesses of the earth. The hand hooks the edge of the floor and drags itself up, and I realize that this is going south very quickly. Havoc doesn't display such theatrics when he is summoned.

"Goddammit," I say. "Havoc, I'm going to make you scrub my toilets!"

Instead of Havoc, a minotaur pulls itself out of the ground which is shifting back to how it was before the summoning. He stands slowly, rising tall above me and faces me with a huge smirk on his bull-like face. His fur is white but for the black highlighting his ears and eyes. His horns rise from both sides of his skull, and there is a deep nick in one of his bovine-like ears, which flickers in my direction. The thick white hair runs down to his chest where his bull-like features fall away to human flesh and bare skin.

"Hey, baby," the minotaur says, and I sigh.

"Hey, Iya. Where's Havoc?"

He puffs out his chest. "He sent me instead."

"I see that. And what is he doing that is so important?"

"Reading a book."

I stay kneeling, which is never the best position for the completely naked Iya. He has no issue with everyone seeing his genitals, and trust me, I can see them just fine. "I see. And did you tell him he is an asshole?" I ask.

"No, he said I'd get to see you, so I gladly came," he says with a grin. "I told him I'd gladly 'come' just for you."

"Yay for me. Go back."

"I refuse," he says, winking at me.

I grumble. Dealing with Iya is never easy. "You are filth. Iya, I'll force you back. Go peacefully."

"Maybe if you do something for me first. Trust me, I'll make it worth your time," he says with a suggestive eyebrow lift that makes me shudder. He doesn't seem fazed.

"Nope."

He cocks his head. "You know you want a piece of Iya."

I stare at him in annoyance. "Iya, I force you to return," I snap, and he's knocked down to his knees.

"Wait! Please! I just want to penetrate you! I will treat you kindly!" The ground opens up, and he claws at the circle as he's pulled back through it and dragged away.

"Well… that was fun. Might have to bleach my eyeballs now," I say.

"How can you control such a powerful demon?" Ravera asks.

"Clearly, I'm struggling because he's an asshole," I say.

"Iya the Minotaur… he's a very high-level demon," she says, clearly impressed.

I raise an eyebrow. "Oh no, I wasn't talking about Iya."

"The demon you are trying to summon is higher than that?" she asks with wide eyes.

She clearly doesn't understand what I can do. I walk over to the corner where I have the one thing that will get Havoc to listen. I pick it up and toss it onto the summoning circle.

"A Hershey bar?" Sam asks, rightfully suspicious.

"Yes, a Hershey bar. The asshole wants a Hershey bar," I say. "Havoc, get your ass up here."

Chapter Two

I touch the summoning circle and feel Havoc grudgingly give in. The lights go out, and the candles around the room light instantly as Havoc appears before me. I stand and look up at the tall demon. Unlike Iya, Havoc looks human. It is rare for a demon to have a human-like appearance, but the higher the level, the better chance they appear and act human. But there's something about his aura or the way he carries himself that makes everyone aware that he isn't human.

He doesn't need to have the head of a bull for people to know that he's a demon. He's dressed in all black, his coat covered in black feathers that reach down to the ground. His hair is a rich black, which contrasts sharply to the white horns that rise up, twisting softly. His eyes are slit like a cat's and the most vibrant blue I've ever seen. He's an attractive man that women can't seem to get enough of. He holds a pale hand out, and I set the Hershey bar in it.

"This better be good, I was enjoying myself," he says as he tears the plastic wrapping. His eyes are on the two humans and the witch who is close to losing her mind.

She panics, knowing exactly who he is, and rushes for the door. He shifts into a black raven and flies over to the door where he shifts back. To her, it appears as if he moves that quickly, but I know otherwise. His ability to shift into a raven is smooth and effortless, unlike how a were shifts. When they shift you can see their body changing, morphing, but

Havoc's change is almost instant. And when he appears again, he is always fully clothed, sword still at his side. I once asked him how he keeps his clothes when he shifts and he asked how I could light fire with my words and we just never questioned it again.

Magic is weird.

Ravera slams into him and cries out when she realizes her exit is blocked by his presence.

"Where oh where are you going, little witch?" he asks as he grabs her chin and yanks it up. He runs a finger over her lips as he stares down at her. She struggles to string some magic together, but his aura is so suppressing she can't even get the words out. Her familiar, a cat, jumps out of her purse and starts clawing at him.

"How cute," he says as he picks the cat up by the scruff of the neck. It growls as its tail whips around in anger. I walk up to them, return the cat to Ravera, and then push her away from him.

"Havoc," I say in warning as I keep a hand pressed firmly against his broad chest.

He grins at me, clearly aware of what he's doing. He just likes to play dumb. "What? I could tell you were annoyed with her anyway, what's the harm in a little fun?"

"Honestly, not much, I was enjoying it. *But* the last person you played with, pissed their pants, and I had to mop the floor afterwards."

Havoc laughs, and the detectives jump, startled. They had been dead quiet, trying to pretend they didn't exist. Hoping to get Havoc's mind off them, I hand him the candy bar he left behind when he shifted into a bird. He bites into it as he stares Ravera down.

"What do you want, child?" he asks as he shifts his attention to me. "Did you miss me? That has to be it, right? Everyone misses my gorgeous face."

"Immensely." I'm not sure my voice could get any drier. "These detectives want to know if you can read something for them."

Sam holds out the paper with a shaking hand and when Havoc takes it from him, he whimpers which makes Havoc grin.

"Havoc, stop torturing them," I say.

"Hmm…" he mutters as he looks around, but I notice that the menacing aura falls significantly so they can actually function. Once the humans remember that they can breathe, they let out a huge sigh of relief and Ravera stops shaking. Havoc peers down at the paper and scans it.

"Out loud."

"So many rules," he says. "It's a contract… it's written in Dulan but… Old Dulan. Which I don't know."

"Can you figure it out?"

"Hmm… I suppose I can decipher some of it. It's a contract through an organization called… Velmah de Rizen."

"Velmah de Rizen…" I think about it for a moment. "They were an organization back in the late 1700s who started by burning witches at the stake. As nonhumans started increasing in society, they began burning anyone they suspected of not being a human. They claimed they were Hunters but they refused to conform to a society which had begun to welcome nonhumans. Their idea for saving the world was to hunt them down and kill them. It was like a cult at the time, wasn't it?"

Havoc holds up a finger and nods. "Ah yes. I remember them. They had you tied up a time or two because they thought you were weird," he says, then laughs heartily at the memory.

"And you just watched both times," I remind him.

He grins, flashing his fangs eagerly.

"How old are you?" Sam asks as he thinks about the math. Thankfully, he seems poor at it because he doesn't come up with an immediate answer.

"Doesn't matter," I say. "So, what is the contract for?"

"It is for a person to join the organization by the name of… Victor Belmont," he says, eyes still scanning the document.

I raise an eyebrow. "Belmont… he's dead. Has been dead since 1810, so why would Ether have this?"

"Was Ether human?" Sam asks.

I shake my head. "He was not. He was a werewolf."

"This organization is no longer active?" Ian asks.

"No, I killed all of them around two hundred years ago," I say.

Havoc gives me a sharp look.

I sigh. "Havoc killed like three of them, I killed all of the rest."

"Liar. I tore their heads from their torsos and bathed in their blood," Havoc says, like it's a fond memory.

"No, you saw a pretty lady and was off wooing her when they all attacked me while I was in bed. You arrived *just* after I'd taken care of them and you killed off the three scouts wandering about. Remember that?" I grimace at the thought of him wandering off with women *again*.

The demon stares at me thoughtfully. "Hmm… I do remember that lass. Her breasts were nice and round, but her nipples were huge! You could have hung your coat on them! I was trying to do that when you kept calling for me to help, but I had to see."

"Did it work?" I ask, curious despite myself.

"She smacked me, but I think the coat hung there for a few moments first."

I can't help but snort, slightly amused. "Lovely." The detectives don't seem impressed. "Anyway, to answer your question, they should all be dead."

"Could someone be killing again in their name?" Ian asks.

"If you don't mind, I want to see the bodies."

"They're spread out throughout the nearby districts."

After the war between humans with abilities and humans without was over, there was also a shift in power. Each state still has law enforcement, like the police, who help keep peace, but there are no longer cities to protect. The cities shifted and changed into districts, where each has what is referred to as a boss. The "boss" of the district is generally whoever is fit to run it, usually someone of magical descent. They can run their districts as they please as long as they aren't radical. The boss is generally the most powerful person in the area. People respect power because it keeps them safe from things outside of the district. The district bosses of each state belong to a council which meets when decisions have to be made. If one boss is not fit to run, the council can usurp them and find a new boss that will be a better fit.

"Show me the closest body," I say.

"We will need to get you permission to see the body."

"Fine, get it as we head there," I say as I grab the broom and sweep away the chalk.

"Aren't you sending him back?" Ravera asks.

"Why's that?" Havoc asks as he starts walking for her.

"Come on," I say as I wave to Sam and Ian. They head through the door as Havoc smiles at Ravera, who is no longer looking at him in fear. It is definitely a different emotion. Probably lust. I grab him by the hair and yank him after me. "Come on."

"This pretty little lady was just about to give me something I wanted," he says.

Ravera always has enjoyed playing with things she shouldn't touch, and Havoc is more than happy to grant that wish.

"Don't care. Seduce girls on your own time," I grumble.

He laughs and follows after me as we step into the café. Everyone looks up at the sight of Havoc, but most are used to him, even if they're still secretly terrified of him. Or terrified he'll set his eyes on their girlfriend.

"Yoko!" I call.

"Coming!" she says as she peeks out of the kitchen. "Hey, Havoc!"

"Hey doll," he says with a wink. "Want to come home with me?"

"Still engaged," she says as she holds up her hand as proof.

"You're just worried that if you go home with me, you'll realize how insignificant your fiancé is," he says.

"Um… I'm standing right here," Baron, Yoko's fiancé, says as he rings someone out.

"Did I ask where you were standing?" Havoc asks.

Baron shifts uncertainly. "No, but—"

"Why did you choose such a weak creature?" Havoc asks curiously, even though Baron is taller and broader than him. Even so, I know that Havoc is more powerful.

Yoko shakes her head, used to Havoc's harassment. "I should've chosen you? You sample women like appetizers, and then throw them away like trash."

"I do, don't I?" he asks with a grin.

"That's really not something to be proud of," she says as she picks up a tray.

I wave Havoc toward the door. "Yoko, we're going with these two, we'll be back in a few hours. If you need anything, call."

"Going out for a happy ending?" Yoko asks, and I laugh. The other two are not as impressed.

Together, we head out to their vehicle, and I get into the back seat. Thankfully, Ravera decides she's had enough and heads off.

"Miles?" Havoc asks.

"What do you want?" I ask.

"Chocolate," he says.

I pull another chocolate bar out of my pocket and hand it to him. He rips it open and begins to break off each square, savoring every bite. Sometimes I feel that if it was between saving my life and a chocolate bar, there wouldn't be a debate. Or a pretty woman. I'd be left there to die. Ever since I gave him his first piece way back when, he's had an odd addiction to the stuff. He says that there's nothing that tastes like it in the demon world.

Quite honestly, I'm not sure why I leave my life in Havoc's hands when I really think about it.

"You seem very concerned about this organization," Sam says as he looks back at me from the passenger seat.

He has no idea what he's getting into if the organization has returned. "We can pray that it's a copycat because if it's not, we all need to worry."

"You think you'll be able to tell by seeing the body?" he asks.

"I can hope."

"So… you are a mage?" Ian asks, and I see him glance at me in the rearview mirror.

"I am."

"So when you summon a demon such as… him, you can control him?" he asks.

"Of course. I would never summon a demon I couldn't control. Any mage with an ounce of magic can summon. Someone with the lowest level of magic can even summon someone from a much higher level than them if the demon wants to be summoned. You have to have a stronger spirit than the demon in order to summon it if the demon doesn't want to come over. But if you are low level, you can possibly summon Iya, for example, because Iya loves to make messes. He would come because he wanted to, but the summoner wouldn't be able to control him."

"How would you get him to return?" Sam asks curiously.

"Find someone strong enough to force them to."

"Generally you?" he asks.

"Yes."

"But what makes demons different from the others?" he asks.

"Demons are very powerful, and most are very mischievous. Not all are bad, but they do like to cause chaos," I say. "But what makes them different is that they generally have a mind of their own. The more human-like ones are smarter, which makes them more deadly. They are power hungry and bloodthirsty, so it's good that demons stay in their realm and can only come up when asked of them."

"Why is that?"

"They can't live here alone. They need to feed off the spirit of their summoner."

"Wouldn't that kill the summoner?"

I shrug. "Hasn't killed me yet."

"So, once you send Havoc back, someone else could, hypothetically, summon him and ask him to kill you, and he'd have to?" he asks.

"Gladly," Havoc says with a grin.

"Shut up. Technically yes, but no one can summon Havoc besides me until I die," I say.

"Why is that?" Sam asks, seeming to be genuinely curious in me for some reason.

"Because we made a contract. He will serve only me until I die and in return, he gets my soul," I say.

"Why would he want your soul?"

"I am a very high-level mage. My soul is where all my magic comes from. He will become even more powerful once I'm dead," I say.

"Why did you agree to such a contract with him?" Ian asks Havoc.

Havoc thinks about it for a moment as he examines his last piece of chocolate. "He's powerful. He's the most powerful human I've ever met, and it intrigued me. I also didn't know he would live this long. In the era he was born in, people rarely lived past forty. It has been hundreds of years, and this decision still haunts me."

"You dislike it?" Sam asks.

Havoc looks over at me and smirks. "A demon usually dislikes any contract he's been forced into. But do I dislike Miles? In some ways, I do. He has so much power that he could control the world, yet he sits there and runs a coffee shop. He's not even the boss of this district. So much power he wastes, and that disgusts me."

"Good," I say. "I like to see you disgusted."

"I like seeing you tortured."

My gaze turns sharp, and he turns his attention back to his chocolate bar, noticing he has struck a nerve.

The vehicle draws to a stop outside a hospital and I'm glad, or I may have sent Havoc back at this very moment. Ian parks in a visitor spot before getting out. We follow him into the hospital as he moves toward the elevators which will take us down to the morgue. The four of us step inside and ride the elevator down to the basement. As soon as the doors open, Ian heads over to a guy that is walking down the hallway. He begins to discuss my presence, but the other man just stares at Havoc, so I'm not sure if he even comprehends anything being said to him.

Carrying himself with confidence, another man walks up, but he keeps to the far side, away from Havoc.

He smiles at me, clearly knowing everyone else and wishing to not know Havoc. "I'm Lieutenant Johnson. You think you can help us with this case?" he asks as he holds his hand out. He looks to be in his forties with a buzz cut and a military appearance. His clothes couldn't get much neater if he'd ironed them on himself.

"Maybe," I say.

"What was your name again?"

"Miles and this is Havoc," I say.

He looks nervous, and I can tell Havoc is eating it all up. He loves fear and anxiety and can feast on it for hours.

"Nice to meet you," he says as he shakes my hand.

Havoc holds his out, and the man is now regretting every decision he's ever made. He hesitantly holds it out, and Havoc takes it and pulls the man toward him. "Why the quiver?" he asks as he cocks his head.

"Havoc," I snap, and he drops the man's hand. "Don't mind him, you'll get used to him. Everyone is always like this the first time they meet him."

The man remains standing stone-still for a moment before taking a breath. "Okay…" he whispers. "Um… right this way."

He leads us through the door, and Havoc follows closely behind me. The medical examiner has the body waiting on a table for us, so I walk over to it and peer down at it. He hands me gloves, but I wave them away since I can't do as much with gloves on. Ether West's head was nearly cut off at the neck but for a small strip of skin connecting it to the back. His skin is pale, showing signs of having been dead for only a short period of time. Definitely not nine days like the familiar had told me. Carefully, I examine the body but besides the cut across his neck, there are no marks or wounds.

"Were there signs of a struggle?" I ask.

"Not much. There were a few things knocked over in his house, but he clearly hadn't shifted into his were form or fought them," Johnson says.

"It reeks of magic," I say.

Havoc looks over at me surprised. "The Velmah de Rizen didn't use magic. They were against nonhumans."

"This one does," I say. "It's old magic."

"I'm intrigued," he says as he stares down at the body.

I move my hand over the body until I find the point of the spell in the middle of his chest. "I'll break the spell, but something is going to happen," I warn them.

"Like what?" Sam asks nervously.

"Not sure, but we'll find out," I say as I hold my hand over the body. "Es… ven… ellsar," I whisper.

I can see my magic wrapping around my fingers like string. It's almost red in color but only noticeable to my eyes. It reaches down to the man, touching his chest as I feel resistance. A darker magic, almost black reaches out of his chest, bumping and clashing against my own, but I'm stronger. I feel the snap of the magic as it lets go and notice a red glow on the man's chest where the emblem of the Velmah de Rizen is burned into his skin. More like it was there before but hidden. They didn't want anyone without magic to figure it out.

"It's their emblem," Havoc says.

"Yet, it's different," I say as I point to a flare on the base of the R.

"It looks the same," Havoc says stubbornly.

"The R is different."

"I think it looks the same," Havoc repeats.

"Havoc, it's different. Look at the R."

"It looks like a fucking *R*," he says. "It's the same."

I set my hand over his eyes and push a vision into his mind of the last man we saw who had this brand burned into his chest. Visions aren't a common thing for a mage to manipulate, but for some reason I've always been good at them. I can make anyone see something that I have previously seen. It makes me a bitch to win an argument against. Whenever Yoko tells me that I didn't tell her to do something, I just force her in a headlock and shove the memory into her brain. For years, she's worked on a solution to protect her mind from me but so far, she hasn't accomplished it.

I pull my hand back, and he looks at me with a stubborn expression on his face.

"It's different," I say.

His lip twitches like he wants to say something else. "Barely."

I shake my head. Only Havoc, even after being forced to see the original, would still refuse to agree with me. "The original was burned in with an iron brand. This is clearly magic, and the symbol is a little different."

"Something else is a little different," Havoc says with a laugh as he motions to the doors that hide the bodies. The doors begin to rattle and shake, as if something is trying to escape through them.

"A necromancer?" I ask in confusion. "The spell was set by a necromancer…" That doesn't sound right. Necromancers aren't generally into spells such as this one, but perhaps there was a mage and a necromancer.

Havoc reaches over and turns the handle on the first door.

"What are you doing?" I ask, since it clearly looks like he's planning on letting whatever is inside, out.

"It knocked. It clearly wants out," he says innocently.

"Yes, to kill us," I say.

He shrugs. "I still don't see the issue."

I wave my hands in a motion around his entire body. "*This* is the issue."

He gives me a huge smirk that fills his annoyingly handsome face. Why I let myself still be drawn in by his looks, I'll never know.

"The only issue I'm guilty of causing is every woman, whose eyes have ever touched me, to have a wet dream. Oh, and you as well." He's so confident all the time.

I look at him with narrowed eyes. "I have *never* had a wet dream about you," I lie.

He grins at me. "Oh really? Lying is a sin."

"I think… we have more pressing matters at the moment than wet dreams!" Sam says.

Havoc waves him off. "Oh no, this is a pressing matter. Lies are very pressing matters. So, Miles, how many wet dreams have you had about me?"

"Not a damn one." More than I can count.

"Seriously guys, what the hell is going on?" Sam asks, voice rising a little.

"We're seeing a liar in the making," Havoc says.

"Don't flatter yourself," I say.

His smirk seems to take over his face. "I don't have to."

The door to the drawer Havoc unlatched slams open, and a hand extends out from within. It flails for a moment as the medical examiner screams something. That's when the hand hooks onto the edge of the drawer and begins dragging itself out. Its body falls out, slamming to the ground in a heap of limbs and hair. Its head snaps back as it sees us and slowly rises from the ground. I hear a commotion farther down as another body drops off a table.

"Oh my god. Oh god. Oh god," the medical examiner whispers as he falls back.

The body rushes toward us, and I set my hand against its head the moment it's within reach, arms grabbing for me. With the necromancer so far from his work, it's easy to break his spell. So I let my magic invade the corpse until I feel a string of magic that isn't my own. Then I allow my magic to grab it and sever it, leaving the body to drop to the ground.

"Why?" Havoc yells.

"What?"

"Why couldn't I tear them apart?" he asks, and I notice he has his sword drawn.

"Because they may be loved by family who probably wouldn't be too happy seeing them diced up," I explain. Honestly, why do I need to explain this?

"You care too much."

"You care too little," I say as I do the same to the second body. Then I walk back over to the humans who are staring with wide eyes.

"S-So what are you thinking?" Lieutenant Johnson says as he straightens up. He's easily composed and I like that about him.

"I don't know. I need to think about it," I say.

"You need to think about how many wet dreams you've had about me so you can give me a legit answer?" Havoc asks.

I ignore his very presence. Something I should have done the day I decided to bind him to me. I was young and dumb and slightly infatuated with the dangerously handsome man.

"Would you be interested in meeting with our department tomorrow morning?" Lieutenant Johnson asks as his eyes flicker over to a corpse.

"Sure," I say. "I'm done here."

I follow them out of the hospital to where I feel a strange fluctuation of magic. I can tell that no one else senses it because the two detectives are still chatting away. It feels similar to the magic that I just snapped inside the building, but a little stronger. I wonder if that means the necromancer has come out to play.

"There you go, Havoc, have fun," I say as the ground begins to shake.

"Earthquake?" Ian asks, uncertain.

"Nope," I say as the landscaping falls away and hands begin to stretch out from beneath the earth. Skeletons rise up out of the ground with one thought in their mind—if they still had a brain that is. It means the necromancer is around here somewhere, and he is not happy about me breaking his hold on the corpses.

"Light my sword on fire," Havoc says as he steps forward, sword raised.

I call the name of fire and suddenly the crotch of his pants is burning as I try to keep my grin in check.

He howls something as he smacks at his pants until the flame is out. Slowly, he turns to me and presses the tip of his sword against my neck. I glance down at it before raising an eyebrow.

"What the hell, Miles. What the hell?" Havoc asks.

"You said your sword, and you're always talking about your mighty sword that you love to penetrate all the ladies with. A simple mistake really," I say as I hold up my hands like I'm innocent.

His eyes narrow and then he gives me a nod. "You're right. It is like a mighty sword," he says approvingly as he brings his actual sword away from my throat. "That you have wet dreams about."

I think about setting his entire body on fire, when Havoc grins and runs forward as the skeletal humans, animals, and beasts rush for me. Havoc reaches them first, sword swinging as he brings it down through them. They have no defense against him and crumple to the ground as ash as I try to pretend that I'm not watching the way his body moves.

Chapter Three

Havoc is riding on my shoulder as a raven, watching the café as I examine our stock.

"*I want more chocolate*," he says, but in his animal form only I can hear his voice inside my mind.

Lucky me.

Our bond allows it, but no one else can hear him which is both convenient and annoying. Convenient for times when he's too far away to see but annoying when I don't want to be forced to hear his voice.

"Don't have any more," I say.

"Then go find me more," he says as he pecks the side of my head.

"Dammit!" I snap as I bat at him. He flies to my other shoulder as I pick up one of the charms I was working on.

"*Who is that?*" he asks as he digs his talons into my shoulder.

I look over at the door as a beautiful woman walks in. I can instantly tell that she is a succubus because she has the attention of all the men in the room. Of course, her charms won't work on Havoc or me, but Havoc has a weakness for beautiful women.

"That's Belle," I say.

"*Belle looks lonely. I bet she's looking for a 'beast' under the sheets*," he says as he shifts. Because he was on my shoulder when he did so, he slams into me, throwing me into the table I'm working at.

A few people jerk back startled, but the rest are used to his appearance even though they still look nervous. He strolls up to her with a grin on his handsome face, his cloak of feathers fluttering around him, white horns contrasting with his dark hair. "Good evening beautiful. Why don't I take you somewhere other than this ugly little place?"

Her eyes light up, and she's instantly excited. "I would love to."

And they're gone.

A blessing really, even if it causes me slight irritation. I'm sure the irritation is just because it's *Havoc* and not anything else. There is nothing about him that I could ever want, so I'm sure it's just because it's *him*.

Havoc *should* be fine. He generally comes back without disturbing much of the peace as long as he has a woman to follow around. I help around the café for a bit when a woman walks up to me with a nervous smile. Of course I already know that the smile isn't directed at me.

"Is Havoc around?" she asks.

She is one of his past one-night stands and clearly wants a second. Most do. None ever get it.

"Nope. He's out with another woman," I say, feeling no obligation to feel sorry for her or make Havoc look like less of a dick.

She looks hurt and it annoys me.

"I told you last week that he never sleeps with the same girl twice and you still went with him," I say.

"But if I could just see him. It's more than just lust," she says as she dramatically grabs her chest.

"That's what they all say. He's not here," I say as I shoo her away. They all think that they'll be the one to capture Havoc's heart. But in the hundreds of years I have known him, he's never slept with the same girl twice and has never generally liked anyone enough to enjoy their companionship. I suppose our relationship is the closest thing Havoc has to anything of substance.

After I finally convince her to leave, I close up the café before heading upstairs to the second floor that I use as an apartment. I could have a bigger house with the money I have stored away, but I like the hominess of this place. There are two bedrooms, a kitchen that connects to the living room, and a bathroom. I have lived here for about seven years now and have found that even though it definitely isn't the most extravagant place I have stayed in, I probably like it the best. Well, besides the time that I stayed with the Queen when she thought I was a dog because I couldn't get a stupid illusion off me.

***

We were invited to the police station to go over some details, but so far, all we've done is sit and wait.

Havoc is staring at the detectives, making them nervous and scared. He just can't behave no matter where I take him.

"Havoc," I say.

"Hmm?"

"Knock it off."

"I'm bored. You're over there playing on your phone, why can't I play a game?" he asks as the detectives try to look anywhere but at Havoc.

"Havoc," I snap.

"Hmm?"

"Shoulder."

"I refuse."

"Then knock it off," I say.

He grins as he stares at me, challenging me, but I just stare back, so that when Lieutenant Johnson walks in, Havoc and I are having a staring contest like two ten-year-olds.

There are two new detectives who have joined us apart from Lieutenant Johnson, Sam, and Ian. They had, at some point, been introduced, but I definitely don't remember what they said their names are.

"So, please go through all the deaths, locations, honestly, anything suspicious," I say, hoping a briefing might jog a suppressed memory about this organization.

"I don't understand why these two are involved," one of the new detectives says. "No one wants to work with nonhumans."

Havoc kicks the man's chair so hard that it screeches across the floor and the man teeters backwards, arms flailing against a losing battle before he hits the ground on his back.

"What'd I tell you!" the man yells from his new location on the floor.

"Havoc. Shoulder. *Now*," I hiss, and he shifts into a raven and grudgingly flies to my shoulder where he bites my ear and twists it hard. I grab him in my hands and hold him in a death grip. "We are here to help because I know more about this organization than any of you."

The man sits back down in his seat but is glaring at Havoc who is trying to peck my nails off, so I start squeezing.

"Miller, you can leave if you can't work with everyone on the team," Johnson says sternly. "I already have your data here, you're just around if we have questions."

Miller shuts up, and Lieutenant Johnson slides the list of names of the deceased in front of me. I don't bother telling him that I've already memorized all of their names.

“All their deaths were in the same manner as Ether West,” Johnson says.

“We can assume all of them are marked by the necromancer, even if we can’t see it,” I say.

“Should we have witches in the area check?” he asks.

“It could be unsafe.” I toss Havoc back onto his chair and he shifts to his human form before glaring at me. “So, I’ve done some research, and as I thought, all members of the Velmah de Rizen were human. Which contradicts with this because a human can’t do a spell such as the one placed on the bodies.”

“So the goal of the original organization was to eradicate all nonhumans, correct?” Johnson asks.

I’m thoughtful as I nod. “It was.”

“So, these murders are similar to how the organization used to eradicate nonhumans,” Sam says. “The only difference is the way it was covered up was by someone with magic.”

“They could still be trying to eradicate nonhumans,” I say. “Depending on who is behind it, they could be using the organization’s name as a way to instill fear and get nonhumans to stop trusting humans. They could also belong to the organization but have a more specific goal.”

“Like?” Sam questions.

“Power. A witch, wizard, necromancer, whatever they are, is only powerful when there is not a higher power. They could be erasing anyone more powerful or who could pose a threat.”

Johnson taps his pen on the table. “Do you think that is what is going on?”

I lean back in my chair as I think about it for a moment. “Honestly? Yes. People have been power hungry for years, but each district has a boss who keeps that power down. But if you kill the boss, you take over the district. Simple as that."

"But they didn't target the boss," Johnson says.

"Bosses are very powerful. It'll take a lot of work to get to them. They'll have to start lower and break down the tower the boss stands on in order to reach them," I say.

"So you think they're eventually aiming for this district's boss? Do you think we need to take this matter to her?"

Explaining things to our district boss would probably be the right thing to do in case there is something more going on. "Wouldn't hurt."

"But if they're going for the most powerful, your demon said you are more powerful. Wouldn't they target you instead?" he asks.

"They could. But a lot of people don't know I'm here or about my power. They'd rather target someone who would cause more of an uproar. Did any of you bring the ring I asked for?"

"Here," Sam says, passing me a plastic bag with Ether's ring. He was wearing it when he died, and I didn't think to ask for it back at the morgue.

He gives me a soft smile that widens when I say, "Thanks."

"What are you doing with that?" Johnson asks curiously.

"I'm going to try to See what happened that day. By using the ring, I should be able to see a vision that could tell me how he died."

"How long will that take you?'"

"I can do it this afternoon."

"Let us know when you find something," Johnson says.

"Understood."

***

“I think you’re starting to think you’re a little more powerful than you are,” Havoc growls at me as we walk toward the café. He’s still furious that I yelled at him for screwing with the detectives.

“Am I? Or are you just being so reckless I have to treat you like a child?” I ask curiously. “You know I don’t mind you screwing around with people but not when we’re in a serious meeting.”

He glowers at me, clearly pissed, and I sigh.

“You’re never happy with me, Havoc. What do you want?”

“I want free will.”

“When I give it to you, you refuse to listen and destroy more than you help.”

He doesn’t look happy. “If you weren’t so weak, I would listen,” he growls. Then the ground rumbles as it opens up, and he drops back through the gateway into the underworld where he will remain until I force him out. So be it.

I walk into the café where the succubus from last night is waiting. “Where’s Havoc?”

I don’t have the time or energy to deal with her. “Don’t know.”

She bites her bright red lip. “I want to see him again.”

“He only sleeps with women once.”

“Trust me, he’ll sleep with me more than once,” she says with a purr as she reaches for me.

“I’ve never seen a succubus grovel. It’s not attractive,” I say, and her black-lined eyes narrow.

“Come here,” she says, and I can feel her power as she tries to grab onto me like she plans on seducing me, but I brush it off with my magic and walk past. She stares at me aghast, and I smile sweetly at her.

“Not gonna happen, sweetheart,” I say. “Yoko, I’m going to try to See something, so please don’t go into the back room,” I say.

“What are you Seeing?”

"Porn," I say.

She doesn't miss a beat. "Gay porn?"

I give her a grin. "Like five guys going at it."

She taps her chin with a finger as her eyebrow lifts. "Hmm… mind if I join?"

"Immensely," I say.

She laughs. "I'll tell Baron."

"Thanks," I say as I pass through the doorway and head into the back room. As soon as the door is shut, I light the candles with a wave of my hand. I draw a magic circle around me, different from the one I use to summon, and kneel down. Carefully, I hold the ring in my left hand and close my eyes.

With a deep breath, I allow my magic to flow out of me. Winding its tendrils around my fingers, it reaches the ring and wraps around it, consuming it. And suddenly I'm seeing things through the "eyes" of the ring.

I'm in a house I've never been in. The first thing that grabs my attention is a man sitting in a chair in the corner. He's reading a book when he hears something that makes him set his book down and look around…

Back in the café, someone enters the room I'm in, distracting me enough that I start to pull out of the vision. I look over at who has walked in, but the pull from the vision was abrupt, and the sever between the vision and now isn't complete yet, so the room seems fuzzy and I feel disoriented. I can make out that it is Baron walking toward me, so I quickly dispel my magic, planning on starting over once he has left.

"Baron, the sock on the door means I'm busy—"

When he walked in, my mind was hazy from being in two places at once, so I don't notice that he grabbed my sword from the corner of the room until he drives it straight into my stomach. Pain tears into me as I gasp. I stumble back as I look up at Baron in shock and realize, now that my mind is cleared, that he's being possessed. He draws the sword back, pulling it out, as unbelievable pain crawls over my body. I press my hand against the wound and fall forward. I hit the ground on my hands and knees, but in an attempt to stop him, I crawl toward him. I catch his leg as he pulls the sword up, ready to chop my head off.

I try to slide my hand under his pants so I can touch his flesh, but his pants are so goddamn tight I can't get my hand under them.

"Why are you wearing skinny jeans!" I yell as I yank his sock down and touch his ankle. I can feel the foreign magic winding around his own shifter magic, choking it down. I grab onto the other magic and cut the hold it has on him, causing him to stumble back in confusion. He looks around as he tries to decipher what is real in this moment.

That's when I feel an alert through the barrier I have placed around the café. It speaks of an intrusion, so I sit back and try to focus. I feel them, at least fifteen no… twenty coming toward my café. Coming for me. But I'm not the only one here. No… no, not all of my friends… Yoko… Baron.

Pushing the pain aside, I clamber to my feet and grab my sword which Baron is still holding. He's standing in a daze, clearly confused, but lets the sword go without a fight. I hold a hand against my stomach as the blood pools out, coloring my hand. I push through the door and stumble into the hallway as I use the wall to guide myself into the café.

"Get out! Everyone, get out now!" I yell, and they know that when I tell them to do something, they do it. People are up on their feet and running toward the door without hesitation. Someone trips over a chair, and Yoko rushes to help them before turning to me.

I'm at the cabinets, yanking them open and grabbing for bottles. As I rummage through the shelves, I'm leaving blood streaks on everything as I grab an al-siv potion that Yoko made. I don't bother making a paste out of the powder since as soon as I press it against the bloody hole in my stomach it sticks. The moment it touches my skin, the pain is blocked and my mind clears.

"Oh my god, Miles. What happened?" Yoko asks.

"Go check on Baron," I say as I point to the back, and her eyes go wide. She turns and rushes to him as I head the other way, through the door and out into the alleyway as someone in black walks toward me.

I draw the symbol for fire in the air then push my hand forward as the fire races along the ground and grabs onto his body. He screams as he falls back, smacking at his clothes as he tries to put the fire out. I start moving, but there are five behind me and at least seven on each side. I feel dizzy, and even though I've blocked the pain, my body isn't handling the wound too well.

As they come up on both sides, I draw the symbol for earth and raise my hands. I can feel my magic dig deep under the cement, grabbing the earth below and drawing it up, tearing a few of them to the ground before someone blocks the attack. I turn down the alleyway and stumble as my legs threaten to give out. Desperate for a break, I fall against the wall before sliding down to my hands and knees. Quickly, I draw Havoc's summoning circle using the blood that's all over my hand. I seem to have a surplus of it.

"Havoc!"

Silence.

"Fucking Havoc!" I yell.

Silence.

Giving up on him, I realize that I'll take anyone. "Iya!" I shout, hoping for anyone, but I hadn't drawn the symbol for Iya, and if Iya isn't close by, he won't be able to pass through Havoc's summoning circle.

My mind is too fuzzy, I can't reach him and force him up. He'll have to willingly come to me.

I look up as I see people moving toward me, so I send flames racing at them. When I notice someone making their way toward me from the side, I moan and push myself up to my feet, forcing myself to move.

"There are plenty to kill, Havoc. Please! It's your favorite thing to do! And I'll let you kill them all! I won't hog even one of them!"

I start running as I realize that if I don't do something soon, I'm going to die. I can taste the blood in my mouth and even with Yoko's potion, the blood hasn't stopped leaking out of my stomach.

Just as I'm considering alternatives, Havoc appears in front of me, and I slam into him. He grabs me before I fall back, but his eyes are looking beyond me at my pursuers. And they light up as a grin explodes across his face.

"Why didn't you call me sooner? You're up here keeping all of the fun to yourself," Havoc says, and I nearly run my sword through his heart in pure anger.

"I *did* call you," I growl.

He rotates his arms, like he's loosening up before the fight. "Did you? I thought I heard a little rat squeaking something, but I didn't realize it was you. I was over there setting out rat killer."

"I'm going to shove my sword so far up your asshole, all you'll be able to do is squeak," I growl.

"Don't try to inflict your gay fetishes on me," he says as he sees the people coming at me. Eagerly, he rushes forward to kill them.

I fall against the alleyway wall as I watch him. "I don't have a fetish for impaling people with a real sword," I say before realizing that those words might be the last words out of my mouth. My dying words. "I'm better than you," I shout after him. There. Those dying words are better.

There are two werewolves, a high-level witch, and a druid. The werewolves reach Havoc first. He rushes in and the wolves avoid him, leaping to the side to get away, but Havoc is quicker, driving his sword into one's heart before swinging around and attacking the other wolf. It's all starting to look like a blur to me, but a moment later both weres are on the ground.

"Actually, you're not, or you wouldn't come crying to me." Havoc looks back at me like he has time to fuck around. "'Save me, Havoc. Save me!'" he mocks.

"At least my hair is nicer," I say. God, now my dying words are about my hair.

A witch comes running toward me, so I call upon the wind and push it at her. But instead of pushing her away, I wrap it around her, compressing her lungs while Havoc cuts down the other two and turns to me.

"Thank you," I say as I look around. Hell NO! My dying words definitely can't be me thanking this wretched creature. "There are still fifteen," I add.

He quickly walks up to me and yanks my arm away. "You were stabbed? Who got close enough to you to stab you?"

"I was in a vision with the ring, and Baron had been possessed... He stabbed me."

Havoc growls as he bares his fangs. "Come on."

I nod as I push off the wall and start walking in the direction that has been cleared of people hoping to kill me.

"Two ahead," I say, and he rushes ahead of me as I hold my stomach hard. The block I applied is wearing off, and the pain is starting to take over.

Havoc tears them down, then looks back at me and grins like he's proud of himself. He's thrilled he's allowed to kill for once.

"Good job," I say as I follow him. "This way is clear." I turn and start coughing. I hold my hand over my mouth and wipe the blood off my lips.

My legs feel shaky, and my entire body feels so heavy that when I stumble, I let myself fall against the wall and stare at the ground.

"What are you doing?" Havoc asks.

"Just… looking at the rocks. This one that looks like a rock is rather nice."

"Miles!" he snaps.

"Coming," I say as I start walking.

"Don't act so weak. You're fine," he says as he gives me a pat on the head like I'm a pet.

I nod and keep walking toward him. I can feel too many surrounding us. Havoc is strong, but I don't want him to get hurt. And if I die, it'll make him weaker without a host.

"Havoc, I return you to the underworld," I say.

"What?" he asks as he looks back at me in alarm.

"There are too many. Go back," I say as I wave at him like he's a feral cat I'm shooing off.

"You don't think I can handle them?" he asks, sounding quite annoyed. I'm over here submitting to the idea of dying so he can live, and he's annoyed at me!

"If I die, you'll be completely vulnerable."

"Why would you die?" he asks, confused.

"I have been stabbed *through the stomach*!" I yell, but it hurts to yell, so I shut up.

"So?"

"Please allow me to strangle you before I die," I say as I close my eyes.

He's fighting against my command for him to return to the demon realm, I can feel it. I'm too weak, I can't control him, and he's realizing that. I look up at him as he narrows his eyes like he's unsure of what to do and then he rushes off.

For a moment, I waver and then sink down to the ground. I can hear Havoc fighting as I see someone draw close to me. Reaching up with my hand, I try to call for my magic, but it's hard to get the wildness of it to tame down for my shaking hand. Havoc rushes over and tears them to the ground before they can reach me.

"Miles."

"Hmm?" I ask as I look up and notice that it's just the two of us.

"Those still alive ran off… but more are coming. We need to go."

I nod.

"Miles. You're not hurt that badly, right?" he asks as he pulls open my jacket. The blood has soaked down into my pants even with the makeshift bandage. "You've lived this long and you're really going to let something like this bother you? How could you have screwed up like this? You could take care of these men in your sleep. I told you not to trust others. This happened because you trusted that disgusting werewolf."

"It's not Baron's fault," I say.

He grits his teeth but reaches down and lifts me up into his arms. I lay my head against his chest as I feel like I'm floating somewhere between a sea of pain and oblivion. He holds me against him with one arm, while trying to support me and the sword with the other.

"Now I have something else to have a wet dream about," I say as I reach out and squeeze his muscular arm before closing my eyes.

"Miles."

"Hmm?"

"You're a fucking idiot."

"Thanks," I say.

"You're going to die."

"…'is but a scratch."

He moves quicker as he holds me tightly. "Shit," he hisses as he starts to run. I've never heard Havoc sound panicked before, especially when it pertains to me. It strikes me as odd, but I can't focus enough to linger on it.

He cuts down another man before stepping into the café, surrounding me with familiar smells.

"Yoko!"

"Don't lead them here," I say.

"Shut up," he snaps as he rushes into the back room. "Yoko!"

"Havoc? Miles! Is he okay?"

"He's dying. I need a healer *now*."

"There are no healers around here. I can get him to a doctor."

"Is he… going to be okay?" Baron asks.

"Come any closer, and I will rip your limbs off and skin you alive," Havoc growls.

"Havoc, please," I whisper.

"Quickly," Yoko says, and I'm carried from the café.

I sink down into his arms as he cups his hands over my stomach and holds me against him.

"Stay awake… dammit, Miles. Stay awake."

CHAPTER FOUR

When I wake, I'm connected to far too much equipment. I feel numb, but I can't focus on anything. When I move, pain tears through me, making me moan. Havoc, in his raven form, is perched on the footboard of the hospital bed. He's watching me closely but doesn't say anything. Or maybe he does, and I can't understand it.

***

There's a ruckus, making me open my eyes. Raven Havoc is perched on my leg while watching a man cower in the corner. He puffs out his chest and caws at him very triumphantly. I reach a hand out and barely touch his tail feathers, causing him to look over at me.

"Don't be mean," I whisper as I try to grasp his tail so I can drag him back to me. I can't get my fingers to work very well though, and his tail feathers slide through my grasp.

He hops a little, like he's preparing to kick some ass. "*I don't like him.*"

I keep my eyes closed until someone else comes into the room.

"Good morning," the doctor says as a nurse unties my gown. "I'm glad to see you doing better today."

The nurse touches my stomach, making me cringe. She jerks back like I have shot her, and I quickly see why. Havoc rushes to her as she scrambles away, clear terror on her face. I grab for Havoc and catch his wing so I can drag him toward me before he can do anymore damage to the hospital staff. He claws at my hand as he tries to get free so he can pluck the poor woman's eyes out.

"Sorry about Havoc," I say.

"Heh heh…" the doctor mutters, and I'm not quite sure what that means, but it didn't sound good how he said it.

After the quickest check-over ever and eyeing me from a distance, they leave me alone with just Havoc. I let go of him, and he ruffles his feathers before perching on my thigh.

"Thanks for staying with me," I say.

He looks over at me and then looks away.

I try to reach out to poke him, but he's too far away. "What's wrong?"

"*You're not supposed to be so weak,*" he grumbles.

"Sorry, Havoc, but I'm still human. If it wasn't for you, I'd have died."

"*Should've let you die.*"

"Yeah, yeah," I say. "You said that last time, yet I'm still alive. I'm starting to think you like me."

If ravens could glare, Havoc is glaring, but it doesn't have the venom it normally holds when he's angry at me.

***

We last about twelve hours in the hospital before Havoc can't take it anymore. You know, because it's all about Havoc.

He jumps off the bed and shifts into his human form. "We're going home," he says as he reaches over to me and yanks the IV out of my arm.

"Fuck," I say as I glare at him.

"Just be happy you don't have a catheter in because I'd be yanking that out next," he says as he yanks the monitors off me and picks me up.

"What are you doing?"

"Suck it up," he says as he carries me out of the room. I throw an illusion over us so no one stops us. If they tried, Havoc would probably make the whole situation worse, so I just let him do as he pleases. Out in the parking lot, he points to a man getting out of his car. "We're taking that car."

"Yes, let's steal a car," I say sarcastically.

"That was my idea, don't take the credit for it," he says as he walks up to the man who is shutting his door. "Give me your keys."

The man looks at us in pure terror and quickly hands him the keys. Havoc pops the trunk as he carries me over to it.

"I swear to god if you are planning on putting me in the trunk, I will chop your nuts off while you sleep," I growl.

He walks on by the trunk and opens the back door. "I don't know what gave you that idea."

He stuffs me inside like I haven't nearly died from a stomach wound. In response, I try to kick him in the balls which misses him and jars my stomach. "Fuck…"

"Stop whining," he says as he gets into the driver's seat.

The car roars to life, and he starts driving it as I try to remember if he even knows how to drive. I decide that I don't care enough and close my eyes. Not until he turns off the car, do I open them again. Slowly, I reach for the door and push it open before swinging my legs out so I can drop down onto my feet. I have to hold onto the door to steady myself as he comes around and grabs my arm roughly, like it'll help to drag me in. I just let him, but I only make it to the stairs before he gets fed up with how slow I'm going and picks me up. He carries me upstairs and sets me on my bed before staring at me.

"Weak," he grumbles.

"You're a sweetheart," I say. "If I'm so weak and you hate me for it, why didn't you let me die?"

There's another moment where emotions unlike anything Havoc ever wears touch his face, and then he instantly covers them up with anger. I find it strange and want to say something, but I know it'll make him angrier. Is he upset that I nearly died? That's very unlike him and couldn't possibly be the case.

He scowls at me and leaves the room. So lovely now that I don't even have a nurse to assist me if I need anything. Can't imagine I'll get some water either. Instead, I push away thoughts of Havoc and decide to try to sleep away the pain

***

When I wake up, I'm thirsty. I don't have to look far for Havoc since he's perched on my footboard, staring at me, which I can't imagine is very entertaining. But it's how I know that Havoc secretly cares for me.

"Would you please get me some water?"

He shifts and stares down at me. "Do I look like a slave?"

"Yes, but that's fine, I'll get it myself," I say as I push the covers back and sit up. I must sit up too fast because the pain touches me, and I grimace. I sit here for a while, trying to decide how badly I want water. After a few minutes, I decide that I don't want it bad enough and lie back down.

I doze for a bit but when I wake up, the first thing I notice is the glass of water. I eagerly reach for it as Havoc watches me.

"Is Yoko here?" I ask, believing that to be the only reasonable excuse for a glass of water.

“Human, I have decided that I will… *care* for you until you are better *only* because it sickens me to have my master in such a weakened and pathetic state,” Havoc declares from where he sits in a chair. I don’t know why it makes me so happy that he cares. He usually pretends that humans are nothing but a nuisance, so it’s nice seeing that our years together have chipped away at the wall he puts up before everyone else. “What do you want to eat?”

What’s easy that he can make without bitching too badly? “Lunch meat sandwich. First drawer in the fridge.”

He gets up and leaves, and I stare at the ceiling while I wait. It’s not long before he returns with a sandwich. It’s not on a plate and looks pretty maimed as he holds it out to me. I take it and notice the unreasonable finger marks in it, but at least it’s something edible.

“Thank you,” I say as I take a bite before realizing he left the plastic on the cheese. He grins at me as I take it off and expose the single slice of meat balled up in the middle, but I just close the sandwich back up and eat it. “Delicious, thank you.”

“I was going to rub my balls on it, but then I thought you might enjoy that,” he says.

“Yes, because every gay man loves balls rubbed all over their sandwich,” I say sarcastically.

“I thought so,” he says as if confirming his hypothesis. Of all the demons in the world, why did I choose this one? And why do I have to like him?

There’s a knock on the door. “It’s me,” Yoko calls.

“Come in,” I say, and she pushes the door open.

“Hey, Miles, how are you doing?” she asks with Baron behind her, and I realize I have just done a horribly stupid thing.

Havoc is on him so quickly Baron doesn't have time to react. Havoc grabs the larger man by the neck and lifts him two feet off the ground and slams his head into the wall.

"Havoc, stop!" I say, but I'm still so weak, I can't control him. I can see Baron's body tense as he starts to shift and I know that if he shifts, he'll just escalate everything far too quickly. "Don't shift!" But if Baron doesn't do anything soon, Havoc will hurt him.

I throw the covers back and rush to my feet. Quickly, I move across the room and grab for Havoc, knowing my skin on his will help me stop him since my magic will be stronger.

"Havoc, please stop!" I say, and Havoc, in his anger, swings his arm around, pushing me off him. I stumble back, tripping over my own legs before hitting the ground on my butt.

Havoc stops moving and looks back at me as Yoko rushes to my side. Before she can reach me, he moves between us and pushes her away. "Get out! Get out!" he yells. "I'll kill both of you if you don't leave."

Yoko looks at me and I nod, so she grabs for Baron and rushes out. Before she completely leaves, she turns back to me. "Um… I brought you some soup and stuff… I'll leave it on the counter."

"Thanks, and I'm sorry," I say as I watch her shut the door.

Havoc is just standing there staring at the closed door, expression unreadable. He's hiding his emotions from me again, as he's known to do. Sometimes, I just wish more than anything that I could tell what he's thinking. He's never been dealt a good hand. Demons rarely are. He's been abused by masters, treated like a pet or a slave. But he's been mine for so many years, I thought that he'd eventually open up to me. I *want* him to open up to me.

"Come here," I say, and he flinches. "Havoc, come here."

He slowly turns around and looks at me as I sit up.

"Come *here*."

Tentatively, he walks over to me.

"Sit down."

He kneels down in front of me and looks me right in the eyes, and for a moment, I see a glimpse of guilt in them. And for once, he's not immediately covering it up with anger.

"Havoc… thank you for protecting me. I would be dead right now if it wasn't for you. And I thank you for being with me for all these years. You have been the only person who has ever been there for me since I was young. I honestly care about you more than anyone else, but sometimes you let your anger take over your mind and don't think reasonably. I need you to. I have already explained to you that Baron had been possessed."

He looks away from me. "He pissed me off."

I look at the head-sized hole in the wall. "Clearly. Can we try having you ask me before you do something reckless?"

"Fine. I'll consider it."

"Thank you."

Having been abused for years by previous masters, it took him a long time to trust me. And being a master who has never hurt him, he's opened up to me more than he's ever opened up to anyone. But I think it also makes him more possessive over me and act more rash when things like this happen. Maybe it's a fear of losing me and getting a different master or maybe it shows how much he really cares about me.

***

"I fixed the hole in the wall," Havoc says when I open my eyes.

I look at the wall and see that his "fix" was him taping a piece of computer paper over it. "Lovely."

"I also made you soup," Havoc says.

"You did?" I ask, surprised. "Thanks."

He holds out a bowl of chicken noodle soup that Yoko must have brought. Hesitantly, I take the bowl from him and dip the spoon into it. I take a sip of it and try not to gag. He must have forgotten that you're supposed to mix water with it.

He grunts something and then leaves, so I grab my water glass and pour it into the soup. It tastes pretty normal after that, though the added water made it cold. So I use magic to touch fire to the bottom of the bowl and reheat it. I finish eating and slowly get to my feet and start walking toward the bathroom.

The door slams open, nearly hitting me, and I stare at the new hole in the wall from the door handle. "Where are you going?" Havoc asks.

"I need a bath. I have dried blood all over me and feel disgusting," I say.

"I'll help you."

I sigh. I can only imagine how *that* would go. "I'm fine."

"You are weak and can die easily," he says.

"Not too easily. I did just survive a sword being stabbed into my abdomen," I remind him as I slowly walk into the bathroom and shut the door in his face. I turn the water on as he pushes the door open and lets himself in. "I'm fine."

"You can't even bend down. How are you getting your socks off? You can't tell me you don't want me to see you naked. You love being naked with men."

"Says the person who sleeps with any woman who looks your way," I say.

"Do you know how long it has been since I've seen a woman naked?" he asks, clearly mortified about the answer.

"Four days."

"Four FUCKING DAYS," he says.

"There's something called 'porn,'" I say.

"Ha! Me? Havoc? Have to resort to watching porn? Don't make me laugh!"

I sigh. "You're in here, so help me," I say as I unbutton my shirt. He pulls it off and tosses it then whips my pants down as I look at him, startled.

"Just in case you were curious how quickly I could get a woman's pants off," he says.

"Um… thanks. I'm so glad to now have that knowledge to forget," I say as he takes my socks off. All that's left is my underwear, and while Havoc has seen me naked, I'd rather remove my own underwear.

Before I get a say in the matter, he yanks them down and blatantly looks at my groin.

"Huh."

"What?" I ask.

He shrugs. "Nothing!"

"No, I want to know what the 'huh' was about."

"I just thought you'd have a raging hardon being in the same room as me," he says.

"So you think for the last however many years, whenever you're in the room I have a stiffy?"

He nods. "Sounds about right, honestly."

I sigh and step into the bathtub before sitting. "You can leave now."

"Fine, fine. If you fall, it's not my fault."

He leaves, so I'm left getting into the shower in peace. I *really* don't think I could handle letting Havoc wash *any* part of me. That's all the fuel he'd need to make my life hell.

I'm still tired, but I want the dressing to soak so it's easier to remove. I've been trying to leave it off for longer periods of time, but I still hate removing it.

I pull the shower curtain open and jerk back, startled. "Holy shit!" I cry as I look at Havoc leaning against the sink. "I thought you left!"

"I did. It's not my fault your much inferior ears couldn't hear me stomping my way into the room. Did you jerk off while thinking off me in there? Is that what took so long?"

"No, I actually just tried *not to die*," I say as I grab a towel and wrap it around my waist before stepping out and sitting on the edge of the tub. I'm getting water everywhere, but I just need to sit down since I feel light-headed.

Havoc walks over to me and kneels in front of me before pushing my arms back. "Are you taking this off?"

"Yeah," I say as I grab an edge of the dressing and pull it free. Havoc reaches out and runs a finger down my chest toward it and I still myself.

My mind is gone from the wound and fixated on that gentle touch. His hand slides down my wet skin, making heat rise in me and my cock begin to harden.

Nope! NO! No way am I going to let him keep doing this. If I got hard while he touched me—and I already know I'm going to—he would never let me live it down. I can't just sit here while he… tantalizes me and expect my body not to react.

"Thank you! I'm done! All good!" I say as I stand up and push him away.

This man is going to be the death of me.

***

I sit in the café and watch the customers as Yoko and Baron rush around. Havoc glares at Baron every time he looks our way, but so far he hasn't confronted him again or tried to punch his head through a wall. Instead, he stands by my side and glowers at anyone who looks at me with anything other than a smile. But a beautiful witch has just walked in, and Havoc's attention has been averted. Someone could come up right now and stab me fifteen times, and he probably wouldn't even notice.

"I hope I'm never attacked when there's a beautiful girl around," I say.

He nods. "Me too. The real issue would be if it was the beautiful girl attacking you." Even while talking, he never looks away from her. I mean, she *is* beautiful and he hasn't screwed her yet, so she has two things going for her. Well… three things. She's also a woman.

I sigh and rub at my face.

She walks over to us and smiles at me. "I was told you sell illusion charms?" she asks.

"I do. What do you want them for?" I ask curiously. I don't know her and don't want my charm helping her steal something or screwing someone over.

"My familiar."

"You want them to appear invisible?" I ask curiously. Some witches create charms for their familiars so that they can fit in without people knowing they are a witch. A lot of times, familiars wear them while a witch goes to work so they can go with them without being noticed.

"No… I don't mind people seeing her. She's just a bit… distracting," she says as she snaps her fingers. The cat-like creature trots up to her from where she'd been sniffing another familiar but with the scales and fangs, she looks like something out of a child's nightmare. "Everyone's scared of her, and I keep telling them she's super sweet, but they don't believe me." It stretches and shows off its wicked set of teeth. It even creeps me out and I've seen some shit.

"I see, what do you want her to appear as?"

She smiles, hopeful that I'll be able to fix her issue. "Just a cat would be fine."

"I can do that. Havoc, can you help her find a charm that will fit on her familiar's collar?" I ask, since he'll clearly be spending time with her tonight, he might as well start early.

He leads her over to the area, and she looks through them as she smiles at Havoc. I can never understand how the man could be so ruthless, yet when he sees a pretty woman, he can change long enough to get her in his bed. Then he's back to being ruthless when he tells her that he never wants to see her again.

She comes back with the charm, and I take it from her. I pick up a brush and open the ink before dipping the thin brush into it and drawing a symbol of Illusion on the back. "There you go. Yoko will ring you out," I say.

"You did it already?" she asks curiously.

"Yup."

"I heard you were good, but I didn't know you were that good," she says.

I grin. "It's a simple spell."

"Thank you."

"Yes, thanks for coming," I say. "Feel free to come again."

She will. She'll be here tomorrow asking for Havoc.

She smiles, looks at Havoc, and then heads to the counter. Havoc doesn't follow her, though, but stays with me.

I stare at him in shock and realize that some drama is needed. "Havoc… Havoc! Oh my god, Havoc!"

Startled, he looks over at me. "What's wrong?"

“Are you ill? What are you doing?” I ask as I touch his forehead. “Oh no, he’s dying. Someone help!”

He smacks my hand away. “What?”

I jab in the direction of the witch. “There’s a woman… she’s getting away! Hurry! Gotta catch them all.”

Havoc glares at me.

“Oh. Wait… have you already slept with her?” I ask. “Sometimes I lose track.” I know he hasn’t. I have an amazingly good memory of who he’s slept with and I dislike them all.

Not that I’m jealous or anything. Ew. Gross. No.

“No, I haven’t. I can’t leave. I have to take care of the invalid.”

“Oh, trust me, no one can attack me in the time it takes you to finish,” I say.

He looks at me in shock. “Oh trust me, I can keep those girls satisfied *all night long*.”

“Uh huh… yup,” I say. “Keep telling yourself that.”

He gives me a playful grin. “You’re evil.”

“Thank you.”

He snorts and shakes his head, but he doesn’t leave my side for anything.

***

After a day in the café, I decide that reading a book would be a good idea. Havoc, on the other hand, clearly doesn’t if his amount of pacing is anything to go by. He walks up and smacks my book out of my hands. It slams against the wall, putting a dent in the already damaged surface.

I glare at him as he stares down at me. “Fix the wall,” I snap.

He yanks the paper off the wall, away from the hole Baron's head had created, and carries it over to the new hole and presses the tape against it. "Fixed," he growls.

"Alright. Now what do you want?" I ask.

"I haven't had sex in *thirteen* days because of you."

"Sorry about your luck?" I ask. "Are you running out of women in this town? I mean, you have to have fucked through the city by now, right?"

"Let me fuck you," he says.

"Ha! What?" I ask, believing I've heard him wrong. Maybe my stupid desires are now making me hear things wrong.

"You spread your legs for any other guy who looks your way, let me fuck you. I want to fuck something," he says.

"Yes, I'm such a slut," I say sarcastically. "I haven't even slept with a guy in a year."

"All the more reason for you to have sex with me," he decides.

"What's wrong with you?" I ask curiously. "Are you ill? Are you dying, perhaps?"

"What is wrong? Are you honestly asking that? My *balls* are going to explode."

"There's a quick fix to that," I say as I mime jerking off.

"Yeah, it's called having sex with you."

My body is wanting to get behind this, but I know that I can't. It'd be absolutely stupid to sleep with him even if I really want to. Oh fuck, do I want to. But I can't. He just wants sex and I have and will always want, something more.

"Come on."

"Really? Have you ever even slept with a man before?"

"I have."

That surprises me. I always assumed he was completely off limits because he was only interested in women. I swallow hard as I fight against my body that is raging a war with my mind. It's just sex, right? And he's offering. It's not like we're committing to something.

But that's the problem, isn't it? I've always wanted commitment. Seeing him running off with all of those women already bothers me. After sex? How much more will it bother me?

I return my attention to the conversation. "And?"

"Women are easier," he says.

"Then go find a woman."

"I don't want them."

"You want me?"

He looks away from me and I'm confused by the gesture. "Shouldn't you just be overcome by joy?"

"I'm just trying to figure you out."

"I just don't want to leave you alone while you're so weak. That's all it is," he says as he looks up at me.

"Are you sure?"

"Stop asking me questions! No wonder why you never have sex! You bore them all with conversation first! Just tell me how much you want my mighty penis!"

I snort. "Oh, Havoc."

His eyes narrow. "What?"

I shake my head, positive I'll never figure this man out. "Nothing."

He pulls me out of the chair and proceeds to drag me over to the bed before pushing me onto it. I should fight him, slip away, go back to the chair. Instead, I let him pull me after him. "So?"

I look up at him as he leans over me. He's watching me closely with those inhuman blue eyes. He is a gorgeous man. There is something he exudes that makes everyone look his way. What makes me hesitate is knowing that he sees nothing in sex but the act of pleasure. This will be the biggest mistakc of my life—and I've done some stupid shit—but what's one time going to hurt?

"I don't care. I guess I might as well see why all these women grovel at your feet for you to come back to them. I'm still a little sore, so just don't get too carried away." I'm such an idiot. Such a fucking idiot. I'm letting my body talk. My desire talk.

"Oh, you'll be even more sore when I'm done with you."

"Funny," I say as he yanks my shirt off, nearly deskinning me in the process.

"My god! Let me live through this experience!"

"You could put on an illusion of a woman," he realizes.

"Alright," I say as I throw on an illusion of a ninety-year-old woman, and since my shirt is off, I make sure the breasts are touching my belly button.

He wraps his hands around my throat to give me a shake as I laugh. I drop the illusion as he glares at me.

"I was very close to strangling you with those tits," he says. "They'd have wrapped nicely around your throat."

I laugh harder as I reach up and push his jacket off. Then I slide my hands up under his shirt, running my fingers over his bare skin. Pulling his shirt off, I marvel at his muscular stomach. Not that he does anything to acquire it but eat chocolate. I run my finger down his muscles as he grins at me.

"I've seen you eyeing me when I don't have a shirt on," he says.

And I know I have because I've always wanted to run my fingers over him and feel every inch of him.

"I'm just checking to see if they're painted on because you honestly don't do much in the way of working out," I say.

His hands stop on my shoulders. "I am regretting this decision more by the minute."

"Really? I'm kind of enjoying it," I say as I lean forward and bite his nipple rather hard. I feel like he deserves it after all of the pain he's put me through.

"What the fuck?" he says as he pushes my head away.

I laugh, and he climbs on top of me, sitting on my legs so I'm pinned down. Then he grabs my arms and holds me down as he stares at me.

He pins me down with his gorgeous eyes. "My nipple has to be bleeding."

I can't help but grin at him as my cock hardens. Clearly, there's something about him pinning me down that turns me on. "Let me lick it for you," I say as I stick my tongue out.

He leans down and captures my mouth as I feel his tongue caress my own. My erection is pressing against my pants, and I would very much like to free it, but he's still sitting on me, so I can't move. He pulls his mouth off me and kisses my throat before biting it.

"Ow!" I snap.

"Pay-back," he explains.

"Uh huh, sure. Now let's see this penis you're so proud of," I say as I reach for his pants.

"Oh no, you always unveil the best thing last. Keeps everyone from being disappointed about what comes afterward," he says as he nods at my groin.

"Funny," I say as I watch him unbutton my pants. He slides them down slowly as he watches me. While kissing a line down my stomach, he pushes my pants down my thighs, making sure to miss any of the sensitive areas as he follows the pants and underwear's descent with his lips.

"You're a tease," I tell him as he slides back up my body, and I feel my cock rub against his bare stomach, making me realize how badly I want him naked. It feels surreal. How many times have I dreamed of this happening? Maybe this is nothing more than a dream again.

I grab his pants and unbutton them before hurriedly pushing them down. I have seen Havoc naked before. Honestly plenty of times, but never like this. His gaze is intense, making me remember how unhuman he is, and for some reason, it excites me. He slides one hand down my stomach and between my legs, rubbing my inner thigh, just taunting me, but never once touching my aching cock.

"Do you even have lubricant in this place? I mean it's been ages since you've gotten laid," he says.

"I just assumed you brought your ten-gallon jug of it," I say.

"Nah, I used all of that already," he says as he reaches over me and yanks open the bedside table before grabbing some. "The plastic is cracking, it's so old. Do you want me to wear a condom?"

"It's not like we need to with what we are. You can't even get a cold from a human."

"Good because I'm positive these things are expired."

"Probably," I say as he captures my lips again. He pushes our cocks together and the feeling of his skin against mine makes me moan as I grab hard onto his ass. I slide my hand between us and take his cock in my hand as I run my finger over his skin, causing a sharp intake of breath from him. I rub the tip with my finger before sliding my hand down until I reach his balls and he groans against my lips.

"I'm a little nervous having you anywhere near my nuts," he admits.

I grin deviously as I give his balls a gentle squeeze. "Why's that?"

He groans as I slide my hand up his length and nip his neck. "Because I don't trust you," he says as he slides a hand down between my legs. He moves his finger between my ass cheeks, rubbing my hole slowly with a wet finger before pushing inside of me. It is almost like a succubus has finally caught me in a spell. No matter how much my brain is telling me this is an awful idea, I'm not backing away.

He grins. "My, what lust is radiating off you," he says. "I've never seen you lose composure, Milliant."

"Why don't you stop bragging and actually show me something worth my time?" I ask before biting his lip between my teeth and pulling it.

He grins, and I kiss him hurriedly as I slide my hand up his cock to the tip, then down to the base. His thick dick is as hard as mine is, telling me that even with all of his teasing, he's as into this as I am. His finger moves in and out of me before a second is pushed inside, opening me up. It feels tight as he stretches me, but I want to feel more of him. He kisses my lips as our cocks brush against each other, and I need him. I want him in me and touching me and grabbing me.

"Please, put it in," I say.

He smirks at me, and I smack my hand against his mouth.

"Don't be an asshole. Or I will fuck *you* instead," I say.

"I'd like to see you try," he says.

"Would you? Because I happen to remember that I have control over you," I say.

"Hmm… I will continue on," he says as he pulls his fingers away from me.

"Good boy," I say.

His cock, wet with lubricant, brushes between my legs as he settles against me. I feel the tip of his cock push against my entrance as I feel myself slowly open up for his size. He's larger than I'm used to, but he's careful not to hurt me. He slowly pushes into me as I grab onto him, feeling like he's completely filling me up. He slides a hand down my leg that's hooked over his waist as I moan, and he kisses my throat. He pulls out slowly before pushing in hard, and I dig my fingers into his back. He reaches down and rubs my cock as he thrusts in again. He hits me just right, and it makes my entire body feel numb with pleasure and desire. I moan, and he captures my lips with his own.

He moves inside me, touching my body in a way I feel like it has never been touched before. Like he knows every spot that will please me until he's driving me crazy. I dig my fingers into his back, knowing that I can't last much longer, but I don't want it to end. As his hand moves over my cock, I groan as I come. I feel myself tighten around him and it makes pleasure course through me as his thrusts become quickened, telling me that he's close. He grabs onto me as he comes inside me, and I hold onto him, knowing that this is probably the last time I'll be able to pin his body against mine.

He pulls out of me and lies down on the bed. He rolls me on top of him and wipes a shirt over my butt, rubbing the lubricant off before throwing it on the ground.

"Better have been your shirt."

"Nope. Yours."

"Of course."

For a short while, he holds me there on top of him, my head against his chest, and we fall into an easy silence. I try to push down all of the thoughts swirling around in my head and just focus on the now. I know I've made a mistake, but I've always been a stupid man when it comes to Havoc.

But until morning where I'm forced to face what I've done, I'm going to enjoy every moment of this.

Chapter Five

The door opens and Sam walks in. He smiles when he sees me and walks over to the counter to where I am reading a book.

"Did you know that you can bring a drowned person back to life by blowing tobacco smoke up their rectum?" I ask as I hold the book up.

He looks startled and a little worried. "You… can?"

"No. These are just stupid things they used to believe in," I say.

"They seriously used to blow tobacco smoke up the butt?"

"Yes. They'd even have little stations set up near large rivers for it."

He looks amused. "Interesting."

"I'm sure that's not why you came here. Did you need something?"

He gives me a soft smile. "I just wanted to see how you were doing."

"Much better than I was," I say, returning his smile. "Thanks."

"That's good to hear—" That's when the door slams open and Sam jumps, startled. I am so used to Havoc's ridiculous entries that it no longer fazes me.

He eyes Sam, instantly making him nervous. But instead of going toward Sam, Havoc comes over to me and pushes me out of my chair. I look at him confused about what he's up to as he sits in the chair, then grabs my waist and pulls me onto his lap. I awkwardly sit on his lap as I try to figure out what the hell is going on and why I'm suddenly sitting on Havoc's lap like he's Santa Claus.

After we had sex, things went on like normal. But being with Havoc has always made me happy, when he's not being annoying or irritating that is. I didn't expect more. But now… this? Who knows what he's doing now by pinning me on his lap. Being weird like usual.

"Sorry for the interruption, what were you saying before I walked in?" Havoc asks.

He's such a child. It's like he's trying to claim me even though he doesn't *really* want me. Right?

Sam shifts nervously. "Um… I was actually going to ask Miles out to dinner, but now I feel like that would be awkward."

"And why would that be awkward?" I ask sarcastically as I struggle to remove Havoc's death grip around my waist. His hands are locked together like he's praying, and I can't get them unlocked for the life of me.

"Haha…" Sam says nervously.

I turn to Havoc, which is hard to do when I'm pinned against him. "You're such a child, let go of me." I claw at his hand, but even that doesn't help.

"I'm just seeing what you're doing. Is that not allowed?" Havoc asks.

"I'm talking to Sam. *Clearly.*"

"Why?" he asks as he glares at Sam. Sam is eyeing the door and questioning if he can just disappear through it.

"Because I want to," I say. "We're good. Go see if Yoko needs help."

He tips my chin up and kisses me on the lips. Literally just tries making out with my face as I sit there in surprise. Then I slide my fingers into his hair and yank his head back.

"Knock it off!"

"He reeks of lust; he wants to fuck you," he decides.

“So? Isn’t that my decision, not yours?” *Especially when you’ve acted like nothing has happened between us.*

He grins at me, and it makes me realize that Havoc just got a little crazier. Everyone he sleeps with he throws away, so why is he doing this?

“Havoc, go into the other room,” I say as I decide that if I can’t unhinge his hands, I can squeeze through them. I start sliding down Havoc’s lap as his hold tightens and I’m left hanging from his grip. His arms are around my chest, my shirt pulled up enough to show everyone my stomach. “Havoc, I swear to heaven and hell. Let me go.”

He pulls his hands free, and I hadn’t realized how much I’ve been pulling against them because I fall to the ground with a thud. Havoc laughs as he gets up and just leaves.

Why I ever wanted to be with that man, I will never know.

“Don’t ever dabble with demons,” I say as I get up. “The power of summoning another being stronger than you can imagine, with emotions and desires such as his, is… purely stupid. A wise man, even if strong enough, summons a lower demon. They are less intelligent and less deadly. Only a fool makes a contract with one like Havoc. And I’m a fool.”

“I don’t see you as a fool. You clearly can control him,” Sam says.

“See, it’s a relationship of give and take. Complete control, and Havoc would hate me so much he’d look for loopholes, figure out ways to screw me over. Kill me if he could. But because I treat him like a human and give him enough room to do as he wants, he listens to me.”

“I understand.”

Right here is a normal man, a handsome man who is nice and kind. A relationship with him would have to be better than me longing for something I’ll never have.

Even so… if there's even a chance… "Anyway. Sam, thank you for the offer of supper but with everything going on right now, I'm going to have to decline. I would like to try and keep my mind focused," I say.

"I understand."

"But thanks for the offer," I say with a smile.

"Well, I need to get going."

"I'll see you tomorrow. Lieutenant Johnson wants us to help him with something."

"Alright, see you then."

He leaves but before he's even completely out of the door, Havoc is beside me.

"What?" I ask.

"Just making sure the asshole left."

"Go find some woman to bother."

"You'll have to do," he says as he tips my chin up like he's going to kiss me again. When I don't lean into him, he cocks his head and gives me this sexy grin that makes me want to climb into his arms and let him do dirty things to me.

"What exactly are you doing? Marking your property? Playing with something new? I thought you never had sex with the same person twice?" I ask.

"I don't," he says as he kisses me. This time I lean into him. I slide my fingers into his hair as the kiss deepens. Just as soon as I tell my brain to stop this nonsense, I let myself get swept back up into his touch. I could kick myself for letting this happen again and again.

I pull back and glance up from his lips to find his eyes watching me. I press myself into him and can feel his cock against mine.

"If you don't sleep with the same person twice, then we are keeping this the same way?"

"Of course. I will never sleep with you twice."

***

When I wake up, I notice Havoc is staring at me. I roll over to look at him as he grabs me and shakes me.

"What exactly are you doing?" I ask.

"I feel sick inside," he moans.

"Demons can't get sick."

"My body is rejecting this."

Mine should be too. "Me?"

"Yes."

"Then get out of my bed," I say, even though I don't want him to go. I have this stupid war raging inside me as I try to convince myself that it's just sex. I can keep sex and emotions separate. "You're in *my bed.* And let me remind you that it was your idea to have sex *again*."

His hand slides down and cups my ass, ears clearly not working or listening.

"Nope, not going to happen," I say as I push his hand back.

"I have already committed a grave sin by having sex with you twice. I might as well get my fill," he says as he pulls me toward him. Even though I want to give in and get my fill as well, I know it'll make it harder to convince myself this is just fun sex.

"Nope, I've had enough of you for one day and I just woke up. I have things to do," I say as I get out of the bed.

Havoc looks over at me and growls. "You're rejecting my offer? I have women groveling at my feet for a second fuck from me, and you reject a third?" he asks.

"I have things to do, *Havoc*."

His eyes narrow. He's growing irritated, and I can tell he's trying to draw me in with some weird aura that has all the women coming back, but it doesn't even touch me.

I walk up to him and for a moment I can tell he thinks he's won until I grab his chin. "Do not forget who I am, Havoc. When I say I'm busy, that means I am busy."

He growls at me, and the lights in the room dim before growing dark. "Then I will find someone else to fuck."

This is why I shouldn't deal with him. This is why I need to pull back now. "That is your option," I snap as I walk from the room. I don't want to walk away, I want to go back to him, talk him into staying with me, but I can't. I need to walk away while I still can.

He grumbles something as I head into the bathroom, but he's clearly not done because he follows me inside. I grab my toothbrush as he watches me with his arms crossed like that will persuade me to jump into his arms and onto his dick. I brush my teeth as I stare back at him before spitting the toothpaste out and heading through the door. I get changed and walk downstairs with Havoc still following.

My phone rings as I walk down into the café. "Hello?"

"Miles, this is Lieutenant Johnson, we need to speak with Rehna, but we're having trouble getting in touch with her. We're not sure if something happened, and that is why we can't reach her," he says.

Rehna is the boss of this district and has been for about forty years now. She mostly stays to herself unless her people need something. She prefers to work from the sidelines, allowing people like Johnson and Sam to handle the minor issues. A lot of people appreciate her for that since there are tales of districts with bosses who suppress their people. "Alright. I can help."

"I'll pick you up at ten?"

"That's fine," I say as I head over to the counter and grab a cup and pour myself some coffee. My café is already in full swing at eight in the morning. Today is Baron and Yoko's day to run the place since I took care of it the previous day, so I'm free to help Johnson.

I grab my list of orders from behind the counter and head back to my workroom.

When ten comes around, I walk toward the front door, and Havoc falls in line behind me. He's still annoyed with me and wants to make sure I know he's annoyed by glaring at the back of my head, even as we get into the vehicle waiting for us with Johnson and Sam inside. Instead of sitting near me, he yanks the front door open and barks for Lieutenant Johnson to get in the back. He hesitates, but a smidgen of him is scared of Havoc, so he complies while acting like he totally doesn't care.

"Head to Wicker Woods," I say, and Sam complies as Havoc turns his annoyance off me and onto Sam.

Now he's thinking the reason I refused to sleep with him is because of some feelings I have for Sam. Which doesn't even make sense. Then again, Havoc rarely makes sense. Sam is terrified, but I don't care enough to help him and continue playing on my phone.

"W-Where do we park?" Sam asks.

I glance up. "Just pull over somewhere."

He quickly does, probably with the hopes of getting out of the vehicle quickly. I get out of the car and walk toward the woods as the rest fall in line behind me to get as far away from Havoc as they can.

Havoc sighs as loud as he possibly can, in case I've forgotten about his pouting.

"You're such a child," I say as I grab Havoc by the arm and pull him up beside me. "Knock it off."

He growls but walks beside me.

"Havoc," I say sternly. "You know if we enter the woods with any ill intentions, she will not see us. Why are you annoyed with me?" He looks over at the others, so I grab his arm and pull him back. "Excuse us for one moment." I drag him back toward the car so no one can hear us talk, and face him.

"Is it him? He the reason why you don't like me?" he asks as he nods at Sam.

"If I liked him, I would have gone out to dinner with him," I say. "You only want sex from me, so what does it matter, Havoc?"

"Because I don't like sharing."

"Havoc, for three hundred years I've been yours, and you've been mine. Why do you think that has changed? You have been the only one there for me since the beginning. Look at it through my eyes," I say as I set my hand over his eyes and toss him back into my memories of when I was twelve.

I walk into the room my master has led me into and stop suddenly. I can feel the power rippling all around me and it makes me feel ill, but Master Geoff is smiling. He's enjoying it.

In the middle of a summoning circle is a demon kneeling before us. He raises his head as he notices Geoff's presence and grins. His fangs are instantly noticeable, and I want to step back and flee, but I also want to reach for him. Grab him. Touch him. I'm mesmerized by the power the demon holds. He rises to his feet and towers over me. But I'm not scared of him or at least not as scared as I should be. Instead, I am awed by his power, and I feel a hunger to hold onto that power.

"Kneel," Geoff growls, but the demon is unfazed.

He's naked, covered in welts, wounds, and blood, but he has no intention of listening.

"Kneel," *Geoff orders, but the demon doesn't even flinch. "Milliant, watch and learn. You can control any demon, no matter how powerful."*

The demon is bound, but Geoff grabs a whip and begins beating him. It's wound in magic so with each strike, it pulls away patches of skin. But the demon never flinches and I marvel at his strength. How can he not show any pain or fear of this horrid man? But what I notice even more is that with each hit, Geoff grows angrier that he is getting no reaction from the demon that is bound to the circle. My entire essence reaches out for him, wanting to grab onto something for the first time in my life. His eyes touch mine, and for some reason I smile. The demon's eyebrow rises as it tries to read my reaction.

Geoff continues to beat the monster until he's bleeding, but still the demon won't kneel. For some reason, I feel my feet move on their own as I walk up to the demon and set a hand against his chest as my eyes stay captured by his. He's watching me carefully and with my skin against his, I can feel the power the demon possesses, and I want it all for myself. I want to wrap my spirit around it and claim it.

Geoff hits me with the whip, and I fall away from the demon with a startled cry. I look over at Geoff a moment before he begins beating me. "You dare allow yourself to be captured by the demon?" he growls.

But he doesn't understand. I wasn't captured by the demon. I'm drawn to it. I want to control it, set it free, so it can do my bidding and tear Geoff apart, piece by piece. The demon starts laughing. He understands my sick desires as Geoff beats me to submission.

I look up at Havoc. "None of that has changed," I say. "None of the feelings I felt that day have changed. I have never desired anyone as much as you and I never will. You are mine now, whether you like it or not. Are you happy?"

"Can we go back and watch him beat you again?"

I snort. He's such a sarcastic ass. "If we can watch him beat you first."

He just laughs.

"Why do I even *care* about you?" I ask.

"I honestly don't know," he realizes as he acts like he's thinking very hard. "Ah, that's right. Because I'm unbelievably handsome."

I quickly hold a hand over my mouth. "Don't make me vomit."

"I can't wait until you cease to exist, and I can feast on your soul."

"I'm going to make sure I die somewhere you can't reach me," I say.

"You're not allowed to see other men."

"Don't be difficult." And don't make me believe there might be something more there.

He glares at me as I turn to the woods and start walking into it. I hear the flap of wings and look up as two gryphons descend before me. They're beautiful creatures with lion-like bodies and bird-like heads raised far above me. Havoc instantly draws his sword, but I calm him with a hand on his chest. There's a woman on one of their backs, who is watching us carefully. Her skin has an unhuman shimmer to it, and her hair is so light it looks transparent. I know that she is a celestial being, but that is the extent of what I know about her. She started tagging along with Rehna before I knew her, and the rumor is that she could keep Rehna from ever aging. Rehna's body is human, so she should have continued to age, yet she never has. I also saw Rehna heal remarkably fast the last time she was attacked in my presence. Rehna herself has no healing abilities, so I wouldn't be surprised if this being has been caring for her.

"I wish to speak with Rehna," I say.

She gracefully slides down off the gryphon and walks over to Sam. Even though she's completely naked, her long hair hides her bare form.

"Is your hair taped over your tatas or something?" Havoc asks curiously.

She slowly looks over at Havoc and I realize I should probably get a shock collar for him or something like that.

And of course he's not done. "I mean… I was watching real close as you slid off that bird thing and not even a glimpse of a nipple. It was impressive."

She cocks her head slowly like she doesn't understand Havoc, and I sigh. But honestly, none of us understand him either.

"I apologize on his behalf," I say as she turns her head away and returns to Sam.

Havoc leans in close to me so his mouth is next to my ear. "You think you can summon the wind just to give me a sneak peek?" Havoc whispers.

"She is a divine creature, and you are treating her like she's a sex toy!"

"She's *naked.*"

"Shut up," I hiss.

I look over and see that everyone is watching us, so I just smile and wave her on, hoping she'll continue or put some clothes on or *something*.

She runs her fingers over Sam's face but doesn't stop walking. Her hand slides off and the tips of her fingers touch Johnson's face as she moves to Havoc. She hesitates with him but keeps walking until she touches me.

The moment she touches me, she stops and turns her attention to me. Her free hand reaches up until she has one hand on each cheek and is looking right up into my eyes.

"Let me into your mind," she says softly. My ears don't recognize her language but somehow, my mind is able to comprehend her words. Which must be some kind of ability on her part because I haven't invested too much time in a magical translator.

"Tell Rehna it's Miles," I say.

"Rehna knows who it appears to be. But appearances can be deceiving. Let me into your mind," she says.

Fuck.

"You might not like what you see," I warn her.

"I have seen a lot. Let me in your mind."

I hate opening up my mind, even though I know I could kill her without moving a muscle. She knows it too, and that's why the gryphons are nervously pawing. I drop just a fraction of the barrier on my mind, and her eyebrows twitch. She leans forward and softly presses her lips to mine. I drop into her mind the moment she goes into my own, so I know what she's looking at. I need to make sure it's not something specific, but it's not. She's flipping through the memories that make up my mind like she's flipping through a book. The only time there's hesitation is when she reaches one of my darkest memories. I can feel her flinch when she touches a memory with Geoff. Then when I sold my soul to Havoc. Another when I murdered twenty people in thirty seconds. Then when I killed Geoff. She winds through my memories until she reaches the moment we are now at, and I realize my entire lifetime has just been reduced to thirty seconds.

She pulls her lips away and looks up at me. "His death brought me happiness," she says.

"Ah, me as well," I say as she drops her hands.

"Follow," she says as she steps away on bare feet and slides back up onto the gryphon's back.

"Why did you get a kiss and none of us did?" Havoc asks.

"Even I'm kind of jealous about that one," Johnson jokes.

I give Havoc a wink. "I'm special."

Havoc huffs.

The gryphon begins to walk, and we fall in behind it. The ground has turned from thick brush to a stone path as we are led straight to a shrine. A small animal-featured boy opens the door, and we step inside the completely furnished shrine.

Rehna is there to greet us. She's a woman who looks like she could be anywhere from twenty to forty. She's very average-looking, yet everyone is drawn to her. In some way, it feels like her power is what makes her attractive to others. She is a paladin, but most of her power comes from her exceptional abilities with a lance. It doesn't matter how long the lance is, when she is wielding it, she moves with the grace of a dancer. She also knows some small spells such as a barrier, but nothing extensive.

"I apologize for all of the inconveniences," she says as she hugs me. "One of my own had been possessed and tried to kill me."

"Same here," I say, and she looks at me in surprise. Her green eyes are wide as she watches me. Her hair is pulled back tight into a bun, telling me she had probably been sparring before we interrupted her.

"Who even knows your whereabouts?" she asks. "Most people don't even realize who you really are."

"That's what we're going to figure out. This is Danny Johnson. He's with the special units part of the police department as well as Sam Diaz. They are trying to find answers to the fifteen deaths, all nonhumans or users, that occurred on September 10 at the same time. They found a letter on each body dealing with the Velmah de Rizen," I say. "Do you know the name?"

"Vaguely," she says. "They were killed, were they not?"

“Yes, I believe that Havoc and I had killed them all, but someone is now using their name.”

“Copycat?”

“Not exactly. It’s different. They’re magic users that are now targeting nonhumans or users. It makes no sense. Valmah de Rizen was dedicated to eradicating every nonhuman. But now they’re made up of nonhumans?”

She looks thoughtful as she tries to comprehend what’s going on. “So… could there be a significance to the name and organization? It could be something as simple as instilling fear in those who know of the name.”

“I suppose, but there have been other radical organizations which were more resented and more widely known,” Johnson says. “Before this, I had never even heard of them.”

“Unless they don’t care about causing fear in anyone but those old enough to know who they are,” Rehna says.

“That’s true,” I say. “My interest was only piqued because of the organization. You have already been targeted once. It will likely happen again.”

“Do you think they want me gone just because of my position?” she asks.

“Most likely.”

“Are they targeting other district bosses?” she asks.

“I’m not sure,” Johnson says. “Right now, we are in the dark about a lot of their actions. We have just now enlisted Miles’ help because he knew about the organization.”

I see Havoc’s body grow stiff as his attention turns to the forest. I close my eyes before kneeling and touching the ground with my hand. I can feel the forest compress, like it’s trying to hide itself from a malice that is invading it.

“Havoc,” I say, and he leaps onto my outstretched arm as a raven. I pluck a feather out, and he glares at me.

“*Ow that hurt, dickhead,*” he says into my mind as he pecks my head and rips out a chunk of hair. Not because he needs it for a spell like I do but because he’s an asshole. Then he spits the hair out and leaps into the air.

“What’s going on?” Rehna asks.

“Shh,” I say as I place the feather between my lips. With it there I can wind my magic around it, allowing me to see through Havoc’s eyes as he searches the trees. It’s easier because we are bound together and already have a link between us. Suddenly, the ground begins to quiver, and I pull the feather out from my lips.

“Necromancers,” I say as I walk out of the shrine.

Everyone follows me as Rehna shouts for those in the area who can’t fight to get into the building.

“No sign, Havoc?” I ask out loud. Even though he can’t hear me from this distance, the link we share through our minds allows him to know what I am saying and allows me to hear his voice in my mind.

“*Nothing. They’re hiding,*” he says.

“They have to be strong to be affecting us from here,” I say as the ground begins to break. Earth rises up, and I hear roots cracking as the dead are forced through them.

“*Should I return?*”

“No, I can handle it here. Find them,” I say.

“*Understood.*”

The cracks in the ground spread as I watch a hand reach out of the dirt and drag itself up.

“What the hell?” Sam whispers.

The dead are rising all around us. Humans, wolves, horses, gryphons, weres, anything that has ever died in these woods is at the necromancer's fingertips. I pull my sword from where it rests at my side and slam it into the ground. Fire races out from it, tearing through the skeletons, and turning their bones to ash. But that spell only works around twenty feet of me and I can't use it multiple times without draining my magic. It's also hard to keep the flame hot enough to burn the bodies the farther it spreads. The other issue is the bodies that haven't been rotting for hundreds of years. On top of that, I have to deal with the shrine, the people I want to keep alive, and the trees. I'm sure Rehna wouldn't be impressed with a massive forest fire.

Hundreds more come to join, and I realize that this can't be the work of one necromancer. I move toward a dead man that is running at me and cut his arms off with my sword before grabbing his skull in my hand.

"Vehath," I whisper, and my magic snakes down my fingertips, right onto the skeleton's skull as it finds the death magic that allowed it to rise and live again. It winds around it, proving stronger, and chokes it out. The necromancer feels me instantly and drops the hold on the dead man, but I get a glimpse of where they're at. It feels like there are four of them from what I can tell so far.

"Near a river, Havoc. The river has a fork in it around a large boulder," I say.

"*Understood*," he says.

I turn back as an undead werewolf rushes at me. I slide back as I raise my sword up and swing. It catches the werewolf on the side and rotting flesh falls from its body as it slams down to the ground. I rush forward and drive my sword through the bones, severing its head from its neck. Rehna has her lance and is swinging it flawlessly through the air, tearing through the bones like they're paper.

"Rehna, protect me," I say.

She nods, so I close my eyes and cut my hand with my sword. I let the blood drip down onto the ground, and the earth eats it. I slam my sword down and then kneel, so I can grab a connection to the earth.

"*Disha fel veyon dethcka*," I whisper.

"Miles, don't!" she yells as she runs for me.

"I will not hurt their souls," I say, but that's probably not why she's telling me to stop.

"That's black magic," she says.

"I am stronger than the black magic I use," I say as I keep reciting the spell in my mind. I say it aloud once more and then slam my hands down. I can feel the black magic swirling around me, mixing with my magic as it invades the earth and races along it, tendrils reaching up and grabbing onto the dead that were still moving toward me.

I look up and watch as the undead that are fighting the gryphons, weres, and protectors of the shrine stop moving, and all look at me. I can still feel the necromancers' magic inside of them, fighting against mine, but I am winning.

"You dare attack me when I am stronger than all four of you?" I ask. They can hear me through the bond created by my magic. And through it, Havoc can feel their location. "Whoever sent you is either a fool or does not understand my power."

An undead man closest to me looks up. "What if the one who sent us does know your power and knows he's the only one who can control it?" it says. I can tell it's one of the necromancers speaking to me through the dead man, but the words send a strange chill down my body.

I growl as I stare the undead down. I can feel the spirit of one of the necromancers flickering out, telling me that Havoc must have found her. The moment her life is extinguished, some of the undead drop to the ground as bone and ash.

"I have lived hundreds of years since I last saw him. He does not know my truc power," I growl.

"He does, and he'll take the rest of what keeps you human and use it for his own," the undead says.

"Then why's he hiding behind people like you?" I hiss.

"The time isn't yet right."

I can feel it the moment Havoc kills the necromancer talking to me, but that's fine. I have no further need to hear about my nightmare come to life. I have heard enough. Within minutes, all four are dead and I urge the deceased back to their resting spots. The earth closes, and I drop my hold on everything and stare at the spot where the undead who'd spoken once stood. Havoc lands before me, breaking my contact with the ground, and I look up at him. His clothes are bloody, and he has a hungry look in his eyes as I let my head fall against his chest, completely exhausted. Black magic has a way of consuming the caster, and I used too much of it.

"Well, old friend, looks like our nightmare has come back to life," I say.

Havoc sets a protective hand on my back as he looks out into the woods where the four necromancers lie deceased.

Chapter Six

Havoc is reading a book in the library when I walk in. He doesn't even bother to look up at me as I approach, so I push his book away and sit down on his lap with my back against his chest.

"Hmm… thought you didn't want me anymore," he says.

Oh, don't I know that I shouldn't be doing this.

"You're such a child. I never said that. Just because I didn't want to have sex then, it didn't automatically mean that I hated you," I say as I turn my head to look at him.

"No one has *ever* turned me down," he says, voice thick to the point it's almost a growl.

"How are you so childish?" I ask. *And why do I still want you?*

"Hmm…" He leans toward me and kisses me on the neck softly, and I can't help but lean into it. "So… do you think Geoff is alive?"

"I'm not sure alive is the correct word. We did a pretty good number on him," I say.

"You're upset."

If Geoff is honestly back, upset wouldn't cover it. "A bit. I thought that nightmare was over with."

"How'd you come into Geoff's possession?" he asks curiously.

"I burned down the orphanage I was in," I say. "He heard about it."

"On purpose?" he asks. "I mean I always knew you were a bit devilish, but even I wouldn't burn down an orphanage."

"God, no. I had trouble controlling my emotions. The man in charge was an asshole. He took my friend and nearly beat him to death so I, accidently, burned the entire place down while watching. I didn't kill anyone, though. It was as if the fire burned around each of us. *That's* the moment Geoff decided I had potential."

"I want to see," he says.

"Are you sure?"

"Yes."

"Alright," I say as I reach back and set my hand against his eyes. I throw him right into the moment, allowing him to see it as if we are living the moment as it happens.

It's so dark in the room they've placed me in. It's been days since I've seen anyone and I'm hungry, but I've at least stopped crying. I was so scared I'd killed someone, but Diana snuck by to tell me everyone was okay. I still feel a little sick though. I knew I had an affinity for fire but... I never imagined I could do something like this.

I close my eyes and the door opens, startling me. Cliff is there and I flinch back, but he grabs me by the hair and drags me out. "Here. Just take him," Cliff says as he pushes me forward. I fall onto my hands and knees as I try to blink away the brightness.

"Get up," says a man I don't recognize.

I stand up and look at him. He's a tall man with short, dark hair and piercing gray eyes. He looks as average as any other man, but there's something about him that instills fear in the pit of my stomach. My body tells me that this is a monster I should fear, but I don't know why. He doesn't look like a monster. The smile on his face looks almost kind compared to the hell in here. He reaches out and cups my chin, and I instantly feel the magic bubbling through his fingertips. I can see it moving and jerking about, but it's dark, almost black. I shy away from him and thrust up a barrier. He watches me for a moment, and then his soft smile turns to a grin.

"I'll take him," he says.

"Good. Don't ever bring him back," Cliff says as he pushes me forward.

"Come along," the man says. "What's your name?"

"Milliant," I say.

"What a ridiculous name," he says as he takes me home.

For a few days, he allows me free roam of his mansion, and I walk about it in a state of confusion. I have never even seen a home such as this one. I cannot believe that I am allowed to move through it freely. I wander a bit but am nervous and mostly stay to my room. The room is larger than the house I'd lived my first six years in. And all around me are so many things filled with magic that I can feel my own magic bustling inside of me.

"Milliant, come along," Geoff says, and I follow him into his work room. "I will teach you everything I know, if you're worthy. Do you think you're worthy, Milliant?"

"I don't know," I admit.

He smacks me across the face, startling me. "Answer again."

It's not as if I've been shy to hits and harsh words, but I thought he'd be different. "I will try to be, sir."

"Better."

"Take your shirt and pants off," he says, and I'm so scared of him that I do so without hesitation.

"Lean against the wall," he says, so I do as I watch nervously. He has a brush in one hand and ink in the other. Then he begins to paint symbols on me. Lines that stretch from my hands to my chest, over my

neck, and down my legs. I'm confused, but I still know that what he's doing has to be some type of spell.

He whispers something, and I watch him nervously. My magic is bristling uncertainly along my skin.

"Do you know what I just did?" he asks.

"No," I admit.

"I just locked your magic away, so it doesn't consume you. You've gone too long without learning the right way to use it. This will allow you to learn simple spells safely first."

"Yes, sir," I say.

"And if your magic ever gets out of control, all I have to say is Silvé," he says.

Pain tears through the markings, and I scream as I drop to the ground. As quickly as the pain comes, it's gone, and I'm left kneeling on the ground, staring at him with wide eyes, full of fear. I thought I feared Cliff. But that is nothing compared to the fear I now feel for Geoff.

I yell the word for fire at him and he grins at me, making me realize that I just did a very stupid thing.

"Silvé," he says, and I fall to the ground as pain consumes me.

It feels like someone is taking a knife and shredding the skin he'd drawn the ink on. He looms over me while grinning, and I realize that I have left one hell and walked into another. But this hell has a monster in charge.

"Stop," Havoc says, and I look over at him. "I don't want to see you tortured."

I laugh. "It's alright. I thought you were into BDSM."

"Only when I'm the one doing the torturing. The only one who should be allowed to beat you is me," he says as he pushes my head down, forcing me to lie over his legs, and begins smacking my ass.

"Oh my god, you asshole," I say as I reach up and grab the white horn snaking around his head and yank it down.

"Ow, you little fucker," he hollers as he dumps me onto the ground and then pins me there with my arms above my head.

"Like that'll stop me from doing whatever the fuck I want," I say as I bring my foot up and let my toes slide over his groin.

He looks down at my foot and then up at me and raises an eyebrow. I smile at him, and he leans in to kiss me as he releases my arms. Instead of letting myself be pulled into the kiss, I bring my hip up, throwing him forward, and then hook his arm and draw it down as I flip him onto his back and sit down on his stomach.

"Oof… you little shit," he says.

I look down at him as I grin. He reaches for me, and I shake my head. "No touch, big boy," I taunt, and my control over him forces him to put his hands down at his sides as he looks up at me with a raging glare.

"You think you're fucking cute, don't you?" he asks.

"Of course," I say as I ruffle his black hair. "What do you want me to do?" I lean forward until my lips are half an inch from his. "Do you want a kiss?"

"Not from you," he says defiantly.

I grin as I lean close enough to kiss him. Instead, I take his bottom lip between my teeth and pull it gently. "Funny."

"Let me go, or when I do get loose, you're not going to enjoy it," he growls.

"So scary," I say as I slide a hand up my shirt as I rock my hips on his stomach. "I'm. So. Scared. Of the *big*. Bad. Demon."

I know I'm being dumb, but sometimes, I just can't help myself.

I push my shirt off and drop it onto the ground before leaning back against his knees and unbuttoning my pants. He's watching me intently as I pull the zipper down and begin to work my pants off my hips. I slide them down one side then the other as I put my feet in his face. I take my briefs with them, so I'm sitting naked on his stomach.

"Too bad you don't want me to touch you," I taunt as I run my hand down my stomach and over my cock. "Because I could use a big, hot, cock right now. Not yours. But you know, if there's one around," I say.

I can feel his hard cock against my ass, eager to join in. "Let me go."

"Nope." I lean forward and lick his throat. Then I bite it before sitting up. "Not going to happen. What is this nasty thing jabbing me in the back? Put your legs down," I order, and he fights it, but it's a losing battle. All too soon, he's lying completely flat on the ground, so I slide my butt over his groin until I'm lying on his legs and unbutton his pants. "How embarrassing." I release his erection. "Your words are all 'no, I'm not enjoying this. No, I don't like you' yet look at how hard you are." I lean forward and go to lick the tip before looking at him, startled. "I forgot. You didn't want me to touch you… sorry." I slide over his erection, letting it brush my thigh as I sit back down on his stomach.

"I never said you couldn't touch," he says.

"But… when I tried to kiss you… you said not from me," I remind him.

He grimaces.

"Oh well, I'll pleasure myself," I say as I get up and head into my bedroom.

"Come back here right this moment!" he yells.

I grab the lubricant from my drawer and return as I watch him. "Or what?"

"Or when I get loose, I'll fuck you so hard you won't walk for a week."

I snort. "You're not that good, I'm afraid." I sit down on his stomach again, and as he's watching, I pop open the lid of the lubricant and squirt a nice pile right on his forehead. I laugh at the murderous look on his face.

"Whoops," I say as I wipe it into his pretty hair with my finger.

"You think you're so funny."

"I don't think I'm funny, I know I am. Oh, how I wish I didn't have to pleasure myself alone," I say as I slide a hand between my legs and push my finger inside of myself. "Hmm… it feels so much better when I do it without you."

I slide down his body and take his cock in one hand before lowering myself between his thighs. Then I run my tongue over the tip as I watch him, eyes locked onto his.

"I would suck you, but you said you didn't want my mouth anywhere near you," I say.

"Can… Can I take that back?" he asks.

"What back?" I ask as I wrap my mouth around him and swirl my tongue around the head of his cock before pulling off. "You don't like that though, right?"

"Miles?"

"Yeah?" I ask as I look over at him.

"Come on…" he says pleadingly.

"Come on, what? What's wrong?"

"Please let me join in."

"You are joining in," I say. "You're a comfortable seat." He is looking at me with such lust that I can't help but grin.

He sighs. "Why are you so gorgeous?"

My eyes flicker over to his in surprise. "Submitting, are we?"

"Yes."

"Good," I say as I slide up onto his waist and take a hold of his cock with one hand.

I press down on it as I drop my hold on him. His cock slides deep inside of me as he reaches out and runs his hands up my legs, but he leaves me in control as I move on top of him. Pleasure ripples through my body as I notice him watching me. His eyes slide over my body as I grin down at him.

"I feel like I should ignore you more often," he says.

"Do you?"

"Oh yes, I do," he says as he grabs me and rolls me underneath him.

He pushes in hard, and I moan as I arch up into him. He captures my lips, kissing me hard as I grab onto him. I dig my nails into his back, drawing my fingers over his hot skin as he thrusts into me. He hits that spot inside of me that makes every touch feel like ecstasy.

He slides his hand down my stomach, grabbing my cock as he rubs me with each movement. I arch up into him as he kisses and nips my throat. But the pleasure is too much, and I feel my body reaching its limit as I moan against his touch. I feel my body tighten around him as he reaches his climax, fingers digging into me, breath heavy. He covers me with gentle kisses as he pulls out of me.

"How have I known you for this many years and not known that you can actually be sexy?" he asks.

"Because you've been too busy chasing women," I say as I lie down on top of him.

"Take me to a time when you interacted with me, I want to know what you saw when I only saw a scrawny, useless child"

"You're awfully greedy," I say as I cup my hand over his eyes and close my own. And then I'm living it again. I'm right there, experiencing it as if for the first time.

I can't stop thinking about the demon. I want to feel his power again. I want to combine it with my own and destroy this place.

Geoff hits me hard across the face, and I look up at him. "Fucking pay attention."

Destroy Geoff.

"Sorry, sir," I say as I look at the candle and light three of the eight candles on fire.

"Good," he says. "Now the two end ones."

I do with just a word.

"Alright, I'm going to town, I want these chapters read while I'm gone."

"Yes, sir."

"And practice the details of your symbols. They look like shit."

"Yes, sir," I say as I look down at the symbols I'd drawn. I can't tell what is wrong with them, but I am far too afraid to ask.

As soon as he leaves, I open the book and start reading, but I get this odd nagging feeling deep in the pit of my stomach. I look back at the door and take a deep breath before turning again to the book. Geoff will be gone for at least two hours. That's plenty of time.

Quickly, I rise to my feet and rush through the door. I check outside to make sure Geoff is actually gone and then head down the stairs into the basement. There's an incantation on the door, but it's easy for me to break, and suddenly I'm inside the room. The demon is sitting on the floor when I walk in. Hearing me, he looks up at me from where he's confined to his small circle. Only enough room for him to sit, not even lie down.

"Come here, come here," he says softly.

I'm drawn to him unlike anything I can imagine. I can't stop moving toward him. Only when my foot is right before the spell circle, do

I stop. He's chained to the wall, telling me Geoff doesn't completely trust the circle.

"Come here... please... come here," he says as he reaches for me.

Drawn to him, I reach out for him and hit that barrier. Pain tears into my hands, and I jerk them back. I hear a noise behind me and quickly look over at the door as Geoff stares at me.

"I'm surprised you actually hesitated before coming down here," Geoff says, and I realize he's going to kill me.

The demon is laughing behind me as he sits back down.

"I'm sorry. I'm sorry. Please, I'm so sorry," I say.

"Are you? Then you should have listened," he says as he grabs my arm and drags me from the room as the demon laughs.

"You were laughing so hard," I remind him as I pull back and stretch. "I need to go check on the shop."

"What did he do to you?" Havoc asks quietly.

I look down at him and grin. "You feel guilty?"

"Slightly," he says, but his face tells me that he truly does feel bad about it. "Tell me what happened."

"Hmm… He put me in a room and summoned a demon. He let the demon try to kill me but made sure it wouldn't completely kill me. It terrorized me until I pissed myself. And after that, I've always had a healthy fear of demons." Besides this one.

"It deterred you for a little bit, but you kept coming back," he says.

"Yes, I got smarter." I stand and pick my clothes up.

"Did the markings from his ink disappear once he died?" he asks curiously.

I drop the illusion I always keep on myself. By now, it is so familiar I tend to forget that it is even there. But when it drops, the black lines run around my wrists and up my arms to my chest.

"Would they still work if he's alive?"

"One way to find out," I say.

"Hmm… That's something I don't want to find out."

I pull my clothes on, and he gets up and follows me into the bathroom where I clean up before heading down the stairs. Just as I reach the door, he grabs me and tips my head back so he can kiss me softly on the lips.

"I'm sorry for laughing," he says.

"What time?"

He gives me a gentle smile, but there are other emotions hidden beneath it. "Just one of the times. I like you so much, I'll let you pick."

I grin and press my lips gently against his, relishing in the soft touch before pulling back. "I'm supposed to be working."

When we walk into the café, Yoko stares at me with her eyebrows raised. "What?" I ask.

"What… happened to you?" she asks.

"Uh… not much?" I ask before realizing that I haven't put the illusion back on.

"You and Havoc now into adult finger painting?"

I laugh, and Havoc sets a hand against my chest when I start to walk away. "Hold on, hold on. What is this… adult finger painting and how have I never heard of it?" Havoc asks, intrigued.

"It's where you have sex while finger painting each other," Yoko says.

"What a *splendid* idea," he says as he stares at me.

"No," I say.

His eyes get wide, showing his excitement at the idea. "Then we could hang our artwork all over this café."

"No."

"This shall be fun."

I adamantly shake my head. "No."

Havoc is not deterred. "Who knew you had a smart mind in that pretty little head of yours," Havoc says as he pats Yoko's black hair like she's a dog.

Yoko dodges the touch. "I'm not sure if I should be flattered or offended."

"Just ignore him, and you don't have to decide," I say.

She turns back to me. "So… do you wear an illusion all the time? Like right now, you're definitely not twenty-six, yet you look it."

"This is how I looked when I was twenty-six."

"Wait… how did you look when you were in your eighties?"

"Never got there," I say. "Stopped aging at twenty-six."

"How?" Baron asks as he pokes his head out of the kitchen. His superior hearing allows him optimal access to listening in on all conversations.

"Now that's a secret."

"That even I don't know," Havoc says.

Yoko pushes my shirt up and looks at the markings Geoff left on me. "I've never seen anything like these."

"Yeah, I don't really understand them myself," I admit.

Havoc slides between us. "You're getting too touchy."

Yoko looks over at him, raises an eyebrow, and then grins. "Am I?" She slides both hands under my shirt and pinches my nipples.

Havoc doesn't think it's funny, but Baron laughs as Yoko slides her hands down to my butt and squeezes it. Havoc pushes between us and breaks us apart.

Yoko willingly steps back, but she's grinning now. "So, what's this going on between you two? Did the lady killer finally get tamed?"

"Of course not," he mumbles before quickly looking at me like he's worried he's hurt my feelings. "I'm not…"

"Don't hurt yourself," I tease.

He opens his mouth like he wants to say something but bites his lip. Yoko's already forgotten about him, more interested in something Baron is doing. "I'm not like… looking around… or anything. Heaven and hell, you guys are just being evil today."

I can't help but grin at him and feel a little good inside that the question made him so flustered.

"You guys want to play a board game?" Baron suggests.

The café is pretty dead, and on dead nights, we usually do something to entertain ourselves. So Yoko pulls out the board game Life. She lays it out as Baron checks on the remaining customers. I take a seat as Havoc stares at the board.

"That's right, you've probably never played this with us, have you?" Yoko asks.

"Probably not, he's always whoring around," I say.

So I quickly explain the concept to him, being as vague as possible so he loses.

"Basically I need to dominate all of you," Havoc says.

"You can try," Yoko decides.

"Don't underestimate my domination powers." He spins the dial. "Get married," Havoc says in disgust. "As if I'd ever get married."

"You need a spouse," Yoko says as she pushes the little people toward him.

"A single spouse? Ha! As if I would do that," he says as he gathers up a handful and begins filling his entire car with women. When he runs out of room, he just lays them on top.

"There. I am… *married*," he says like the word is disgusting.

"Wait, you forgot Miles," Yoko says as she picks up a little blue guy and lays it on top of the pile of women.

"Eh… I forgot."

"I feel so loved," I say as I spin the dial, but I do notice that by the end of the game, his "Miles piece" is the only one still in the car with him.

Chapter Seven

There's a hard hammering on the apartment door, and Havoc rushes from the bed, sword drawn, ready to cut down whoever is knocking.

"Settle," I mumble as I push the blankets back. "A killer wouldn't knock first."

"Killer or not, they disturbed my sleep," he growls.

I grab my sweats and pull them on as I reach out with my magic to see who it is. It's Baron and he feels panicked, so I rush through the hallway and pull the door open.

"What happened?" I ask.

He's completely naked, chest heaving, with two naked women behind him who seem to be in as bad of sorts as him. Speaking about naked, Havoc is naked as well, still holding his sword as he stares down at them with narrowed eyes.

"My pack… was attacked," Baron says between gasps.

I look at him in alarm. "What? Someone came after you?"

He looks upset as he rubs at his face and I notice that he's filthy. "We were in Everett Woods… some kind of… beast just… attacked us. It was… acting like it was sick, wavering and stumbling, but it was too powerful. I barely got everyone out alive. Thankfully it didn't follow us, or we might not have made it. It was really weird, because the woods… it appeared dead. All the trees had lost their leaves, there were no other animals…"

"What?" I ask. That is worrying. "Come in, take a break, I'll get my stuff. Everyone from your pack is back?"

"Yes, Lunar took the wounded to the hospital. The three of us were the only ones mostly unharmed," Baron says.

Hana, a smaller wolf who I've spoken to a few times says, "I… I think it was the forest spirit."

That makes me stop and look back at her. That would make sense though, wouldn't it? That would be the reason everything in the woods would be dead. Either the woods has died and affected him or something affected him, and it was doing something to the woods.

"Okay," I say. "Grab something to drink. Let me get my stuff." I go into my room and pull on my clothes. Havoc dresses himself as well, as he watches me.

"What do you plan to do?" he asks.

"I'm not sure yet. I guess to start we need to figure out what's happened to him."

"Will you kill him?"

"Only if I have to," I say as I button my pants. There aren't many forest spirits left and it would be horrible to have to kill one.

Havoc sets a hand on my shoulder and gives me a gentle squeeze. "If his land is dead, he's going to die."

"I know," I say as I button my jacket. "But I hate nothing more than seeing another spirit die. Too many have died already."

I fasten my sword to my side and pull on my necklace of charms before heading out to the others. "Are you guys staying here or coming with me?" I ask.

"I'll go," Baron says.

"I'll go as well," Hana says.

"Yeah," Yuna says.

"Alright, thanks," I say as I walk up to Yuna.

I tip her head back as I pull out a small compact filled with ink. She watches me closely as I dip my finger in it and draw a symbol onto her forehead. Then I draw another on her chest and run the line down to her belly button. Then one on each hand and foot.

"This is a barrier and when it breaks, you will feel a snap. If that happens, you will become vulnerable again. That means I want you to retreat," I say.

"Understood," Yuna says as I move on to Hana, and then Baron.

"Do you guys want clothes?" I ask. "Havoc, go get them clothes while I finish up."

Havoc retreats into the bedroom and returns with my clothes since I'm sure he doesn't want to get his dirty. The girls grab them, but Baron shrugs before giving in and putting some sweats on. We head downstairs to my car and get into it.

As I drive, I call a druid I know. If the forest is suffering, he would be the only one who could help it with his connection to the earth.

"Hello?" a groggy voice asks. He is the boss of a nearby district and is always eager to help. I could tell him a weed in my front yard is dying, and he would rush over to assist it.

"Evan, I need your assistance. I've heard that Everett Woods is dying. I'm going to see what's happening, but when I'm finished, I may need you to help it," I say as I slow at a red light.

"Dying? The entire woods?" he asks. I can tell his shock by the inflection in his voice.

"Yes."

"Okay… I'll be there."

***

When we arrive, I can already feel that something is amiss. We're still half a mile from the woods, and the night is dark around us. Everett

Woods was once a forest, but since then, it has been whittled and cut away by the growing civilization, so it is now nothing more than a forgotten patch of trees. But the forest spirit who'd once protected the area, is still confined to the small woods, struggling to keep what is left alive and safe from industrialization.

"Are you sure this is a good idea? Shouldn't we get Rehna to help?" Hana asks nervously.

"Miles can handle anything better than Rehna," Baron says, but Hana and Yuna look doubtful.

Baron pulls his pants off before shifting into a werewolf. His shift is quick and fluent, since he does it so often, but to someone witnessing the shift for the first time, it is a disturbing transformation. It definitely isn't as quick as Havoc shifting to a raven. Once in their other form, werewolves look similar to wolves, other than having a larger frame. In this form, Baron's back comes up to my mid-stomach. His hair is coarse and his fangs are noticeable, even when his mouth is closed. His nails are sharp enough that a swing of his paw could disembowel someone.

The others follow his lead, thankfully after taking their borrowed clothes off so they don't rip them. Werewolves can't shift their clothes with them, so when they shift back, they are always naked. I suppose they could shift with the clothes on, but they'd look quite ridiculous. Havoc, on the other hand, can shift with his clothes and sword and be completely dressed when he shifts back. Don't ask me how. It's magic.

I don't have to wait long before a truck pulls up next to my car, and a man gets out. He looks to be in his forties, although I don't really know how old Evan is. He has dark blond hair that curls around his ears. Right now, it looks like an absolute mess as it sticks up in the back. He is wearing black plastic-framed glasses which contrast sharply with the light color of his hair and beard.

“My entire body aches,” Evan says as he walks over to me. “It’s like the earth around us is just… dead.”

“I can feel it too,” I say as I look in the direction of the woods.

“I’ve never felt such a thing,” he says as I take his hand and start drawing symbols on it. “I can put a barrier around myself.”

“Not if the land is barren,” I say, and he looks at me in surprise.

“You think it’s barren?” he asks. Druids pull all of their magic from the earth, so if the land is now barren, he couldn’t pull any magic from it. He would be as defenseless as any human.

One time we were working together in a high rise building, and he literally showed up carrying a potted bonsai tree so that he was still connected to the earth. He walked around that entire day carrying it. Even as his arms began to tire, he refused to put it down because he knew I would never let him live it down.

“You forgot your bonsai,” I say.

“No, I didn’t,” he says as he reaches into his pocket and pulls out a miniature ficus tree.

“Seriously? If I touch a plant, it just dies and you’re carrying one around in your pocket?”

“Talent,” he says as he whips open his jacket and reveals a necklace made of air plants.

Everyone takes a moment to just stare at Evan. “You’re acting very proud of yourself, but that’s just embarrassing.”

His eyebrows knit, like he’s confused. “Embarrassing? No, no it’s not.”

The consensus seems to be that it is embarrassing. “Eh… um… Sure! Now let’s go.”

I start jogging with the weres next to me. Havoc shifts into a raven and flies above us without getting too far from me. I cast a spell on my eyes so I can see in the dark as if it is still daylight and do the same to Evan.

The woods has been reduced in size over the years, but nothing prepares me for what I come upon. The trees are lifeless, nothing but empty husks. All of the leaves have fallen to the ground or hang lifeless, faded and brown, from the branches. The grass is dead, and the ground is blackened. Miasma creeps up the barks of the trees and is so thick the air feels hard to breathe.

"Gods," Evan whispers as he walks up to a tree and sets his hand against it. He jerks his hand back like it's hot and looks pained. "It's all dead… I can't feel any plant life for miles. What could have done this?"

"A ritual of some sort," I guess. "Evan, do you wish to stay behind? You'll be completely defenseless in here."

"No, I have my bow and your barrier. I'll manage."

"Baron, rush to Evan's side if his barrier breaks and get him out."

Baron nods as I take a step into the woods. I feel the forest spirit's presence in an instant, and Havoc shifts beside me, sword drawn, eyes bloodthirsty.

"He's coming," I say, and I see the weres' bodies tense up.

I take a step forward and see the forest spirit walk out from behind the trees. I have only ever seen him from afar, but he had always seemed tolerant of people in his woods. He has never looked like this. He's the size of a horse, with the body of a white wolf. Red scales run down from under his chin and over his stomach. He has two tails, and his paws are more like a cat's than a dog's. Fangs stretch out over his lips as he bares his teeth at us.

What is strange is that his white coat is covered in darkness, almost as if the tip of his hair is dripping black paint. His eyes are a strange hue of red, and his coat looks dull. He drags his feet like there are weights on them, and I see that, in a way, there are. Shackles of black magic wrap around each paw. His skin is raw around them, blood dripping from the metal. He growls at us as he moves closer.

"Don't move," I warn the others.

"What?" Havoc growls.

"We can help you," I say as I open up my mind to his.

"*Kill… kill… kill…*" His thoughts whip around in mayhem as I watch him carefully.

"Let me help you," I say again.

"*Kill… kill… pain… kill.*"

I assess the situation but I know what I have to do. "I need to touch him without him killing me. I'm going to try to save him."

Havoc turns to me, apparent concern on his face. "There's no land left for him though. He'll go mad from that alone."

"We'll take one hurdle at a time," I say as I calmly walk toward the forest spirit.

Havoc is enraged that I'm putting myself in danger and doesn't even think about calming down as he watches me.

"Miles, stop this," Havoc growls.

"Shh," I whisper as I keep walking.

The beast crouches down as he slinks toward me, eyes locked on me since I'm the closest. Careful to keep my movements slow, I calmly step into him. Suddenly, he rushes me, and I move to the side to avoid him. As he moves past, I press my hand against him, fingers drawing over his fur.

Pain tears through me, and I jerk my hand back. "Fuck," I hiss.

Havoc rushes in to attack, so I grab him tightly and yank him back before he does something we can't reverse.

I know he's worried about what the spirit will do, but I need him to help me. "We're not going to kill him. New plan. We need to figure out what is causing all of the miasma. I can't even touch him without the miasma burning me. Spread out and tell me as soon as you find it. I'm figuring it's a circle of some kind. I'll keep him preoccupied."

Havoc stares at me in disbelief. "I'm not leaving you," he says sternly.

"Go, I can handle it."

"No."

He's angry at me, but I need him to focus. "Havoc, I order you to go," I snap, forcing him to listen to me.

"Fuck," he growls. "Quick, everyone *now*."

They rush out in different directions, and I'm left with the forest spirit alone.

He's delirious with pain and anger. I put an illusion of myself on a tree and he fixates on it, rushing at it as I move the illusion around. He gnashes his teeth as he reaches it, lips pulled back as he snarls. He strikes it, his claws tearing through it and I'm very glad it isn't me standing there. But now he realizes it's not real and isn't fooled by a second one. He fixates on me and rushes at me as I quickly throw a barrier up around me. He hits it and snarls as he fights against it.

"*I'm pissed*," Havoc says into my mind. He sounds upset and the emotions startle me. He's left me in danger more than once and not batted an eye.

"I know you are."

"*I'm not even going to care if that thing tears you apart.*"

"Alright, but I'll be okay."

The forest spirit rushes after me, so I light a row of fire before him, but he runs straight through it like it's nothing.

Suddenly, I hear the werewolves howling and I know that's my cue to get the hell away. Quickly, I start running, but I know he'll reach me before I make it to the others. His four legs are clearly quicker than my two.

"*You hear them?*"

"Yes. Help me get there," I say as I jump a fallen tree and keep moving. I look behind me as he blindly slams into a tree with his shoulder. Overcome by rage, he attacks it, tearing it to the ground. It buys me a little time as I turn my attention to staying alive.

I hear another howl as I run, verifying that I am heading in the correct direction.

"*I'll entertain him. You get there,*" Havoc says.

Even though I don't want to put Havoc in danger, I know he'll be able to handle this situation better than me. "Be safe," I say. "Stay in that form and out of his reach."

"*Understood.*"

I run as quickly as I can to the sound of the werewolves howling. When I reach an opening in the trees, I notice a magic circle right in the middle. The others are already there as I look at them.

"Evan, do you know what the circle is for?" I ask.

He's standing on the circle, bare feet in the middle as he looks down at it. "I'm trying… I think it's just to kill the land."

"They wanted to weaken the forest spirit. They may want him for some reason," I realize. "Protect me. I'm going to be completely vulnerable."

Baron nods his reply and waits for my signal.

I kneel down and press my hand against it as I allow myself to grasp the magic surrounding the magic circle. With a steady breath, I calm my body so that I can gather all the open threads of magic and demolish them. Beneath my feet, I feel the magic circle hum and then collapse as the magic is cut off, and the circle is closed. When I draw myself away from it, I see that our company is trying his hardest to kill everyone. And everyone is trying their hardest to keep me alive. I also notice that the miasma is not as thick now, and the air feels more breathable. Destroying the circle won't bring life back to the land, but it will remove the miasma that killed the land.

"Okay, back up," I say as I turn to the forest spirit.

He rushes at me, and Havoc moves in to protect me.

"Havoc, get back," I say. "Let me handle this."

He growls at me but steps back, giving me room to move. I step out of the way of the forest spirit as he lunges for me, teeth gnashing as I feel spittle spray my cheek. Angry he missed, he turns and rushes at me, so I hold my hand up and reach for him with my magic.

"Submit," I say into his mind.

I need to break the hold the magic has around each of his paws before even trying to reach his mind.

"*Kill… ki… kill… ill… kill…*"

My magic snakes along the ground like wisps of smoke as it crawls onto the beast's legs. He slows down as I hold him with my magic. Saliva is running out of his mouth as touches of gold begin to wash away the red of his eyes.

"Submit," I say as I move toward him.

He growls deeply as I slowly walk up to him. He strikes out with his claws and tosses his head around. He is panting hard as I reach out and touch his forehead, sinking my fingers into his fur. He cringes back and then lunges forward, slamming into me. I fall back, but Havoc catches me before I hit the ground and guides me toward the beast so I can continue breaking the spell. The beast jerks back and starts backing away from me.

"Submit," I growl, and he drops down to his knees. "Submit."

He falls onto his side, and I kneel down and press my hand against his forehead, tearing away the binds that keep him suppressed. Finally, I drag away the last of the miasma, freeing him of it.

He looks up at me and then drops his head. "Please kill me," he says, voice rich but full of pain.

"No, I refuse."

He's shaking beneath my hand and I want to comfort him. I can *feel* his pain as he says, "My land is gone, there's nothing left. Please, allow death to consume me."

"Let's see if we can bring it back before you completely give up." My fingers sink into his white fur in hopes of encouraging him.

"The forest is dead," he growls as now golden eyes flash over to me. "I know better than anyone that it is dead."

"Let's figure that out for sure first," I say as I get up. "Come on."

He hesitates but slowly rises to his feet.

"Evan, come here," I say, and Evan walks up to us hesitantly. "Do you feel any plant life?"

He takes his shoes off and steps onto the ground. He looks up at me and shakes his head.

The forest spirit growls. "I told you—"

"Wait until I say that I give up before you give up."

"There's nothing," he growls. "If a druid can't do it, you can't."

"Alright, Evan, we're going to try something. It may not work… it probably won't work, but it's worth a try. Come, sit with me."

He sits down in front of me.

"I'm going to feed you my magic, and you're going to find even the littlest scrap of a seed and make it grow."

He raises an eyebrow. "I don't know if I have the power for that," he says hesitantly.

He might be right, but I'm still going to give it the best try that I can. "I will create a circuit between us so the magic will flow through us, allowing you to use whatever amount of my magic you need," I explain as I pull out a marker. I draw matching symbols on our palms and then grab his hands. “Ready?

“Yes,” he says.

I can feel his magic wrapping around me. To my eyes, it almost looks green, like vines. I welcome it and feed my own magic into it as the druid chants something in a language I don’t know. For a long moment, it seems like nothing is going to happen. He might be right and together we’re just not powerful enough. And that’s when I see the black miasma begin to fade away. I can’t help but smile as I watch the earth between us as the ground begins to grow a rich brown. Suddenly, the earth cracks just a sliver, and a small bud of green peeks out before reaching upward a few inches until a single leaf curls out from it.

Evan takes a deep breath. “That’s all I can do… How are you so powerful?” he asks.

I wink at him. “It’s a secret.”

He gives me a half-grin. “I couldn’t even sort through the power you were throwing at me.”

The forest spirit brings his nose down and touches the sapling before lying down and staring at it. “Can you do more?” he pleads.

I’m exhausted just thinking about it. “Not right now. This night has sapped a lot out of all of us, but it proves that you have something to live for. It’ll come back. I promise.”

“I’ll come back every week and help it grow,” Evan promises.

“Are the ones who did this still alive?” the forest spirit asks.

“Yes,” I say. “And I fear you’re not safe here. They needed you for some reason. All of this was to weaken you. I don’t know if it was to kill you or if they wished to control you, but you’re no longer safe here.”

“I will kill them,” he growls, and the hair on the back of his neck stands on end.

"I'm working on it," I say. "But you'll be even weaker without the life of your forest. They'll come back for you, so I ask you to come with me until this is all over."

He looks down at the sapling and then back at me. "I want to help you to repay you for what you've done. But what if they return? This is all I have left."

"They probably will return," I say truthfully.

"You could take the sapling with you?" Evan suggests. "That way it's protected until we know no harm will come again to these woods."

The large beast turns to me, golden eyes watching me closely. "Will you allow me to serve you in order to repay you?"

"You don't need to repay me, and I don't want your service. But if you wish to assist me, then I'll gratefully accept."

"May I ask your name?" he asks.

"Milliant, but you can call me Miles."

He stares at me for a moment as he thinks. "That name sounds familiar. Have we met before?"

"In passing. Your name?"

"Badrick," he says. "I apologize to all of you whom I've caused harm."

"We're all okay," I say.

"I am thankful for that," Badrick says.

"Alright, now let us get you home," I say.

Evan digs up the sapling since he could basically step on the thing, rip it apart, and forget to water it, and it would still grow. I glance at a plant and it gives up on life.

We walk back to the vehicles and only then do I realize that I have a dilemma.

"I don't suppose you'll ride on the roof of the car?" I ask.

The forest spirit looks over at me and cocks his head.

“Right. Evan, do you mind dropping our new friend off at my house?” I ask.

Badrick eyes the vehicles before cocking his head. “You wish me to ride in the back of a truck?”

“Yes,” I say.

He stares at me, then the truck, but he seems to remember that the reason we are covered in dirt and bruises is because of him and climbs into the bed of the truck. He sits down and Evan gives me a look, but I just smile at him.

“See you at home,” I say with a wink.

“Uh huh… great.”

Chapter Eight

I watch as Havoc wanders around the café, pestering everyone he can. Surprisingly, or maybe not, everyone seems to love it. They laugh and lean into him, like they're eager to hear what he has to say next.

I sigh and head up the stairs since I really should be doing something for work instead of staring at Havoc and trying to figure him out. Seems to be a weird pastime.

"What are you doing?" Havoc asks, making me jump.

"You scared me! Where did you come from?"

He cackles, clearly impressed with himself. "Heaven probably."

I snort. "Yeah… yeah… that's not likely."

His smile falls. "What's that mean?"

I shake my head as I try to fight the grin. "No idea."

"What's been up with you?"

"With?"

"Miles… I know you way too well. Like sickeningly well. It's almost creepy how well I know you. I know something's up. Are you going to talk to me? You're allowed to give everyone else the silent treatment, not me. Because I'm special."

I can't hold back the grin any longer. "You're definitely that. I don't know… just been thinking about everything. About us."

"Like us or *us*."

"I'm not sure there's a difference."

"I know. I'm amazing in both instances. Is it because of the hot and sweaty sex?"

I hesitate, unsure whether to voice my concerns. Despite all the amazing sex we've had, we really haven't discussed what it means to us, to our friendship, and it's started to eat away at me, apparently to the point that even Havoc has noticed something off. I decide to take the plunge and just say it. "Maybe. It's kind of… you're the person I care most about in my life. I would be so lost without you. I know we butt heads, but I can't imagine two people who've been together for hundreds of years not butting heads. But I don't want to lose you or our relationship because I don't know where our relationship is going."

"You're worried I'm going to… leave you?"

"No… I'm worried things will become weird between us, when I don't want that."

"Miles, things will become weird. Things between us have always been weird. Isn't that how we work? I mean… have we ever not been weird?"

I step up to him and he pats me on the head like I'm a dog.

"There there, I promise we'll always be strange and weird."

"Alright, I have to be honest… I've been thinking of sending your hairy ass back to the demon realm for treating me like I'm a dog."

He grabs me in a bear hug. "You'd miss me."

"I have no idea why."

"I do," he says as I sink into his hug, even if I'm still trying to act like I don't want it. "Don't worry so much. That's our thing, ya know? Just go with it. Let life take you where it wants. Remember that time we ran into that castle with no plans at all?"

"And you got the hair on your balls singed? Because we had no plans. That's how you're wanting to go about this?"

He loosens his hug slightly and gives me a grin filled with his fangs. "Exactly."

I start laughing. "How about with less ball hair singe?"

"I *guess* if we have to."

"You're ridiculous. Now I came up here to do some work in the quiet."

"*Or* I bet we could find something more fun to do."

"Ooh…"

"Brownies! Make me brownies! All the chocolate."

"I'm not making you brownies!"

He pushes my chin up and kisses me gently. "What about now?"

"Hmm… no. You're not that cute," I say. "Hey, Havoc?"

"What?"

"Thanks."

"Anytime. Especially if there are brownies or chocolate involved."

"I'll make you freaking brownies!"

"Double chocolate."

"Double chocolate," I say as I step from him.

"Don't worry about things, Miles. I've always liked your smile the best. Especially when you're attacking things and covered in blood."

"That's… no… remember me telling you that you're strange?"

"Yet you still like me more than anyone else!"

"I do."

***

My phone rings and I jerk awake. "What NOW?" I growl. I had basically *just* fallen asleep, and now someone is calling. I grab my phone and yank it from the cord as I slide the accept button. "Hello?"

"Miles, I think there's someone in my house," Sam says.

I sit up, startled. "What?"

“*Someone is in my house*,” he hisses.

“I’ll be right there. What’s your address?”

He rattles it off to me as I smack Havoc awake. It just makes him grumble and curl up tighter.

“We’ll be right there,” I say. “Havoc, I need you to fly to Sam’s house. Someone is in his house.”

Havoc looks at me for a moment. “Sam you say? He’ll be fine,” he decides as he slowly pulls his pillow over his head like I wouldn’t notice.

I give him a kick as I get up. “Come on, Havoc, now.”

“Fuck, fine,” he says and grabs his sword as I rush over to the window.

Butt naked, with only a sword, he walks up to me and stretches. Then he shifts and lands on my shoulder as a raven. He preens his feathers as I unlock the window. As soon as I have the window open, he hops off my shoulder and flies out.

“You don’t know the address!” I yell.

He swings around and flies back to me as I plug the address into my GPS. I hit start, and Havoc grabs my phone in his talons and flies off for a second time.

“Now *I* don’t know it!” I yell after him as I can hear an echo of “Proceed to the route. Proceed to the route.”

“*This thing is ridiculously annoying, Miles. You gotta give me a minute, you stupid lady*,” Havoc mutters.

With a huff, I rush over to the computer and pull up Google Maps so I can type the address into it. I press print, and the printer slowly begins to print out the directions. I take that time to get dressed and grab the directions on my way through the door.

I try to read them as I run out to my car but I can’t remember the last time I relied on an actual piece of paper to get me anywhere. While getting into the driver’s seat, I can’t help but wonder how a mage as powerful as myself has to resort to paper directions and running around in a car. I throw my car into reverse, hit the curb, and realize I can't read directions in the dark. I reach around until I find the interior lights.

"How did people live like this?" I groan as I juggle driving ninety while reading the directions.

I zoom right past the road I need to turn on, so I make a U turn and back track to the correct road. My brain is nearly fried by the time I make it to a two-story house on the edge of town. I don't waste time turning the car off as I jump out, sword drawn, and burst through the front door.

Havoc, butt-ass naked, steps up in front of me, holding the severed head of a man in his left hand and his sword in the other. "I took care of it as you fucked around. Did you stop for a manicure or something?"

I take a deep sigh of relief. "Thank you. Where's Sam?"

Havoc slowly looks over at me then quickly looks at the severed head. "Oh man, for a moment I couldn't remember what Sam looked like, and I realized that it might have been *his* head I cut off, but I don't think it is. Right? He has dark hair, right? This chap here looks like he doesn't... I think. I honestly don't know."

I quickly look over at the head, but with all of the blood, it's hard to tell whose head it is.

I stare at him in disbelief. "Havoc... I swear to god, if you've cut Sam's head off, I'll cut your nuts off."

"I'm alive..." Sam whispers as he creeps around a corner. Then he sees the man's head before turning a very pale shade of green. "Holy hell. You cut his head off."

Havoc shrugs like none of this is concerning. "Well, he tried killing me, so yes, I cut his head off. Catch!" Havoc says as he tosses the head at Sam.

Sam stumbles back as the head hits the ground in front of him. "Urgh..." he moans before rushing into the kitchen.

Havoc laughs wildly as he walks over to the head.

"Just… *leave it,*" I snap. "You alright, Sam?" I go into the kitchen and find Sam leaning against the breakfast table.

"Yeah… thanks… I think…" he says.

"Did you call it in?"

"Not yet," he says. "Why would someone come here?"

"I don't know. Were you getting too close to information they didn't want you to know?" I ask.

Sam starts pacing as he throws up his hands. "I don't know. I mean, yeah I was looking into the case, but I didn't have any big breakthrough."

It doesn't seem like we've gotten too close to anything as a team. "Okay. I think to be safe, I'm going to have someone watch over you. Is that alright?"

"Uh. I guess. Just… maybe not Havoc? Maybe someone who can recognize my face. I mean that guy was Asian and I'm Latino and he didn't notice?"

Um… I couldn't tell either. "I totally agree," I say as I pick a marker up off the counter. "Havoc, how could you not have noticed that? Sam, go ahead and call it in, I'll be right back."

I head outside to the driveway as Havoc follows.

"You do realize you're still naked?"

"Completely. It's freeing, but there's an added sense of… difficulty, like… you have to protect *two* things instead of one."

"Yeah, you and Sam."

"Oh… I was talking about my penis. But yes, Sam and me. So… what are you doing?"

"Summoning someone to watch over Sam so I can go home and sleep," I say as I draw a circle, then work on the intricacies of the middle. I set my hand against the circle. "Iya, I summon you."

I barely get the words out before Iya is crawling out of the broken ground. His bull-like face peeks up at me before he clambers through.

"You… *summoned me?*" he asks with his Irish-influenced accent.

"I did," I say as the minotaur-like demon eagerly watches me.

His excitement is apparent even though his expression shows differently. "I missed you too," he purrs with a grin.

"I need you to do something for me," I say.

He reaches out and trails a finger over my chest that Havoc immediately smacks away. "Anything for you."

"You remember the young detective who was in the room the day Havoc sent you here instead of coming himself?"

Iya thinks about it for a moment before making a huffing noise. "He was a very handsome fellow."

"I need you to protect him," I say.

He nods, instantly agreeing. "May I penetrate him?"

I'm not even sure why the question surprises me. "Um… not unless he asks?"

"That's reasonable," he says with a nod. "Alright! I will protect him with my life."

"Good choice, Miles," Havoc says. "Send the horny bull in as a protector."

"He'll be just fine," I assure him as I lead Iya into the house.

Sam looks at me startled when I come in with a half-man, half-bull behind me. The human parts of his body are bulky, and he is barely clothed, showing his muscles. The demon is a brick wall, and that's why I've used him for protection. I once saw him knock someone unconscious just by bumping into them.

"I don't know why I thought you'd bring like… a human bodyguard or something," Sam says. "Haha… foolish me."

"Human, I come to penetrat—protect you," Iya says, and I am reminded again why I shouldn't dabble with demons.

Sam is staring at him with eyes so large I'm surprised they don't dry out. "Were you going to say *penetrate?*"

"No," Iya says, shaking his head. "Unless that is the kind of thing you are into? Then, yes."

Sam turns his attention to me as if I'm some kind of traitor, but a car pulling into the driveway creates the distraction I need to escape. "That's my cue to leave," I say. "Have… fun? Iya, don't… traumatize him."

Iya huffs. "Unless he *wants* to be traumatized, right?"

"Exactly," I say as I head out the door. I don't get very far before Sam runs after me.

"Um… excuse me. Miles?" He desperately grabs onto my arm.

"Yeah?" I ask as I turn to face him.

He stares at me with a funny expression on his face. "I really… uh… *appreciate* all of this, but I think I'm fine without whatever that is. I mean he was going to say penetrate, wasn't he?"

I laugh as I look at Sam. "Iya says exactly what he thinks, but he'd never harm you. I've worked with him many times, and he's actually easy to get along with. You just have to remind him to wear clothes."

"Okay… I'm trusting you." He doesn't look very trusting.

"Good because I am a very trustworthy guy," I say.

Havoc snorts.

"Shut up, Havoc, let's go," I say. "If you need anything, let me know."

Chapter Nine

"Sit on my lap," Havoc says as he pats it like I'm a dog.

I stare at his lap and realize it could be very fun to sit on that lap, but it would also require moving from where I'm curled up on the couch.

"It's a very nice lap. You know you want to," he taunts as he pats it again.

"It *is* a very nice lap."

"Then come sit."

"But… this couch is nicer," I say before snuggling under my blanket as I give him a wicked grin.

While we haven't exactly talked any more about what our relationship is or could become, we've fallen into a familiar routine that has kept me satisfied. We talk, joke, and fuck.

We're like an old married couple but seeing as we've known each other for hundreds of years, it's not surprising that we just know how to get along. It helps that there's no longer the tension between us that came with me being annoyed at him for sleeping with everyone and him snapping back at me. I hadn't realized how much that had driven a spike between us until I really thought about it.

"You're getting that constipated look on your face again like you're trying to remember how to use your brain, but you keep forgetting that you really don't have much of one in there," Havoc says.

I chuck a pillow at him, which he smacks out of the way while grinning at me. There's *definitely* no way I can crawl over to his lap now, even if it promises many joyful things.

"Don't be shy, there's enough room for you with your bony ass."

"My ass is perfect."

"Who told you that? Your reflection?"

"Maybe. Here, you can enjoy it," I say as I turn away from him and pull the blanket back so only my ass is showing. Then I pull my sweats down so he sees just my crack.

He gasps dramatically. "It's beautiful."

"Thank you. My momma made it."

He snorts. "At least she did one nice thing for you."

"She was such a bitch, you know with the whole leaving me behind thing."

"Didn't she sell you for like a bag of potatoes? I mean, I would think you'd have at least been worth a goat or something. Even like a half dead one."

I turn to glare at him. "I'm going to trade you for a half-dead goat."

"Oh, sweetheart, I'm worth *so* much more than that. You wouldn't trade me for anything. You L-O-V-E me."

I sigh. "It's sickening, I know. But it's like after spending hundreds of years with something, you start to love it even if you wish you didn't."

He gives me a wicked grin. "I have been the best thing that ever happened to you."

I think about it for a ridiculously long time. Long enough that his grin begins to fall. "Okay… I know this is going to sound crazy, but it's a tie between you and that coat I used to have. You know that green one."

"The one that looked like baby shit? Yeah, I gave that to the homeless man on the side of the road and he said that it was so ugly he'd rather freeze to death than wear it," Havoc says nonchalantly.

I watch him for a moment as I try to figure out if he's lying. Of course he isn't. "You asshole. I hunted for that coat for weeks."

"And every time you did, I'd giggle a little."

The thought of Havoc giggling makes me laugh. "You're the worst person I've *ever* met."

"Did you forget about your mom who traded you for a chicken?"

"She didn't even trade me for a chicken. She just left me."

"I'd have at least gotten a chicken out of you," he says like the ass he is. "Now come sit on my lap."

"*Really*? You just told me you'd have traded me for a *chicken*."

He throws his arms up in mock exasperation. "It was a compliment!"

I snort. "How was *any* of that a compliment?"

"I told you I'd trade you for an old dried up chicken! Now come over here and warm my lap up."

"Hmm… what do I get in return?"

"Oh, I can give you something alright," he says as he winks at me.

"Ew." I make a show of cringing. "How about you give me something I actually want."

"You don't want my penis?"

"Eh…"

"Tell me it's the best penis you've ever seen."

"I like my penis more."

"Besides your own penis. Mine is the best." The poor man is *so* confident.

I suppose he does have a right to be, it is a pretty nice penis but I will *never* let him know that. "I've seen Iya's penis. It's *huge*."

"Are you trying to make me *jealous*?" he growls. *That* gets him up as he rushes over and sits down on me, crushing me.

I push against him but he grabs my arms and pins them to the couch. "You're killing me!"

"Good. Maybe I'll crush some sense into you," he growls. He leans over so his hair is hanging down and smirks at me. It makes me want to kiss him, but I know I can't give in.

"You know what I could use right now?"

"A nice big hot—"

"Shower! I know!"

"Dick."

"What?" I ask like I'm confused.

"They say in lore that demons came from hell, but if I came from hell then where did you come from?"

"Heaven, of course."

He snorts before leaning down, lips so close to mine I could touch them if I *just* gave in. Oh how I want to give in.

"I see you twitching to touch me," he whispers, voice low and deep. "As if I couldn't already *feel* how much you want me."

"Then kiss me," I say as I lean into him, and that's the moment my phone rings. Sadly, I sink onto the couch as Havoc grabs it.

"Hey sweetheart," he answers.

"Who is it?" I ask, alarmed.

Havoc grins down at me, clearly enjoying this. "You sure you want him? I'm better than him."

I yank the phone from his ear. "Hello?"

"Miles? It's Rehna," she says. "I heard about last night with the forest spirit. Is he still alive?"

"Yeah, he's in the spare bedroom," I say as Havoc teasingly draws a finger down my chest until he finds a nipple.

"You have him in your *house*?" she asks.

"Yeah, I laid a doggie bed down for him," I joke.

“Don’t forget that he is a sacred creature.”

“I haven’t,” I say just as Havoc pinches my nipple. “Ow!”

“What?” Rehna asks as Havoc grins like a fiend.

“Ah, nothing. Stubbed my toe.” I try crawling out from under him to get away, but he keeps me pinned down.

Rehna continues on, despite my struggling. “We are calling a council meeting this evening and would like you to join. All the surrounding district bosses will be there, and we want you and the detectives there as well.”

“I’m being invited to a council meeting?” I ask, thoroughly surprised.

“Yes, be there at six o’clock. Don’t be late.”

“Where at?”

“My shrine.”

“Alright,” I say. “See you then.”

“Yes. Invite the humans as well for me.”

“Yeah, sure,” I say.

I hang up and look up at Havoc. “We are invited to a council meeting.”

He rocks back, crushing my insides even more. “We are? How interesting. You need to state your dominance, so you’ll need a suit.”

“Why a suit?” I ask curiously.

“Men look sexy when they’re wearing a suit.”

“You’re right. I need a suit,” I say as I push him off me. Then I head for the hallway. I knock on the guest room door before pushing it open.

Badrick is lying on the floor, staring at the sapling that’s between his front paws like it’s the Holy Grail.

“A watched pot never boils,” I say.

He looks up, startled. “I was supposed to be watching a pot? I apologize, I did not know.”

I shake my head. “No! I just… it’s a saying. That when you watch something you’re eagerly waiting for, it won’t happen.”

He stands up. “Where is this pot you would like me to watch? What is inside of it?”

Havoc snickers from behind me as I shake my head. “Anyway. So… Badrick, we’re going to a council meeting tonight. Would you like to go?” I ask.

“Yes,” he says. “I will do anything to help find the people who destroyed my land.”

“Great, so we’re going to leave in a few hours… and I have no way to get you there. Can you teleport?”

He stares at me.

“Fly?”

He continues to stare at me. “Are you… trying to make a joke?”

“I am.”

“It wasn’t funny,” he says.

Havoc chuckles. “Told you that you aren’t funny.”

“Thanks for your brutal honesty,” I say to both of them. “So… a truck then?”

“Okay.”

“Well, seeing as I don’t own a truck, let’s go buy one,” I say.

“You do not need to buy a truck for me,” he says. “I cannot even properly watch a pot.”

“Are you going to run everywhere? It’s fine, I’m rich. Now come along. Your plant will be fine here.”

“It’s a maple tree,” he says.

“Your maple tree will be just fine.”

“What if someone bumps it over?”

"No one will be in here. It'll be fine," I assure him.

He nods slowly. "Okay, human, let's go."

"We'll be back in a bit," I tell Havoc. "Can you get the stuff together while I'm gone?"

"Yeah… be safe."

I give him a smile, pleasantly surprised. "Of course."

Badrick follows me down the stairs and into the café where everyone looks up with wide eyes. Honestly, I'm not sure why they are ever surprised when I bring something new through these doors. Then again, none of them have ever seen a forest spirit in my café, so I guess I understand their slight concern. We head out into the street and start walking for the nearest car dealership.

"It smells horrible," Badrick says.

"What does?" I ask curiously.

He sneezes, spraying snot down my leg. "Everything. The air, the ground, the people." He stops suddenly and looks at some flower decoration in front of a store front. "What is this?"

"What? The decoration?"

"It's fake!" he says as he stares at the plants. "Why would you plant fake flowers when you can have real flowers? Are these people ill?"

"You're… not around people much, are you?" I ask.

"No, I am not," he admits.

"Some people are lazy, but they like the beauty of a plant. Or maybe they can't keep one alive, so they buy a fake one," I explain.

"Despicable." He's clearly disgusted.

A woman walks out of a store and stops suddenly, staring at us in terror. She's wearing a short skirt and a bra with just a fishnet shirt over it. If Havoc was here, he'd be ecstatic.

"That poor woman. Give her some money," Badrick says as he stares at the woman.

“Um… why?” I ask as the woman looks at us in concern.

“She has worn her shirt so ragged, there are holes everywhere. You just said you are rich, clothe the poor woman.”

The “poor woman” is now looking down at her shirt before quickly backing into the store she just came from.

“That’s called fashion.”

Badrick is quiet for a moment. “It’s fashionable to wear the same clothes until they are ragged? So, you must think you’re fashionable?”

I look down at my clothes. “My clothes aren’t ragged. I mean, yeah… I’ve had this hoodie a long time, but it’s comfortable.”

“Hm… fashion is confusing.”

“It’s a style… you know what? Never mind,” I say. “Let’s hurry along.” Before I get criticized for anything else.

We walk up to the dealership after a rather harried walk that makes me realize that maybe I need a muzzle for him as well. I’m honestly surprised we weren’t shot after he started questioning a guy who thought the lower his pants were, the more gangster he was.

“Stay here,” I say, honestly wishing I’d left him at home.

“No thanks,” he says as he pushes past me and through the door.

Everyone is staring at the giant dog, and I’m left questioning my patience.

“Uh… uh wel… come?” a man asks, clearly nervous. “How… can I help you?”

“I need a truck for my dog. I just adopted him, and he doesn’t fit in my car.” I wave at Badrick who seems to be giving the man terrors.

“You… adopted him?”

“Of course. Why would I buy a purebred when so many dogs need a home? I really wanted a lap dog but how can you say no to these eyes?” I ask as I grab Badrick’s face in my hands.

He's staring at me like I've lost my mind. "Okay… let's… see what we have. What are you looking for?"

"I don't know. Some type of truck."

"Year?"

"New."

"Brand?"

"Don't care."

"Backseat?"

"Sure," I say.

"Okay," he says warily, like he has a reason to be suspicious of us.

But, being the good salesman that he is, he heads out the door. He takes me over to the newer trucks and starts rattling off nonsense about them which I don't listen to at all.

I see one with a window that opens in the back and point. "I'll take that one."

"You want to test drive it?"

"No thanks, I'm just going to use it when I have to take him around. Badrick, do you fit?" I ask as I put the tailgate down. He jumps up into it and looks around.

"I feel like a fool," he says as he stares down at me.

I nod, whole-heartedly agreeing to this. "You look like a fool."

"It talks…" the man says.

"Alright. How do I pay for this thing? A check?"

"Uh… right this way," he says as he leads us inside. "Have a seat."

I do, and Badrick goes over and stares at a fish tank.

"Miles, why are there fish in this box? Are they stuck?"

"No, that's a fish tank."

"Why?"

"What?"

"Why are they stuck in this box?"

“Because people like looking at fish, but not everyone can live near the ocean where they can see them. So they keep them in a tank. As pets.”

“How horrid. Miles, come help me set them free.”

“They’d die if you set them free. Just don’t worry about it.”

“I am very worried about it,” he says as he stares at them.

When we’re finally finished, I head out the door with the keys and get into the truck. Badrick jumps into the back, and I slide open the rear window. He stuffs his head inside and looks around.

“I like it,” he decides.

“Good,” I say as I drive the truck home.

During the entire ride, I have to answer five million questions and begin to wonder why I thought a window was a good idea. Maybe I can use magic to “break” it so it never opens again. I park it next to my car and get out as the truck starts to bounce around.

“My head is stuck!” Badrick growls as he puts his paws against the cab and pulls. His head is, indeed, stuck in the window.

The smart thing probably would be to help, but instead, I run inside and get Havoc and Yoko, so we can laugh as a family.

“Help me, human, before I crush you between my fangs,” he growls as his paw puts a huge dent in the cab of my brand-new truck. “Then I will keep you in one of those… tanks of fish.”

Chapter Ten

I park the truck outside Rehna's forest and get out. The shrine is not accessible by road, so we'll have to walk the last part.

"Badrick?" I ask as he jumps out of the bed of the truck. "I've been thinking, and I feel like you kind of owe me."

He nods. "Yes, I owe you my life," he says.

This poor innocent creature. "So… this council thing is a big deal. They've never invited me, so I would like to make an impression when I arrive," I say.

"Understandable," he says with a nod of his massive head.

"I'll just cut to the chase. Can I ride on your back?"

He stares at me for a long moment and then looks over at Havoc, who is grinning seeing as he also agreed it was a great idea.

With the longest sigh known to mankind he says, "Fine. I always repay my debts, and if this is how you'd prefer them repaid, then so be it. But this will be my repayment. So, if in the future you need me for something, say… to save your life, I will have to remind you that my debt is paid."

I grin. "That's fine. Everyone will remember how awesome I looked when they share stories at my funeral," I say as I walk over to him and set my hand on his back before climbing on. It takes me back to the good old days when I raised hell atop my black stallion. "Havoc, get a picture of me."

Havoc pulls out the phone I bought him so we won't have to struggle with the archaic tradition of printing directions again.

"I wish you had left me to die," Badrick says, and I laugh before posing for Havoc's picture.

Havoc gives me a thumbs up and a wink. "Got it."

"Awesome. Now get me like a theme song to ride in to," I say. "What about 'Gangsta's Paradise'? I feel like I could connect to my inner gangster."

"I gotcha covered," Havoc says as he starts the song. He hands me the phone before shifting and flying to my shoulder.

"Onward!" I shout over the blaring music a moment before the lyrics cut in to "Amish Paradise."

Havoc is cawing maniacally in his birdlike way of laughing, so I shut the song off.

"Fine, no song," I say. "Let's go."

Badrick bolts, and I grab onto him as he lopes into the woods, moving between the trees with ease, and a part of me realizes how much I miss the old days. Back when I tore across this land with a horse and my magic. No rules. Nothing. Just pure power.

"I miss this," I say.

"*I do too,*" Havoc says. "*My favorite times were always when I pretended like I couldn't hear you, and I'd sit back and make bets with the townspeople on who would win the fight.*"

I look over at him startled. "Is that where you kept getting all of that money? I thought you were like… stealing it or something."

"*No, my dear. I was betting. I was very good at it because no one else would put money on you.*"

"Of course," I grumble. Sometimes, I can't help but question why I've cared about him for so long. "You know what? Maybe I don't miss it because the plumbing sure sucked back then."

"*No internet.*"

"Eh."

"*I like now.*"

"Me too," I decide.

Badrick slows down as he reaches the shrine, and my audience looks up at me. Rehna is the first to react by rushing up to me and grabbing my arm so she can yank me down… or break it. I'm not quite sure which.

"He is a sacred creature, you idiot!" she growls.

Being ripped off Badrick's back makes the whole thing slightly embarrassing as the entire council watches.

"Yes, but we looked badass when we rode in," Havoc says after he shifts back into his human form, his feather cloak rustling around him.

"It was fun," Badrick admits. "Now, do you have coffee? Miles' female human gave me coffee, and I do like coffee."

"What about something soothing, like tea?" she suggests.

He shakes his massive head. "No, it has to be coffee." He eagerly follows after her.

Havoc leans into me. "I don't think they thought we looked as cool as we thought we did," he mumbles as he stares at the gawking council members.

"I don't think so, either. Now I'm starting to wonder if the suit was too much," I mutter as I tug on it.

Havoc looks over at me. "Well… with all the white dog hair stuck to it, I'm starting to think you should have gone for white or at least a pastel."

When I look down, I realize that it looks like I decided to wear a fur suit.

"But you're handsome in about anything. Or nothing," he whispers.

"I thought you looked cool," Evan says as he walks up.

He's wearing earrings made from living air plants which makes him the last person I want fashion advice from. I just stare at him as I try to figure out if he wants to look like an idiot or if that's just how he looks.

"Yeah... that doesn't mean anything coming from you," I say.

"What do you mean?" He looks down at his clothes. "I am very hip."

"Are you?" I ask. "Does your district respect you? Or just... laugh at you?"

"They love me." His eyebrows furrow like he's confused on why I would say such a thing.

"Come, let us begin!" Rehna shouts, and everyone heads inside.

Sam sees us first, and he rushes over to us as Johnson and Iya follow.

"Hey, guys. Iya, are you being good?" I ask.

"I am perfect," Iya says, looking mightily proud of himself. "I stopped an attacker from sticking papers through the door this morning."

"The mailman. You stopped the mailman from delivering mail," Sam mutters as we head into a meeting room.

Everyone takes a seat at a large oval table that fills most of the room.

I recognize everyone at the table but don't know any of them extremely well. There are six council members present, all of them a district boss of the surrounding areas.

"So, I am sure you've noticed the new faces today," Rehna says. "Each of our districts has had a person killed and a paper from the Velmah de Rizen left behind with them. This is Detective Sam Diaz and Lieutenant Danny Johnson. This is currently their case, and they have been in charge of it so far. And this is Miles Shavold," she says using my more current name.

"What is Miles' position? Is he also a detective?" a man named Jacob Stewart asks.

He is a mage like me, so I have followed some of his work. His district deals with the nearby university that he founded and ran. It has special classes for those wishing to learn how to control their abilities.

"No, Miles is a mage who is helping out," Rehna says.

"Is it okay to involve others in this?" a woman named Pepper asks.

"Miles is… quite capable of taking care of himself," a man named Aiden says. Aiden is an incubus I ran into some time ago, but we definitely don't need to get into that story. He has mellowed quite a bit since then. Now he runs a district alongside his harem and acts like an actual adult.

That also means he's not as much fun.

It made people nervous when Aiden became the district boss since an incubus can talk just about anyone into doing just about anything. But, so far, people have really warmed up to Aiden.

"Hello, Aiden," I say.

He takes a deep breath and nods. "Miles… I would say it's good to see you, but I'm not sure yet," he jokes.

I grin and notice Havoc looking between us before allowing a huge smirk to cross his face. "This is that incubus you—"

I clamp a hand over his mouth. "Continue on, Rehna."

"Yes, please do," Aiden says hurriedly.

A few of the council members are curiously leaning toward us, but Aiden quickly waves Rehna on.

"Um… okay, as I was saying, this is the list of people who were killed. Could each of you look through them and try to think of something connecting the fifteen victims that the detectives haven't found?" Rehna asks.

Evan leans forward as he plays with a container holding a plant. "They were all in different districts, right?"

"Some. There were three here in Rehna's district, but only one in Evan's district," Johnson says as he slides a map into the middle of the table.

"Location doesn't seem to matter. The only thing we do know is that it appears like everyone died on the same day, at the exact same time," he says.

I glance down at the map and look at the small circles, each with a name written on it. I stare at it for a long moment before something starts to pull at me. If the circles were connected… no… that can't be. Can it?

Quickly, I stand up and reach across the table. I grab the map and drag it over to me as I look down at it, examining it more closely. God, I hope I'm wrong.

"Someone have a pen?" I ask.

Johnson passes me a marker he had been messing with. I take it from him as I lean over the map.

"What if we've been looking at this wrong? We've been so focused on *who* they killed and how they were connected. What if they weren't connected in the way we are thinking?" I ask as I draw a huge circle on the map with all of the victims inside of it. "What if it didn't matter who they killed, but *where* they killed them. And they were trying to throw us off the right path with all of this Velmah de Rizen nonsense. They knew it was a name that instilled fear. It would cause some panic and keep our focus on it. It kept us trying to find a connection that doesn't exist."

I start to draw lines, connecting the dead until I have drawn a magic circle. When I'm finished, I push the map into the middle of the table. "It's a magic circle. I'm not sure what kind, but this is clearly the start of it."

"Jacob, do you recognize what the circle would be for?" Pepper asks.

Jacob takes the paper and examines it as I think about it. He runs his finger over the circle while mumbling something before shaking his head. "I… don't know… I can't imagine what would take this much area. Or this many sacrifices, but you're right, it really does look like a circle of some kind."

"What about a summoning circle?" Evan asks. "Is it anything like the ones you use to call for demons?"

"I don't dabble with demons," Jacob says as he looks over at me disapprovingly. Like dabbling with demons is a bad thing.

I look over at Iya who is sniffing Sam's hair as Sam leans away from him and Havoc who is playing solitaire on my phone while looking ridiculously handsome.

"No. Havoc, can you think of anything?" I ask.

He quickly puts the phone down. "Hmm? What? Uh… No? Is it a necromancer's circle, since it's clear that a necromancer laid a trap on the bodies?"

I shake my head. "No. Necromancer circles are different," I say. "But… I have an idea. Jacob, you're well versed in magic, come here."

"What are you doing?" Rehna asks.

"Shh, I need to concentrate. Jacob, come here," I say.

He looks between Rehna and me nervously. She nods, so he kneels down next to me and looks at the map.

"I believe I've seen this spell before, but it was a long time ago, when I was a kid. I'm going to make you See it," I say. "Then we can figure out if it's the same."

"Okay… I guess."

I set my hand against his eyes before closing my own and sending the vision from my childhood into his mind.

I'm shaking as I stand over the body of the only person left that I cared about. Geoff is kneeled next to her, holding her as he sobs her name and rocks back and forth with her in his arms.

"We can save her," I say.

"She is dead," Geoff growls.

I shake my head. "But we can bring her back to life. I read it in your book."

"That magic doesn't work," he says. "It was written by an insane man during his last days."

"But... we could try," I say.

He's watching me now, making fear run through me, but she can't be dead. She was the only one kind to me since I walked into hell.

"Get the book," he says.

I race back for the house, leaving him next to her and slam through the door. In my hurry, I run into a servant who scurries back in fear. I mumble an apology as I rush up the stairs and into the library. I find the book hidden in the back, wound in leather. Hugging it to my chest, I run down the stairs and through the front door but stop when I see the scene before me.

Geoff has six servants lying upon the ground around the dead woman.

"Please, let me go," a man cries.

"Don't hurt my daughter," a woman sobs, and I look over at her daughter, bound to the earth by magic.

The magic is stronger than any shackle. It forces her to do as Geoff wants. She's younger than me and is sobbing as she reaches for her mother. Even though there is nothing physically binding them, Geoff's magic keeps them apart.

"Come on now, Milliant. Give me the book."

"N-No... we... we can't use humans," I say as my stomach tightens in fear. "W-What about the animals? There are plenty of animals."

"It won't work with them. Give me the book," he growls as he yanks it from my hands.

I'm shaking as I look at the innocent eyes staring right at me. Like they know this was my idea. Like they know that they're going to die because of me.

"I'm sorry," I whisper. "Master Geoff, please, let them go. I will find you something else."

Geoff swings around and hits me hard, causing me to slam against the ground. He turns back to the book which he begins to read from. He mumbles as he sets to work, placing the slaves in the spots he needs them before grabbing a woman. He drags her forward as a man screams for her.

I quickly look away from the scene as my body shakes. The cries of the man tear through my body as I try to choke back my own sobs.

I want to do something to save them, to use my magic for good. But I know he'll kill me the moment I raise my hand against him. I am not strong enough. I'll probably never be strong enough.

"Milliant, come here and hold her over the body until her blood drains completely," he says.

I'm shaking where I stand, unable to go to him but too afraid to go away. "I-I refuse," I say, wishing my words held more confidence.

His eyes are sharp as he turns them to me. He drops the woman to the ground and grabs me by the throat. "If you refuse to help, then you can take her place," he growls as he throws me to the spot he'd pulled her from.

It feels like he places a weight on my back as it forces me to the ground. My hands slam down and begin to shake as they try to hold my face off the dirt. The weight is so heavy I can barely breathe beneath it.

He shoves the woman's body out of the circle as he draws a symbol on the hands and feet of the person he's trying to revive. Then he looks over at me. "This is your last chance. Die here with them or help me."

The pressure on my back is gone as I look over at the men and women sobbing and pleading for their lives. I close my eyes and slowly stand up as I walk over to him. He grins as he looks down at me. I feel so traitorous going to him when I want to do anything but. Yet I know this is what I need to do if I want to live.

"I knew you would choose as much," he says. "You might act like you care for others, but you only ever care about yourself."

I know he's right, so I take the book from him and read the spell. When I have the words correct, I pass the book back to him.

"Elvé vill niyon," he says as he raises his hands in the air.

Slowly, I begin to say the words with him as he continues repeating them. I can see his magic touch the ground and race along it, reaching for the slaves as my magic wraps around his. The slaves scream in pain and terror. I clamp my eyes shut to get away from it as Geoff feasts on my magic. It feels like he's pulling my magic dry, but I don't open them. I hold my hands over my ears as I try to hide from their desperate screams.

The ground shakes as the noise becomes deafening. Magic is fluctuating around me, making it hard to breathe and think. Suddenly there's a stillness in the air that is so eerie, I begin to wonder if we have killed all life instead of six innocent victims.

"My love!" Geoff says, his voice snapping me back to reality.

My eyes open as Valerie sits up. She looks around slowly, but it seems unnatural. It seems wrong. She doesn't stop moving until her eyes lock with mine. Then she lunges forward, grabbing me as she tears me to the ground and begins clawing at my chest, her nails ripping at my shirt and skin. That's when I realize that I have truly lost the only one I cared for.

I yank away from the memory and look over at Jacob who is looking at me with dread.

"What is it?" Rehna asks.

"A spell… to bring the dead back to life," Jacob whispers.

"Like a necromancer's spell?" Evan asks.

"No… there were no necromancers involved. Just Miles and the dark mage Geoff Valvon," he says.

Everyone looks startled. There isn't a person in the room who hasn't heard of Geoff. The man who rose in power by using his dark magic.

"Miles, you associated with the dark mage Geoff?" Aiden says as his eyes search mine.

No one wants to admit to being involved with such a man. "I was his slave for many years," I admit. "Havoc was his demon. That man taught me everything about magic."

"Are you a dark mage?" Pepper asks uncertainly.

"No… I was able to pull my magic back from the darkness before it consumed me," I say, but I can tell that everyone is now looking at me differently. Suddenly, I'm someone to be taken seriously. Someone to watch carefully. And not just the man who rode up on a sacred forest spirit and got chastised about it.

"So explain the spell to us," Rehna says.

I really don't want to, but I know that in order to understand what's happening, I have to. "A woman we both deeply cared for passed away, and I had read about how to revive a recently deceased human. It was marked as the ravings of a madman because everyone knew you couldn't bring a functioning human back to life. Of course, a necromancer can bring a human back that it can control, but even that won't last long. It would constantly drain a necromancer's power, and the human in question wouldn't be a human. They usually don't retain their memories or any process of thought beyond what the necromancer would give it. But this book promised to bring a human back from the dead while retaining all function, all memory. The human wouldn't be connected to the mage that brought it back to life. It would be able to live freely," I say. "So we tried it. And it did succeed… to an extent.

"The moment she saw me, she tried to kill me. It didn't matter to her that she once felt love and affection for me, all she cared about was my magic. She wanted to feed on it. She tried to dig my heart from my chest with her nails so she could eat it. Geoff saved me from her since he'd put too much time into me to allow her to kill me just like that. We thought her attacking me was just some crazy thought she had after coming back. Once we got her calmed down, we were convinced it had worked perfectly. She spoke like her, acted like her, and knew stuff only she would know, yet she was so… wrong. She was driven by power and would achieve it by tearing out the hearts of those with magic. But it wasn't just… something to eat; every heart she ate made her more powerful. The first heart she ate was that of a witch and suddenly, she could have power over potions. She just fed on magic, all the while, gaining their abilities, their magic," I say. "She wasn't right. She wasn't natural. I was like thirteen at the time, but I knew something wasn't right."

"What happened to her?" Rehna asks.

It was such a dark time in my past that it's hard to talk about. "She… she killed a woman she cared deeply about. When I found her, she was covered in her blood, sobbing and pleading with me to end her life. It was the first time I'd seen her show remorse for what she'd done, and I knew it needed to end. So… I killed her."

"Who do you think they brought back this time?" Jacob asks. He's been writing stuff down as I talk, probably his headmaster side taking over.

"Oh, that one's easy. They brought Geoff back," I say, not wanting to admit it, but knowing it to be true.

Everyone's attention is suddenly on me as my words sink into their minds. The expressions of unease and fear tell me that they understand how serious this is.

"But he's been dead hundreds of years," Jacob says. "You two struggled to bring back a woman whose body wasn't yet cold. And Geoff was a very powerful mage."

I had considered that too. "Yes… I know. But things can be different. They could've had more mages, it could've been the power they forced into it. If there was a mage at each of the victims' homes pouring magic into this, can you imagine the strength they would have? And then we have the question of when a person dies, where does their magic go? Does it go with them? Or does it stay with the body? If Geoff's magic stayed with his body, it could've helped the spell."

"So, you're saying the strongest mage to ever walk this earth, is walking it again but this time, he's feeding off the magic of others, making him even more powerful?" Pepper asks.

"Yes."

The feeling of unease moves across the room.

"I don't think any of this is possible," Johnson says. "You can't bring a man back from the dead, one who has been dead two-hundred years."

Jacob nods slowly. “Yes, well… an hour ago, I thought you couldn’t bring one back from the dead that had been dead an hour, so who knows what is possible.”

Rehna leans forward, looking very thoughtful. “So, say we go with the mindset that Geoff is back from the dead, what is next?”

“Well, he’ll likely want revenge for his death,” I say with a grimace.

“Who killed him?” Aiden asks.

“A group of us,” I say.

“How?” Pepper asks in surprise.

I grimace at the memory. “Um… let’s just say, barely.”

“You nearly got everyone killed that day,” Havoc says as he leans back in his chair.

“Yes, I did.” It was a horrible day, but at least one good thing came from it. “So if Geoff has been brought back the same way, we know he’ll start targeting powerful people. It’s probably why they were trying to capture Badrick. Imagine the old magic a forest spirit has,how powerful that would be?”

“So how do we find him?” Rehna asks.

I shake my head because she doesn’t seem to understand the situation. “We don’t even need to look. Right in this room, are the six most powerful entities in the area. He’s going to find you. Each one of you. And try to kill you.” I’m not sure anyone understands the danger we’re in.

“What about the book?” Johnson asks. “Can we figure out who would have it in their possession? Were there limited copies of it?”

“Honestly, I don’t know. I can’t imagine too many would’ve had access to the book,” I say.

“Do you remember the author?” Jacob asks.

I can't even remember what I ate for breakfast and they want me to remember a name from hundreds of years ago? "Oh man… let me think about that. Hmm… Hans… something."

Jacob taps his finger on the table as he thinks for a moment. "Hans Teller?"

I nod. "Yes, that was it."

"In his prime, he was very famous for his studies and spells but as he got older, he began to lose his mind. His last book was never published. It was his only book where he used dark magic."

"Then I guess I own it," I say. "But seeing as someone's using it, it's probably gone. And his body must be gone too. Since only those of us who were there that day know where both the book and the body are, we have an idea of who is involved."

"Who was with you?" Johnson asks.

"Well, it was me, Havoc, Rehna, Evan, Marco, Harvor, Lanni, and Nicolas," I say.

Everyone looks at Evan and Rehna.

"Well, they weren't hard to find," Sam says as he pulls out a notebook and writes the names down.

"Do you need help?" Iya asks as he towers over him.

Sam shifts uneasily in his chair. "Um… no, just writing the names down," he says.

"I'll hold your paper for you," Iya decides as he reaches for the paper, but before he can touch it, Sam slides it out of his reach.

"I'm fine. Thanks," Sam says, but Iya won't be deterred.

"So, what about the others?" Johnson asks.

"Harvor and Nicolas have passed on," Rehna says. "I spoke to Lanni not long ago, but I haven't heard from Marco in about a hundred years. Is he still alive?"

“He’s alive… but where he’s at, I have no idea. I’ll ask around,” I say. “I’ll go check the gravesite and books while we figure that out.”

Chapter Eleven

"So?" Havoc asks as I park the truck just outside of my café and turn it off.

I swallow a lump in my throat and look over at him. "I have to see."

Havoc has to understand my panic, but it seems like he doesn't want me to go. "Tonight? It's already dark."

"I know, but I have to see," I say as I get out of the truck. "Badrick, I'm going to go check the grave. I'll be back by morning."

"Would you like me to go with you?" Badrick asks as he hops out of the truck.

"No, I'll be fine, but thanks," I say. "Ask Yoko to get you some food."

"Perhaps more coffee," he says excitedly.

He already harassed Rehna until she gave him a pot, he *really* doesn't need more. "No… I think you've had enough coffee."

"No, absolutely not enough," he says as he heads for the door.

Leaving him to feed his caffeine addiction, I get into the car while Havoc gets into the passenger seat.

"Man, I'm exhausted. I believe we got a total of three hours of sleep last night," he says as he stretches. I wish he wouldn't have brought it up because it reminds me just how tired I am.

"Take a nap. I'll drive us there, and you can drive us home," I say.

“I think I can handle that.” He puts the seat back and closes his eyes.

He twitches around for a bit like he has fleas chewing on his ass, and I honestly have no idea how he plans to fall asleep.

“This is uncomfortable,” he decides.

His solution seems to be shifting into a raven before walking over to me and stuffing his head in my hoodie pocket. I watch him in disbelief as he crawls inside. He barely fits, and his talons are sticking out, so I poke one of them. His talons clench onto my finger so tightly, I’m surprised they don’t pierce my skin.

***

It takes me four hours to get there and the entire time, I can’t stop thinking about Geoff. Of all of the years I have lived, the years I spent with him still haunt me the most.

And now he’s back and more powerful?

I feel close to having an anxiety attack by the time I reach the woods I buried him in. It feels like something is trying to crush my stomach. What’s funny is that it’s been so many years since his death, and still, he causes so many emotions to swirl inside me.

As I pull in, I realize that everything looks different now, but I can still remember the spot clearly. Now there are condos nearby, a park off to the side, and trails that run through the woods. No one would guess that the path they take for their morning jog goes right by one of the most heinous criminals of the past three hundred years.

I nudge Havoc awake. He’s still sleeping in my pouch, so I jab him in the face with my finger. Startled, he shifts, tearing my hoodie as he falls against the car horn. The horn blares as he flails around dramatically.

I'm watching all of this in amusement until he sits up quickly and smashes me right in the face. Tears invade my eyes as I cup my nose.

He looks at me with wide eyes as blood starts to trickle down between my fingers. I glare at him as I pinch my nose.

"Who hurt you?" he growls, ready to kill the perpetrator. He's looking around for who might need their ass kicked.

"You did!"

His face relaxes. "Oh… okay. Whoops. Sorry. You're all good." And then he pats my cheek, like that'll fix everything.

I glare at him as I look down at my hoodie, making the blood drip faster. "You tore my favorite hoodie!"

"Yeah… I said 'whoops.' I'm going back to bed," he says a moment before shifting back into a raven.

"No, we're getting out," I snap. I grab a napkin and hold it against my nose as I continue to glare at him.

He ruffles his feathers before jumping up onto my shoulder. With a sigh, I get out of the car and start walking as he hangs onto my shoulder, talons sharp against my skin. The woods are completely dark as we head into them. The insects are busy, and I can hear an owl in the distance.

"What if it is him?" I ask as I check my nose, but it looks like the bleeding has stopped.

"*We killed him once, we can do it again. And this time, we will burn the body and pour the ashes into every toilet around town*," he decides.

I grin. "Why didn't we burn him back then? Seems wise…"

"*Good question.*"

"And?"

He hops a little on my shoulder. "*Yeah, I really don't remember. I think someone was concerned his ashes could then be used for something. Like they thought that he'd be better off rotting… or something. Or maybe we were drunk. I don't know, I have trouble listening to what others are saying when they're not talking about me.*"

"Yeah, I'm well aware," I grumble as I step over a fallen tree.

He caws at me. "*Good. I like how well you know me. It's around here somewhere…*"

"I think… this way," I say as I push past some brush.

"*You know what I was thinking about at Rehna's?*" Havoc asks.

"About yourself?

"*Well, yeah... in a way. I was thinking that I've never had sex in a shrine. Next time we need to have sex.*" He puffs up his feathers, clearly thrilled about this idea.

I snort since I can only imagine what would happen if I got caught. "Yes, I'm sure that will go over well, and I'm just positive we won't get caught. Rehna has eyes everywhere in that place."

"*Well, if you keep quiet, we won't. But I know how hard it is to keep quiet when I'm making you moan my name.*"

"Yes, so hard," I say sarcastically as I notice an area that looks familiar. "Over here."

Havoc jumps off my shoulder and shifts midair, landing on the ground as his feathered cloak flutters around him. I recognize the rock and know that just beyond it, I'll find his grave, and I pray that the earth is the same as it was. Maybe I won't find it raised from someone digging the body up. I rush forward and turn the corner to find the ground completely unharmed. Weeds are growing where the lack of sunlight didn't allow much else to grow.

"Right here?" he asks.

I survey the area, but I'm almost positive. "Yes… Someone could have put the earth back."

I draw the symbol for earth and pull my hand up, causing about three feet of earth to rise up, so I can move it to a new location.

"Wait," Havoc says. "Are you sure this is the spot? I mean, I know that mages with an affinity for earth can easily pack this back down like it wasn't disturbed, but the roots would be broken." Havoc steps into the hole and kneels down. "The roots are thick through here."

"You're right. The only one who could move the roots back through the earth would be a druid. Maybe I'm at the wrong location… but I don't think so."

Just to be safe, I pull the dirt out in a fifteen-foot area, nine feet down, but we are greeted with nothing but earth.

"So… we have two options," Havoc says thoughtfully.

"Either a druid did this, or the body has been gone a long, long time."

"Evan was here with you that day," Havoc reminds me.

I look over at him as I think. "I know, but wouldn't it be stupid if it was a druid to put the roots back? I mean we'd figure out that only a druid could, and then it'd point right at Evan. I think the body was never here to begin with. After I buried it, someone dug it up and took it. Which would make sense if you planned to bring him back to life. You wouldn't want him rotting. You'd want to preserve the body."

"But for hundreds of years?" Havoc asks. "Who would do that? And back then, how would you preserve a body?"

I shake my head. "I don't know…"

"So we're clear that it was someone who helped us bring him down, but why help us kill him, just to bring him back to life? And why wait this long?"

"Fuck if I know. Let's go home," I say, feeling defeated. I urge all the soil back into place, but I can't make the grass grow like Evan could.

We head to the car as I toss him the keys. He catches them without even looking my way.

"Are you good to drive?" I ask him, hoping to get some sleep.

"Yeah, I can do that."

"I'll set my GPS," I say as I mess with it as we walk.

I climb into the passenger seat and sink down. It feels wonderful to be about to relax. I'm so exhausted that I want to shut my brain off and stop thinking for a while. I lie down with my head on Havoc's lap and close my eyes. He sets his hand against my head and gently begins to run his fingers through my hair. Instantly, I think he's doing something mean, but his fingers are gentle, and it feels good. I lean into his touch as the soft sound of the music on the radio draws me toward sleep.

But sleep is stressful and filled with dreams about Geoff which makes me restless. I can't seem to get into a deep sleep, but instead I hover between awake and asleep. Suddenly, a noise tears through the air, and I open my eyes. It takes me a moment to realize the noise isn't in my dreams.

"What's going on?" I mumble as I grab Havoc's knee and squeeze it tightly, thankful for the comfort of his lap after such harsh nightmares. "What's that noise?"

"Oh, I don't know. It might be this cop who has been following me for some reason."

Alarmed I sit up and look behind us. "What? Pull over!"

There is indeed a cop following us with sirens blaring, lights flashing. I look around and realize that we're close to home, and I hope it's a cop we know.

Havoc grudgingly pulls over, and the cop parks behind him before walking over to the window. Of course I don't recognize him, and he looks pissed as he shines his light in on us through the glass.

"Roll down the window," I say. Honestly, this is what I get for trusting Havoc with one simple task.

Havoc looks over at me and gives me a wicked grin, and I know that whatever he's planning will be a bad idea. "Just… put an illusion on the car, and we'll drive away." He says it like doing anything other than that would be ridiculous.

"No, we can't just use my magic for bad things!"

"I wasn't doing anything bad! There's no one around!" He continues to grumble as he rolls the window down as slowly as he possibly can, just irritating the cop more.

"Do… Do you know how fast you were going?" the police officer asks, sounding a little hesitant after getting an eyeful of Havoc's expression.

"Yeah, of course. I slowed down to a hundred and twenty so I could get around the curve," he says like it was absolutely stupid for anyone to think that any other course of action would have been better.

A hundred and twenty? Oh my god. Why did I think he could drive us home?

"So… you admit you were going faster?"

"Of course I was," Havoc says.

That illusion idea is starting to look better by the second. "Havoc," I snap.

"You told me to tell the truth to the cops," he says with a smirk. He loves throwing my words back in my face at the worst possible moment.

I sigh.

The officer shines his flashlight in my face before turning his attention back to Havoc. "Can I see your license and registration?"

"No, I don't have a license," he says. "I'm a raven."

He then proceeds to shift into a raven and starts to caw at the officer. He hops around on the seat and caws at him as the cop just stares at the sight.

"Oh lord," I say, completely mortified. Is this really the man that I want to spend years of my life with?

Quickly, I draw the symbol for Illusion on the car. Then I push Havoc into the passenger seat as the cop looks around in confusion since the car he was just apprehending, disappeared or seemed to. I throw the car in drive before the man can reach out. Just because the illusion is making the car invisible, doesn't mean the car isn't there. I push the car up to the speed limit as Havoc shifts back to human form. He's laughing as he looks over at me but stops when he sees that my expression isn't jovial like his own.

"You idiot!" I snap as I smack at him.

He looks at me in shock. "What? It took you so long to drive us there, and it only took me two hours to get us home."

Two hours? "How fast were you driving?"

"I don't know… like a hundred and fifty. You shouldn't have a car that goes that fast if you don't want to *go that fast*," he says.

"It's like… for emergencies!" I say, exasperated.

"It was an emergency. I'm horny, and you were rubbing your face all over my lap."

I sigh as he grins. "Be careful, or you can fly home," I threaten.

He laughs until I turn my sharp gaze onto him. Then he quietly sits back and relaxes as I drive the rest of the way home. I park the car and look over at him again just to remind him that I am still glaring at him. He doesn't seem to notice, so I head inside. It's about an hour before the café opens, so I walk through the quiet tables, toward the door leading to the stairs.

"How are you doing?"

I look over at Havoc and then look around myself. "I don't… who are you talking to? Is there a pretty woman somewhere?" I make a show of glancing under the table like she could be hiding under there.

Havoc folds his arms over his chest as he stares at me. "No one likes an obstinate asshole."

“I… was just asking,” I say innocently before heading up the stairs so I can dodge this question.

“I’m being serious,” he says as he follows me. “I know… this has to be hard on you.”

“I’m fine,” I lie.

“I know you’re lying.”

“Yeah… well… what else is there to do? A man as powerful as him is now loose and able to feed off power. And you know he’ll come for me. You know he’ll destroy everything I love like the last time,” I say. I catch Havoc’s blue eyes and know that now, more than ever, I have things I could never handle losing.

Havoc doesn’t look worried. Instead, he’s exuding confidence. “You’re forgetting one crucial piece. Geoff picked you because you’re powerful. He bound you with a spell because he feared you. A man doesn’t put a collar on something he knows he can control. He knew you were going to become more powerful than him. Demons can feel power, and I was always drawn more to your power than his. That’s why demons always respect you. You think Iya respects or listens to anyone else?”

I snort. “It’s just because he wants to get in my pants,” I grumble.

“It is not. I want in your pants, and I don’t listen to you eighty percent of the time!”

I sigh. “I don’t know. I’m tired and am being obstinate, so let’s go to bed.”

He gives me a soft smile. “You’re always obstinate. I’m not sure how sleep will change that, but we might as well try it.”

I glare at him. “You can sleep outside,” I say.

He laughs as he follows me into the bathroom. As I brush my teeth, I lean against Havoc, needing to feel that support that has always been next to me but never this close. I drew on that support when I was young and need it just as much now. He is the one thing in my life that never left. Never changed. Always next to me, even when we didn't know each other as well as we do now.

When I finish in the bathroom, dawn is starting to rise. I crawl into bed and turn the light off. Havoc lies down next to me, so I roll over and lie against him.

"You want to have sex?" he asks.

"Nope."

"I have to… touch your naked body and… *not* have sex?"

"Correct," I say as I lie against him and close my eyes. "Rub my back."

"W-What?" he asks like he's mortified.

"Do it."

He groans about it, but instantly starts rubbing my back gently with one hand while the other slips around me and holds me close. I close my eyes and fight to push the nightmares away and focus on his gentle touches. They will come, I know they will come. They always do on nights like this when I want nothing more than sleep to take me.

But my mind is consumed by Geoff. My body is exhausted, but every thought keeps me wide awake as I question how much longer I'll be allowed to even walk this earth. Honestly, I have probably overstayed my welcome by a couple hundred years, but I can't give up. Not now. Not when I finally have things to live for. Things to care about.

Havoc kisses the side of my head, drawing me back to the world and away from my unfocused mind.

"You want me to help you sleep?" Havoc asks, voice soft in the dark room.

"Does it involve sex, because I'm far too tired to have sex?"

He laughs. "In a way, but it requires you to do nothing."

"So you just want me to lie here and submit?"

He laughs as he pulls me closer. "No. I want you to open up your mind to me," he says.

I look at him in surprise. Demons and mages share a connection when bound to each other. It is completely open on the demon's side which allows the mage to control them. But the first thing mages learn when dabbling with demons is to never open their mind to a demon and to place a barrier up which keeps the demon from being allowed to hurt the mage. It also keeps the demon from being able to do things, such as use their aura or their own kind of magic on the mage. If a demon did get inside a mage's mind, a demon could start to screw with it. And when that happens, the mage starts to lose control. Giving a demon control can be a very dangerous thing.

Havoc watches me for a moment. "I'm joking," he says, but I can't tell if he is or not. It's almost like I can hear a touch of emotion in his voice, and I realize that he's upset; that he thinks I don't trust him.

I have heard of demons waiting years, all the while convincing their mage they are in love, so the mage opens up to them. Then the demon takes over the mage's power, consuming them. I've seen it happen more than once and have sworn I would never be stupid enough to open my mind to anyone.

I watch his blue eyes in the dim light of the streetlamp outside and know that I trust this man with my life. I have many times, so why not now? "Alright."

"What?" he asks startled. "You don't have to."

I close my eyes and feel for the string of magic that ties Havoc to me. Almost instantly, I find the binding that holds us together until the day I die. As soon as I have a steady grip on it, I reach for the barrier placed between our minds and let it fall. It's been set for so long that I expect the magic to resist, but it falls away like it was never there. I open my eyes and look at Havoc who is watching me in shock.

"I thought you were a wise mage," he says.

I reach out and cup his face. "You can look at it one of two ways. One: I trust you with every part of my body. Two: I know I'm so goddamn powerful I could smash you like a bug."

He grins at me. "Or three: I think it's a bit of both."

I smile. "Maybe. It just… gives you a little more control of yourself. You'll be able to fight against my hold even if I order you to do things."

"I can feel you better too. I can feel your magic. It feels so raw. I can touch it…" He wraps his arms around me and pulls me to him. "I… I can't believe you did that… I just… can't."

It's strange seeing Havoc at a loss for words, and I realize how much this means to him. He's probably never had a human trust him at all, let alone give him *this* much trust. Maybe he doesn't understand how much I care about him. "Yeah… now you promised to help me fall asleep."

"But now I'm just so shocked that I'm not even tired. I mean like… what? I never expected you to do that," he says. "Aw… does that mean you love me?"

I shake my head at this ridiculous man before setting my forehead against his and closing my eyes. "I have loved you since the day I found out how powerful you are," I say, and he laughs.

"Hm… I suppose I have felt… feelings for you as well," he says, and I can't help but laugh with him.

"That was the saddest sharing of emotions I've ever seen."

"Maybe."

But for some reason, it fits us perfectly. I know that Havoc cares more about me than anyone else, and he knows that I care more about him than anyone else. We don't have to say it out loud to understand that. Instead, we've shown each other our feelings by always being there for each other. Our relationship isn't new, but this side of it is. It's new, unexplored territory for us, but I know that there is no one out there that I would rather explore it with. I snuggle into him, finally feeling secure that this will last.

Since committing myself to Havoc, I've been able to see a side of him that I never imagined getting to see. A lot of our relationship had been bickering and fighting, but now we are finally on the same page. We're starting to understand each other better. We can believe in each other and trust each other.

I close my eyes as I feel a buzz in my mind and then an odd stillness as I drift off to sleep, thoughts of Geoff gone.

***

After a solid night of sleep where I dream about having sex nonstop that *has* to be Havoc's doing, I feel refreshed. Havoc is already up when I wake up, so I take a shower and get dressed before heading down the stairs. It's already after noon, and I could've easily gotten a few more hours, but I know that I need to get up and get moving.

As I walk down the stairs, Havoc grins at me from over a cup of hot chocolate.

"How did you sleep?" he asks, sounding mischievous and not at all concerned.

"It felt like an incubus crawled into my mind and took over," I admit.

His grin grows, so I look away from him and notice that Yoko is giving me a deer-in-the-headlights look.

"What… happened?" I ask tentatively.

She grimaces as she watches me. "First off, it's one hundred percent *not my fault.*"

I stare at her warily. "What happened?"

"*Ohhhh,* don't kill me, please. Just remember that I love you," she says as she wrings her hands.

Now I am *really* worried. "What happened?"

"Well… when I pulled into work today, I drove around back, you know, to park my car. And when I turned into the parking spot, I might have… slammed into your car. But it's not my fault because I didn't *see it,* because it was *invisible.*" She's waving her arms around, trying to emphasize each word as she stares at me with wide eyes.

"No…" I say as I realize that I never took the illusion off it. "How bad is it?"

She shrugs. "I… really don't know because I still can't see it. But my car's front end is pretty smashed up."

"No…" I whine as I rush for the door. She runs after me as I slide through the door. I see her car and grimace as I look at the crushed front end. The headlight is completely busted and hanging off it as it struggles for life. "How fast were you turning in to park?"

"I was listening to a good song! And you know how, when there's a good song on, you accelerate more than you should?"

I drop the illusion on my car as I rush up to it and find it… pretty dent free. "Well…"

Yoko's mouth drops open as she stares at it. "Oh my god. It like demolished my car, and yours looks just fine," she says. "What the hell?"

There's a scuff on the corner that I easily rub out with my thumb. "Huh… well… I guess no harm, no foul," I say as I head back inside, glad that fiasco is over with.

Yoko doesn't seem to be finished with this issue though. "No harm no *foul?* My front end is demolished!" she cries as she races after me.

I look over at her as I reach over and take Havoc's hot chocolate before taking a long sip. "Just take the cost of fixing it out of the money you owe me."

"W-What… money?" she asks meekly. Probably because it's a list so long that it'd take her the entire day to read it.

I shake my head and walk inside. "I'll pay for it, just give me the bill."

She gives me a huge, million-dollar smile. "Are you *sure?*"

"I have to keep you happy. I need to talk to you and Baron."

"Yeah sure… Baron!" Yoko yells.

Everyone looks over at us as Yoko proceeds to disrupt their coffee by shouting until Baron comes out of the back. You know, like Baron doesn't have superior hearing.

"What's wrong?" he asks in alarm. He has a spatula in his hand like he can battle off intruders with it.

Yoko shrugs. "I don't know, Miles wants something."

"Now that everyone is watching," I sarcastically say. "There's a man out there who wants me dead, and he will do anything to make sure that happens. I want you two to stay in here all day today. The barriers I have on this place will keep anyone not welcome out. And you also have Badrick to help protect you. So, until I figure out something else, stay here."

"He basically just wants to enslave us to this place," Yoko says as she glances at Baron.

Havoc gives them wicked grins. "We're going to make you sex slaves and force you to watch me having sex with Miles."

Leave it to Havoc to ruin an important conversation. "What?" I ask in alarm. "Is that like a fetish you have or something?"

He smirks at them. "I'd let them join in, but you're always so stingy. I mean there'd be rules. No one can touch Miles but—"

“Have you thought about this?” I ask, highly concerned.

Havoc looks over at me. “What would make you think that?”

I shake my head and turn back to Yoko. “Can you make me some breakfast I can eat in the car?” I ask. “Havoc, get ready to go.”

“Where are we going?” Havoc asks as Yoko and Baron go back to the kitchen. I can hear Yoko muttering something about a foursome that makes me glare at Havoc.

“Home.”

His thoughts on the subject clearly show on his face. “Oh, you know that Nicco and I don’t get along,” he growls.

“You don’t get along with ninety percent of the population,” I say.

“That can’t be true. What percentage of the population are women with huge breasts?” he asks thoughtfully.

I glare at him.

“Ooh, jealousy is sexy on you,” he says with a grin.

Yoko walks up and sets two plates before us. Mortified, I look at what’s on it.

“W-What is this disgusting-looking thing?” Havoc asks, always the one eager to say what everyone else is thinking but are too polite to say.

Yoko looks startled. “What? It’s a new recipe. Does it look bad?”

Havoc turns the plate this way and that, examining the green thing on it. “It looks like a leprechaun vomited on my plate.”

“Baron said it was good…” she says as her eyebrows scrunch together.

Havoc huffs. “Baron has to say that or he won’t get in your pants.”

“Well, he’s not getting in my pants until we’re married, so I know that’s not it,” she says with a glare.

“Oh my holy, *what?* You haven’t climbed that beast like a tree?” Havoc asks.

She folds her arms over her chest and stands defiantly. "No. We're waiting until we're married."

"He's like… I mean you've seen him with his shirt off, right?" Havoc asks. "I'm not sure I fully like the man, but holy hell, he's sinful to look at. He has muscles where I didn't know you could have muscles."

She's got her "defiant" face on. "Yeah, and so what?"

"My opinion of Baron has changed. He's either a eunuch or a saint." Havoc looks toward the kitchen and begins to yell. "BARON! Are you a eunuch or a saint?"

Since Baron is in the kitchen, I pray he can't hear, but he *is* a werewolf so he pops his head out. "About what?"

"Yoko's virg—"

I clamp my hand over his mouth, and he licks my fingers. "Shut it."

Everyone is staring at us again as the café turns very quiet.

"Oh, he's having a mental breakdown because I told him we're waiting until we're married to have sex," Yoko says.

"Oh. That makes sense. I had one of those when you told me too," he says with a wink before heading back toward the kitchen.

I laugh and release my hand as Yoko gives Baron's back a questioning look.

"You think he's not for this whole waiting thing?" she asks thoughtfully.

"I think it's great," I say. "It shows that you both are really devoted to each other. Havoc, would you wait years for me?"

"No sex?" he says like the words are forbidden.

"Correct."

He cringes and shifts his weight around. "Oh, that question makes me very uncomfortable."

"I'd wait for you," I say.

"Of course you would. You're used to not getting any."

I glare at him which just makes him grin.

"Fine, but there'd be stipulations. Like… you'd have to lick a Popsicle once a day while I jerk off or something," he says. "Why don't we get off this heinous topic and back onto the matter at hand? Like our last meal."

I look down at the green blob and try to figure out what it is. "I'm sure it's delicious just… maybe leave the cooking to Baron," I say to Yoko as I take the plate. "We'll be back later. Please be careful."

"I will," she says. "You too."

I head out the door with Havoc by my side. We are each carrying our plate of death, unsure if we should actually consume it.

"Do I have to eat this?" he asks as he holds the plate upside down. The mess stays attached, even after he shakes it up and down a few times. "*Is* it food? Or is it poison?"

I peel an edge off and stick it in my mouth and gag. There is *way* too much salt involved. I set the plate on the ground and slide it under a bush using my foot. "There we go. Delicious!"

"I'm not sure that's safe. It'll probably turn into an alien and take over humanity." Havoc looks up as Baron comes out the back door carrying the trash.

"Hey Baron, think fast!" Havoc says as he peels the mess off the plate and lobs it at Baron. Honestly, I'm pleasantly surprised that he hadn't left the plate attached before throwing it.

It smashes right into the side of Baron's face, causing him to stumble back.

"Look at those cat-like reflexes!" Havoc shouts, like he's amazed.

Baron starts gagging as he tries to scrape it off his face. "Get it off. I'm having flashbacks. She watched while I ate my piece. Get it off!"

"You guys are so dramatic," I say as I laugh. "See you, Baron."

He looks up and gives me some puppy eyes that shouldn't work on a man his size. "Don't leave me… she has an entire pan of that stuff."

"Pour some coffee on it and offer it to Badrick," Havoc says.

Baron nods slowly. "That's actually a good idea," he says as he hurries back inside.

"I'll drive," Havoc says.

I look over at him while wondering how he could have said something so stupid. "Absolutely not." I get into the driver's seat.

"But it takes so long when you drive!"

"Yes because I drive safely," I say.

"I was driving safely as well. Just put a barrier on the car and an illusion. That way if we wreck it, you'll be safe and no one will see the car."

"What about all of the people we murder in the process?" I ask as I get in the driver's seat.

He shrugs, clearly not concerned about them. "Guess they should've gotten out of the way."

"Of course they should've gotten out of the way of the invisible car," I say as I snap my seatbelt on.

"Honestly this world is becoming overridden by humans, they could be thinned out a bit."

"That's your answer?" I ask as I put the car in reverse. "Cull a few?"

"I mean… look at Baron. If natural selection was still a high priority, Yoko would be with a better man."

"You just got done saying you liked Baron a bit more!"

"I changed my mind!"

"Why do you hate Baron? He's like the sweetest man. Is it because he hurt me?"

He looks away from me, clearly not planning on admitting it. "Of course not. I don't care all that much about that. It's because he's dating such a gorgeous woman."

Liar. "Well, woo Yoko a bit, I'm sure she'll come around and see you're the better choice. I'm sure you'll wait until marriage for her, right?"

"You want me to go woo a woman?" he asks, sounding annoyed. I thought for sure the "m" word would have stopped him dead in his tracks.

"If you're not happy, then you must," I say like it is of highest concern to me.

He glares at me as I grin. "So you want me with someone else?"

It's like he can't admit that he likes me but is annoyed that I'm even joking about being with Yoko. "You started this whole thing by saying that you are the better choice for Yoko."

He looks ready to pout. "I did, but I just said it to make you jealous, and you don't even look like you care," he says.

I shake my head as I steal a glance at him. He's watching me with a look of concern. "Are you being serious?"

"I am. I want you to be jealous."

I laugh. "What do I need to be jealous of? I know you won't go elsewhere—you're stuck with me forever and ever. My contract will never let you go! You're mine forever and ever and ever."

"No!" he cries, but I can hear the humor in his voice.

"You just say shit like that because you're uncomfortable with how much you actually like me."

He grumbles about something and then decides to turn his attention to a different matter. "I can fly faster than this," he says.

"Alright, shift," I order as the car rolls to a stop at a sign.

He isn't given a choice with my command and shifts into a raven as I roll the window down. I grab him and toss him out the window before rolling the window back up. I see him catch flight in my rearview mirror as I pull away from the stop sign.

"*I can't wait until I can feast on your heart*," he growls. "*I will roll in your blood and piss on your grave*."

I laugh as I start to drive slowly and watch as he eventually catches up.

I hear his talons tap against the window. "*Let me in*."

"This is too much fun," I say.

He slams into the window and beats his black wings against it as he looks at me with a death glare.

"Is it nice out there?" I ask as I wave. I roll the window down just a quarter of an inch. "Havoc! This is so much more fun."

He forces a talon through the window and tries clawing me with it, but when he finds that he can't get much more of his body through the window, he retreats.

The wind whips his feathers as he reaches for the mirror which he grabs hold of with a talon and climbs onto. He moves onto the hood and makes sure I'm watching as he raises a talon in the air and holds it above the bright blue paint.

"Don't you dare!" I yell.

"*Let me in*," he says as he slowly lowers it.

Not trusting him, I know I need to give in. "Fine." The moment the window is down, he flies in, shifts, and grabs onto my neck.

"I could strangle you."

"Stop!" I say as I laugh. "I will wreck the car."

"I love that you care more about the car than me."

"That's good. I enjoy doing things you love," I say.

Chapter Twelve

When I pull up to the mansion, I can't help but look at it with a feeling of dread. It was once Geoff's mansion, the same one I grew up in and became the owner of after Geoff's passing. It still looks as haunting and dreadful as the day I left the place. In actuality, it is a gorgeous three-story home that seems to have never aged.

It's my memories of the place that makes me hate it as much as I do.

I pull the car over and look at Havoc.

"I deserve a Dairy Queen," he decides.

Of course that's what he's thinking of even though he'd been tortured in this place. "For what? You haven't done anything."

"For just being so goddamn handsome," he decides as he looks at me.

I stare at him in disbelief. Trying to understand this man is a ridiculous thing to even attempt.

"I should've been an incubus. But… I don't even *have* to be one, so many people just fall all over me as it is."

"You are the definition of a narcissist," I say as I shake my head.

"Thanks, I think so too."

"Come on," I say, knowing that there really is no reason in trying to talk sense into him.

"Large."

"What?"

"I want a large blizzard," he decides.

"We'll see how well this goes and then I might," I say. "Or I'll get you a mini, just like your wittle penis."

His eyebrow reaches for the sky. "Now that's not funny. You know I have a very, *very* nice-sized penis. It's just that it's been so long since we've had sex you have forgotten. Would you like a sneak peek?" he asks as he unbuttons his pants.

"That's all it would be. A little 'peek.'"

"You know why I have sex with a woman once and never again in my entire life? Because then I can enjoy it and never regret it. I don't have to hear them bashing me. The comments. The complaints. Nothing. They just stare at me with adoration and lust. We do the deed. And done. We're both happy. You're like some form of torture that I've become addicted to."

"Yay me," I say sarcastically, even though it makes me feel good that he claims to be addicted to me.

Once the door is unlocked, I step inside and shut it behind me. When I turn around, a man is standing directly in front of me, making me jump.

Havoc shudders. "Fuck, you're so creepy."

"I didn't know you were coming," Nicco says, words thick with his British accent.

"Then, was this your daily time to just creepily stand by the door and make no noise?" Havoc asks.

Nicco slowly looks over at him and narrows his eyes. "I *heard* you coming."

"Then you knew we were coming," Havoc says stubbornly.

I ignore Havoc. "If you would charge the cellphone I gave you, I could call you and tell you I was coming."

Nicco grunts, which is just as good a reply as any I was probably going to get.

Nicco is… Nicco. He's a vampire in a sense. But for the past couple hundred years, I have never seen him leave this house, so I'm not quite sure how he drinks, or maybe he never does. He *looks* like he never drinks. He is gaunt and pale but more gray than white. His eyes are a dull red, and his hair is nearly white. He looks like you can push him over with a feather, yet I have seen him tear the head off an ox.

We came to know about each other when I was about twenty, and I talked him out of eating me. Havoc and Nicco have never gotten along very well since Nicco ate a girl Havoc had his eyes on. She, quite honestly, deserved to die, yet Havoc thought it was in his rights to sleep with her first. So that's when they began hovering around like a couple of roosters, and Nicco tore the head off the ox to prove how strong he was. And then Havoc was pissed because… you know, I really don't even remember. But the girl was soon forgotten as the grudge turned to a fight over the death of an ox Havoc didn't actually give a shit about. So, of course, *that* has been a subject for debate for a few hundred years. The ox, not the girl.

"I see you still haven't wised up," Nicco says to me before leaning in close. He takes a deep breath and quickly plugs his nose before gagging. "You have been mating with it."

"No one says 'mating,'" I say, really not wanting to know how he can tell.

"Fornication is much more in, right now," Havoc says.

Now I could gag. "No. No one should *ever* say the word fornication."

"So you've been fornicating with the creature. Shameful," Nicco says with a tsk.

“’Ello, gov’na, I’m a posh little British vamp’iya,” Havoc mocks. “With all my righteous ideals and my biscuits.”

Nicco slowly turns to look at Havoc. It seems to take years for his head to turn from looking at me to looking at Havoc. Honestly, I want to smack them both and get on with life.

Havoc’s not done, of course. “I mean, why do you still have a British accent? Have you even been to Britain in the last two hundred years?”

Nicco rushes forward and grabs Havoc before slamming him against the wall. He lifts him up about two feet off the ground, which is honestly pretty impressive since Havoc is decently tall.

Havoc just glowers down at Nicco who looks a bit uncertain now that he’s thinking about what he’s just done.

Just like roosters. No brain. Just all dickish action.

I decide that the smart thing to do is to just ignore the entire situation. “Nicco, I’m here to check on a book. Anything unusual happen lately?”

“No,” he says as he lets go of Havoc and rushes to my side like I’ll keep Havoc from ripping him apart.

“Anyone come by?”

He shakes his head. “Nope.”

“Great,” I say as I head up the stairs. I walk down the hallway as Havoc stares at Nicco while grinning maniacally. Nicco keeps nervously glancing back at him.

I step into the library, and immediately sense that something is wrong. Because I stop suddenly, Havoc slams into me, having been watching Nicco and not me.

“We’ve been played, my dear old friend,” I say as I feel the unfamiliar magic in the air.

"That you have," a man sitting in the corner says as he stands up. I can instantly tell that he is a necromancer, and necromancers can control one thing:

The undead.

Vampires are undead.

Nicco is being controlled.

Just my luck.

Nicco stands in the doorway, staring at the necromancer as if hypnotized by him as he walks toward us, but he's not what has my attention. I can hear a soft humming noise that sends chills down my body. I quickly turn, my eyes scanning the library as I look for the direction of the noise, but I can't see where it's coming from.

Nicco walks past me, hesitating as he fights against the hold. He weakly tries to block the necromancer who seems to be wanting to escape the room instead of confront me.

"Get the fuck out of the way," the necromancer growls as he drives a knife right into Nicco's chest. I lunge for him, but before I can reach him, he vanishes through the doorway. Nicco staggers before dropping to his knees. I want to go after the necromancer, but I don't have time to chase him, and I don't have time to go to Nicco, because there's something wrong. If the necromancer is leaving just like this, it means there's something worse in this room, and I can hear it coming. Hear the soft humming in my ear like it's wrapped around me. Consuming me.

"I'll—"

I grab Havoc's arm and stop him from chasing the necromancer. "Havoc, stop."

"What are you doing? You're just going to let that asshole—"

"Havoc… shut up, help me find the source of the humming."

He looks confused as his eyebrows knit. "What humming?"

I look at him, startled. Is it just in my head? No, it couldn't be. I've heard of this monster before… but it has only ever been in tales.

I step into the middle of the library as the humming gets louder. "Havoc… she's in here."

Havoc looks at me in concern. "She? What's wrong?"

I hear a giggle and quickly turn around. Suddenly, there's a woman standing at the end of the room which had been empty just a moment earlier. She looks almost translucent with a white robe on. She's wearing a white veil over her face, allowing me to see only her red lips hidden beneath. The entire room feels colder now that my eyes are on her. That's when I realize that she's not the creepiest thing in the room. The creature by her side, its body wrapped around her legs is.

It could only be described as half-human and half-snake. His flesh is as white as her cloak, his arms wrapped around her waist like a child hugging its mother. He stares at us with bright red eyes, the color contrasting sharply against his white flesh. He has a human-like chest that fades to scales which wrap around his waist. It narrows into the tail of a snake that is wrapped around her feet, the end twitching and swaying with the sound of her humming. It's almost hypnotizing the way it moves as her humming fills the room.

"What the fuck is that?" Havoc whispers, and I force my eyes away from the creature's tail.

I pull my hand up to call the name of fire, but nothing happens. My magic is stilled, defused as she continues to hum. And when I reach for it again, I realize I can't even feel it. There's nothing there. My magic is gone, and in its place is her humming. The humming is consuming my body. It's moving over my skin, rippling around me, devouring my magic as I just stand and watch. I can feel goosebumps crawl up my arms as the sound consumes me.

"Havoc, I can't use magic," I realize.

"What are you talking about?" he asks as he looks over at me.

"Her humming is doing something to it." I look down at my body. Where my magic once wrapped around me as tendrils of red and white, is just noise.

"That's alright, I'll just kill her," Havoc says as he pulls his sword free and rushes at her.

"Havoc, wait!" I yell, but I'm not sure why I stop him. Am I scared of her? Scared of what she might do to him?

And then she starts to sing. It's like I can tell it's a song, and my brain recognizes the noise as words but at the same time, they're something else. Something different. Something foreign yet as familiar as the skin on my body. The noise wraps around me as everything in the room shifts. The ground is no longer ground as the floor begins to move, becoming walls, and then I'm falling.

I scrabble for something to hang on to as the furniture begins to slide across the shaking floor. Her words consume me as I desperately grab for anything to hold on to so I don't fall into the pit of darkness. Books are falling from their place as the shelves scream across the wooden floor, tumbling down onto their faces. I hit hard and realize it's now the ceiling beneath my feet. Slowly, I struggle to stand, but the ground is shaking as I try to find purchase.

My eyes lock onto the snake-man's as he lets go of the woman's legs. He drops to the ground, back hitting the floor as his neck cranks back to look at me. His arms snap back, shoulder blades protruding from his back as he twists his arms until his palms are flat on the ground, elbows bowed out unnaturally. He begins to crawl along the floor, face and chest pointing up as arms reach back so he can scurry along the ground toward me. His tail snaps back and forth as I reach for my sword that is hidden by my side and pull it free from its sheath. I hold it in the air as I turn to face him, but the hilt feels hot. When I turn to look at it, the blade begins to move, shimmering and twisting as the metal turns to scales. Quickly, I drop it as it turns into a snake.

The snake slithers across the floor, moving toward me, and I step down hard on it as I try to call for my magic. Her words are intruding my mind, and I can't remember the words for any of my spells. I'm pleading for it to return, but I can't even remember what my magic feels like.

Suddenly, the ground is shaking again, making the room shift, and I fall back. Painfully, I slam down onto my back as the ceiling becomes the wall, and the desk drops down next to me. I push hard against it as it slides into me, causing me to flail back against the moving ground.

The snakelike man is crawling toward me as his neck snaps to the side so he can track my movements. The shifting and turning of the room doesn't seem to affect him because he keeps moving toward me without hesitation. I rush to my feet and race for the fireplace where I can see the glimmer of a fire poker. My foot steps down, and the room shudders as I hit the floor hard on my hands and knees. I roll as I slam into the chandelier, causing the glass to break and shower down on me. I reach for a jagged piece and grab it as I turn, but the creature is on me. He reaches out to me as his face opens up, jaw extending farther than a human's ever should, and I realize that he is going to eat me whole. Just devour me, and there's nothing I can do.

The creature stops suddenly, body shaking as the song stops, and the woman screams. The room shudders as it flips from one way to the other. Gravity takes hold of me as I fall and slam down onto my back, books and papers showering me as something wet sprays out around me.

I sit up and look up at Havoc who stands before me, sword stabbed right through the heart of the snakelike creature. Its body is shuddering and shaking upon the ground. The woman is at the other end of the room, where she'd been when we'd entered and is screaming. She's holding her head as she rocks back and forth while staring at Havoc in horror.

"You alright?" Havoc asks as he pulls his sword out of the heart of the snakelike creature.

Slowly, I look around. The room is as it was when we first walked in. The books are in place, the chairs are in place, and I'm lying sprawled on the ground while snakeman's blood soaks into my pants.

"Where'd she go?" Havoc asks.

I look up quickly but realize that Havoc is right. The woman is gone, and I can't hear her anywhere.

"What… the fuck was that?" I ask as I sit up. Havoc gives me a hand and pulls me to my feet.

He has an odd expression on his face. "Yeah. I don't know."

"Fucking crazy, right?" That's when I realize that as I was thrown all around the room, I never noticed Havoc being thrown around with me. It wasn't until he killed the snakeman that I saw him.

He stares at me for a second and then shrugs. "Are… are you talking about yourself? Because yeah, you were acting pretty crazy."

"What?" I ask confused.

"I mean I really don't know if this is a good time or not, but I took a video of you," he says eagerly as he pulls out his phone. Blood drips off his sword as he sidles up to me and presses play.

I watch a video of myself as I flip and flop around on the ground like a fish out of water. I jump up, take off running, slam into the desk, and then start flailing around on top as papers fly around me. Then I pick up a stapler and leap to my feet before promptly falling on my face.

"The stapler!" Havoc laughs. "That was the best part! When you were trying to attack the air with your stapler, I nearly died! I even got some of it in slow mo," he says eagerly as he starts to flip through videos. "Want to see?"

I jab him right in the stomach, wishing it was his nuts. "I was having my mind *fucked with,* and you're all 'right now would be a really good time for a video'?"

"Why am I getting that I should say no?" he asks. "I killed the snakethingamajig before it reached you. I don't see the harm in pausing for a moment and taking a video. You were the one that told me to always take a moment and capture precious moments in your life."

Why do I even try? "Fuck you," I snap. "That lady was like… mindfucking me, and you were like 'oh this will make a good slow mo'?"

He shrugs. "Well… don't knock it until you see it," he says defensively.

I glare at him, but he just smiles at me, clearly unaware of why I'm annoyed at him.

"Um… hey, guys. Could you help?" Nicco asks from the doorway.

"Splendid," Havoc purrs. "You're still alive. Just in time for me to kill you."

I leave Havoc and Nicco alone as I pass through the door and jog down the stairs. The necromancer, who seems to have thought that I was going to die upstairs and he had nothing to worry about, is sprawled out on my couch playing on his phone. He seems really into it because he doesn't notice me until I clear my throat. He quickly looks up and drops his phone as he starts to call up the undead, but I'm on him first. I slam him into the wall as I stare down at him.

"You're going to talk," I inform him.

He laughs as he stares at me. "It's too late. We've brought a real god to life."

How could they not understand what they've done? "He is not a god. He is the devil. You don't know that man. He'll never stop. He'll feast on power until he can no longer eat it. Even if that means eating you," I say.

He grins at me. "Then I will gladly offer up my heart."

I drag him into the bathroom while planning on how I'm going to throw in some water torture techniques Havoc might have shared with me as he flails and kicks at me. I toss him in the tub before turning the water on and plugging the drain.

"I'll never speak," he says as he grins.

He doesn't stop grinning even when I grab the showerhead and spray him in the face. I'm not much for waiting at this point, and the tub is taking too long to fill. He just laughs. "He is a god now. He's immortal. He cannot die." The man's not even fighting. He clearly knows he is no match for me.

"Everything can die," I say. "And I will kill him."

He's laughing maniacally, so I spray him in the face again. The water is so hot it's leaving his face red and blotchy.

"Tell me where they are," I say as I pull the showerhead back.

"My god will come when you are ready for him."

"He is not your god," I yell as I hit him with the showerhead.

He grins as he sinks down into the water, and I hear something crunch.

"Fuck!" I yank him forward, but the man is already shaking.

His body convulses as the small capsule he bit down on, falls out of his mouth.

There's a soft knock on the door, and I turn to look at Havoc as he walks in. The convulsing, dying man in the bathtub doesn't seem to faze him.

"I… feel like you're mad at me, and I'm not quite sure why," he says.

I stare at him in shock. "Really? You seriously can't fathom *WHY?*"

He looks very confused. "I didn't kill Nicco since I thought you might be happier to do it yourself."

This man. "What? Why would I kill Nicco?" I ask as I stand up and look over at Havoc.

"Well for one, he betrayed you and for two, he's creepy as *fuck*."

"I'm standing right here," Nicco says from over Havoc's shoulder. Even I jump this time.

"Fuck, he's so *creepy*," Havoc says.

Nicco sighs. "I deeply apologize, but as I was saying while you continued to spew threats at me, I had no control. You know vampires have no control over a strong necromancer. He wanted me to behead you, but I was able to fight that."

I take a deep breath. "Are you alright, Nicco?"

He lifts up his shirt and looks at the big hole in his chest. "Well, there's a bit of a hole, but I think I'll be fine."

"Let me check how deep it is," Havoc says as he stabs his finger into the hole.

Nicco growls and leaps at Havoc as I turn the showerhead on the both of them. They jump back, so I turn the water off.

"Why did you do that?" Havoc asks as he wipes the water away from his face.

"So how long has the book been gone?" I ask.

"Oh… about a month now," Nicco says.

"The necromancer has lived here that long?" I ask.

"He has. He was an alright kid but had horrible taste in music. Do you mind if I eat him before his blood completely congeals?"

"He killed himself with poison."

"Poison won't hurt me," he says as he slips between me and the vanity and grabs the dead man. I walk out, leaving him to do as he wants and head upstairs. Havoc follows along quietly behind me, like I might forget about his presence and the anger still burning brightly in my heart.

I walk into the library and stop, startled. The body of the snakelike creature is gone. "Can you hear if anyone is still here?"

"No… and it was dead, I'm certain of that," he says as he walks over to the spot. There's a footprint in the blood. It is petite and barefoot, clearly the woman's.

"I'm going to go set up a barrier. Get this cleaned up," I say as I head out.

I set a barrier up around the house, but I know without regular maintenance, it'll fall like it had the last time. Hopefully, it will keep people far away for now. After making sure Nicco is alright and then calling Johnson about the body, I get in the car.

Havoc quietly gets in beside me as I drive.

"Are you mad?" he asks softly, like he finally understands the situation.

I ignore him as I keep driving, but as soon as I see a Dairy Queen, I pull off. I park my car and look over at him.

The look of pure relief on his face almost makes me forgive him. He's clearly upset that I'm mad at him. "You're really getting ice cream? I thought you were mad at me," he says as he reaches for the door handle.

"Stay here. I'll get it," I say before getting out. I leave him there and head inside so I can get myself a large banana split blizzard before going back out to the car.

I get in, and Havoc looks at me as I start to eat my ice cream.

"You didn't get me one? That's cold," he says.

"It is really cold. It *is* ice cream, if it was warm, it'd melt," I explain as I stare at him.

"I'm sorry, alright?"

"Are you?" I ask skeptically.

"Yes!"

I glare as I thrust the ice cream at him and put the car in reverse. I back out of the parking lot and drive home as we share the ice cream.

Once home, I head into the bathroom and strip as the shower heats up. Naked, I climb in. There's a knock on the door before I hear it slide open. I step under the water and let the warmth beat down on me, hoping it'll drown out whatever stupid thing Havoc has come to say.

"Can I join you?"

I ignore him, so he seems to think that means yes and takes his clothes off. He pushes the shower curtain back and crawls in with me. Slowly, he reaches out to me and wraps his arms around me and I immediately want to sink into them. I mean… he *is* a demon. They're known for not comprehending situations and finding wicked joy in things.

"I really am sorry. You know I'd never let anything happen to you," he says as he tucks his face against my hair.

"Yeah, well, I thought a lot of crazy shit was happening," I say, feeling like I still need to stay stubborn about it. Partly because I love the concern he's showing me. And partly because he was an asshole.

"I know, and I'm sorry. I should have done something… but you just looked so funny—"

I glare at him, and he holds me to him tightly so I can't get away even if I wanted to. Which I don't. But I refuse to let him know that.

"Please forgive me."

I slide my hand down his lower back and let my fingers brush over his ass as the water beats down on us. "I will… if you let me fuck you," I say as I slip a finger between his ass cheeks.

"W-*What?*"

I rub my finger between his cheeks before pressing against his hole.

His eyes get very wide. "Nope. That area's off limits. Want a blow job? I'll do that. Or want like… that finger painting stuff? Yeah, I bet we'd make a masterpiece with that. We could make money off that."

"Nope, I want to bury my cock right here," I say as I push my finger against him.

He tenses as he stares down at me.

"Nothing goes in there."

"But I'm sad and you… you won't make me feel better?"

His eyes narrow. "Do you usually top?"

"No. That's why I want to," I say as I smack the shower off and get out. I dry off and head into the bedroom as he proceeds to stand in the shower, dripping water. I grab the lubricant as I sit on the bed naked and wait.

Slowly he comes out, like he thinks maybe I forgot about it.

"Come on," I say as I pat the bed.

He grimaces. "You can ride me? We can go to a church and have sex? That sounds like fun."

"I'm waiting," I say.

"Fuck me," he groans.

"That's the plan."

He stares at me and I give him a grin. I watch him grab the towel I used to dry off with before drying himself off. He walks to me, standing naked and gorgeous before me as I grin at him.

"I'm just teasing, we don't have to," I say as I lean against him, my cock pressed against his.

He reaches up and grabs my face, pulling me up until his lips press against mine. He draws me into the kiss, driving me crazy and I know that if he told me to roll over so he could fuck me, I'd do it without hesitation.

When he pulls back, breath heavy, he catches my eyes. "The only reason I want this is because it's you."

"I'm… you'd really do it? I mean, I want to, but I knew you wouldn't go for it. Are you sure?"

"I *do* want to make you feel better."

I smile at him and gently kiss his lips before pulling back. “But only if you’re sure.”

He slides his fingers down my sides and grabs my ass, squeezing it gently. “I’m positive. But you better be gentle,” he says as he pushes me onto the bed. I take his hand and pull him onto my lap.

Honestly, I’m shocked and fighting to not show it. I *did* say it as a joke, since I really didn’t think he’d let me. But if he’s willing to, I’d love to be able to touch his body in a way that no one else ever has before. “Gentle is my middle name,” I say as I run a hand up his side.

“Bullshit,” he says. “I once saw you accidentally nearly cut someone’s head off.”

“I didn’t even nick them!”

He raises an eyebrow.

“I *barely* nicked them.”

His eyebrow rises even farther.

“He ran into it.”

He starts laughing as he leans into me. “You’re so ridiculous.”

I smile as I kiss him. “I’m excited you’re into this. You’re into it, right?”

“Strangely, I’m into anything you suggest.”

I squirt lubricant on my hand before running it behind him between his butt cheeks where I push a finger inside of him.

I wrap an arm around his waist, rolling him onto his back. I grab for a pillow and shove it under his waist, raising it up, before sliding my hands up his muscular chest. “How do you stay so damn muscular when I never see you exercise?”

“I’m just perfect like that,” he says.

“Yeah… sure, we’ll let you believe that.” I run my lips down his chest, kissing a line straight down his stomach as my fingers slide down his side. I draw my right hand between his legs and push my finger back inside him. And just as I'm starting to push a second in, I take the head of his cock in my mouth. He groans as I swirl my tongue around the head before sinking down on him.

My mouth is making him relax as I move my fingers inside him. My cock is aching for attention, but I want to make sure he's comfortable and ready.

I pull my mouth off his cock and my hand out of him before sliding up his body.

"Hands and knees is the easiest position," I say.

"Why has my brain turned to mush?" he grumbles as he rolls over.

"I really don't know," I tease as I look at his perfect ass. I smack one cheek as I realize that I never ever imagined I'd have Havoc in this position. I stroke his cock with one hand as my other slides up his back.

"Thank god your penis isn't as big as mine. I mean it's almost tiny compared to mine," he says.

"You're returning to my shit list right now."

"Ah, forgot. Bare ass in the air makes you forget things," he says as he looks back at me.

I try not to grin as I rub lubricant over my cock.

"Sing me a happy song," he says.

"I'm not singing to you!"

"I am Havoc the Sexy. I do the penetrating!"

"I told you we don't have to do this! Do you want to do it? You can do it."

"I will… allow it this once. Once, you here? Never again!"

"Ready?" I ask as I push against him.

"Yes, yes. Penetrate me!"

"Don't make me laugh!"

He leans into me. "Fine. Fuck me, Miles."

And I nearly lose everything right there, but I compose myself and press against him.

I can feel him slowly opening up for me as I push inside him. He's so tight around my cock that it's driving me mad. I want to just push in, claim him, but I force myself to go slow. I slide my hand around and take his cock, rubbing him gently. "You doing alright?" I ask.

"Sure, fine. Splendid. Am I forgiven? I feel like I should be forgiven for every wrong thing I've *ever* done in my life. Are you all the way in yet?"

"Almost," I say as I keep pushing until my thighs are flush against his. Pressed deep inside of him, I lie against him and kiss his shoulder. "This *is* fun."

"Nope!" he says. "Not in the slightest. Why do you enjoy this? How is this enjoyable? And if your cock was as big as mine, oh god!"

"Don't make me laugh. Are you good? Do you want me to pull out."

"No, it's *tolerable* and just for you."

I slide my fingers down his broad back, dying to move my hips. "I understand, but I don't want to do this unless you're enjoying it."

"Don't make me say words that prove you are even remotely right. So continue."

"Wait," I say as I reach between his legs and stroke his cock. "Are you not hating it as much as you thought?"

When I shift my hips in time to my hand on his cock, he groans. "No idea what you're talking about. Do you usually talk this much during sex? It's usually 'Give me your big, sexy cock, Havoc!'"

"Nope. Never happened." I kiss him again as I pull out a little bit before thrusting in. I move my hand down him as I quicken my pace and I feel his body relaxing as pleasure starts to find him. I know he'd swear on his life that he's feeling no pleasure, but the hardness of his cock tells me otherwise. I pull back, almost all of the way out before pushing in, and he moans as I feel his body tighten around me.

"Did you like that spot I just touched?"

"Nope!" he says.

"Don't want me to touch it again?" I ask as I thrust inside him.

I must have hit it again because he ducks his head down and grips onto his pillow. I slide my hand over his bare back as I move inside of him, feeling the heat rising in my body. Quickly, I move my hand over him, rubbing and stroking. His body tightens around me as he groans and cum hits the bed. Pleasure is so close to me as his body tightens on my cock that I push into him as I reach my limit and come inside him.

I pull out, and he rolls me under him.

"Yeah, I'm not satisfied with how this finished," he says as his hand slides between my legs and a wet finger finds my hole.

"Yeah, but I'm done," I say. "I had my fun."

"I'm not. It's not my fault demons can keep going," he says with a grin that makes my body ache for him, even though I'm pretty sure I don't need another around. But as he rubs me, his mouth finds mine and I know that I will *always* be drawn into whatever he wants, especially when it makes me feel this good.

When he finally finishes, I'm exhausted and collapse onto the bed. He stares down at me from where he straddles me.

"If you tell anyone about what I… let you do to me, I will do something horribly bad to you," he says.

"Sure, sure," I say as he grabs me in his arms and pulls me to him.

"I'll spank your ass so damn hard." He gives my bare ass a smack as he pulls me on top of him.

"No! Not my ass!"

He snickers as he wraps me up in his arms and holds me tight. "How do you talk me into everything?"

“I don’t know, I’m just good like that,” I tease as I kiss him.

“It’s like I’m addicted to you and there’s no reasonable reason for why,” he jokes.

“Uh-huh! Because I’m amazing, duh.”

He snorts, but he doesn’t let go of me as he runs gentle kisses down my cheek and over my lips until sleep finally reaches out for him. And I’m left remembering a time when it was just sex and wonder when these caring gestures became so normal. I curl into him and he gives me a half-asleep squeeze, like he’s not planning on ever letting me go.

Chapter Thirteen

I walk downstairs and see Yoko and Baron huddled around Havoc's phone as they laugh.

"Give it to me, give it to me," Havoc says as he tries to reach between them to grab the phone.

"NO! It's not over yet!" Yoko says as she holds it out of reach.

I lift my hand up while speaking the word of fire, and the device bursts into flames. Yoko quickly drops it and watches as it continues to burn on the ground.

Everyone stops laughing and looks over at me.

"I topped Havoc last night," I announce.

Havoc glares at me. "You *heathen*."

"You said you wouldn't show anyone, and I would keep my mouth shut," I say.

"Are you two like an old married couple by this point?" Yoko asks as she stretches. "And what do you have against cats in boxes?"

"What?"

I look down at the phone that is nothing but a heap of melted junk at this point.

"Havoc was showing us some videos of cats jumping in boxes," Yoko says. "What did you *think* he was showing us?"

Havoc gets a wicked grin on his face that makes me realize that I just dug a big grave. "Yes, Miles, what was so bad you had to burn up my phone for?" He taps his finger against the table. "And when I kept up my end of the deal? But now the deal is off. Everyone, want to see a hilarious video of Miles? Allow me to use your laptop, and Miles can say nothing about it because he turned into a traitor."

"Havoc. Please," I grovel while wondering if pleading would even do anything. Maybe I should try suggesting any of his strange fetishes. He wants to have sex covered in paint? Sign me up.

Havoc slides Yoko's laptop over to himself without a glance at me.

"Yoko, tell him he can't use your laptop," I plead.

Havoc clicks something. "And there. *Enjoy*," he says as he stares right at me.

"I'm sorry."

"I need a new phone. Chop chop."

"Oh. My. God!" Yoko says before screaming out in laughter. Everyone in the café is staring at us at this point, and I would like to crawl in a hole and die. "The slow mo! Havoc, this is priceless. This would ruin Miles' reputation!"

"Goodbye, I am leaving in search of a better life," I say as I head out the door.

Havoc jogs after me to catch up. "That was fun. We not only got to make fun of you, but you also made a dick of yourself. But I obviously like your dick, so I guess we're all good."

"Funny," I say. "Let's go. I'm going to drive off into the sunset and hope everyone forgets about me."

"Not going to happen," Havoc says, but he follows me outside and over to my car.

I get into the car as he slides into the passenger seat. "So where are we going?"

"Aiden's," I say. "Rehna found Lanni and Marco. The old team is coming together for a lie detector test to see who stole the book."

Havoc looks thrilled. “Oh, I *love* Aiden’s place.”

I look over at Havoc and raise an eyebrow.

He glances over at me with wide eyes. “I mean, yuck, perky little titties everywhere. How heinous.”

“That’s right.”

“I only need my little snuggleworm,” Havoc says as he leans over and kisses my cheek.

“Yeah, don’t ever call me that. Or talk to me like that again,” I say.

“Alright. All I need is my fuckhead. Is that better?”

“Surprisingly, yes,” I say.

He laughs. “Hopefully, they don’t look through all my videos and find the one of us having sex.”

I slam on my brakes at a stoplight and look over at him. “Excuse me?”

“What?” he asks as he looks around like I am alarmed by something *outside* the car.

“You took a video of us having sex?” I growl.

“Oh yes! It’s alright, I captured all your good sides. And I mean *all of them*.”

“How about you ask next time?”

He’s giving me one of those cocky grins that always gets me. “I see no reason I can’t enjoy a video of you every now and then.”

“I’m sure it just gets drowned out in your sea of videos,” I grumble.

He grins at me. “I love how jealous you get. I never knew you were such a jealous person.”

“Yep, jealousy is just dripping off me,” I say sarcastically as I turn the corner.

“It’s really cute on you. How’d you become cute? What have you done to my brain?”

"Nothing that I know of," I say. "Basically everything that's happened has been your idea so far."

He thinks about it for a moment before his eyebrows knit. "It has… hasn't it? You poisoned me!"

I snort. "Yes, poisoning is usually my forte. I didn't poison you… this time."

"Wait, what?"

"Huh?"

"*This* time?"

"I have no idea what you're talking about."

He snorts. "We did butt heads occasionally when you were younger. Although, I surprisingly got along with you a lot better than any of my other masters. I just had so much fun picking on you."

"Picking? Or torturing?"

"Po-tay-to po-tah-to."

"No… no it's not! I took great care of you!"

"What about the time you made me sleep with your horse?"

"My horse was cold!"

"You're such a liar!"

"What about the time you left me alone with a hell hound!"

He grins at the memory. "I just remember looking out the window and there you are, running as fast as your stick legs could carry you."

"I was a child."

"You were at least fourteen. By that age, you should have been married and had fifteen kids."

I snort. "Yeah, on top of everything else I had going on."

"We have so many good memories of each other," he says with a smile.

"Actual good memories? Or your evil memories?"

He smiles at me. “Aren’t they the same thing? I’m joking… I lived a lot of my life chained, shackled, or caged. The first time you took those shackles off me… it was unbelievably freeing. I’m not sure you even understand.”

“Really?” I ask as I look over at him. “I’d been terrified that I fucked up somehow and you’d eat me. And when I let you free you snipped something at me.”

“Maybe… but I also couldn’t let you, a mere human, know how much it meant to me. Even the humans who’d been kind to me kept shackles on me for added protection. It gave them another layer of control. But I was yours for about two days and you took them off.”

I reach over and rub my fingers over his wrists that have long since healed up. Your wrists were constantly bloody and looked very painful. I couldn’t possibly have left them on. I didn’t know you lived with them on for so many years.”

“Miles, you are a different breed of mage. Most don’t think that demons deserve any kindness, especially back then. The demons were jealous and mystified whenever you came up in a conversation. Some wanted to use you and others wanted to figure out how to become your demon. But you’re all mine and I don’t share.”

“Huh… that’s interesting. I thought all demons wanted to eat me.”

Havoc leans back in his seat and taps his finger on the door. “Miles… don’t drop your barrier for Aiden,” he says thoughtfully.

I look away from the road for a moment to glance at him. “Really? Why?” While I haven’t known Aiden as long as many, I still trust him.

“Well… someone there is probably involved with all of this, and this could be what they’re waiting for. You drop the barrier to your mind, and who knows what’ll happen. That woman who shall not be mentioned again, in case it leads to you remembering the videos I took, was already able to get in your mind with the barrier in place.”

"It was her music that got in there," I say, but it still doesn't fully explain how.

It takes about forty-five minutes to reach Aiden's house. I pull the car over and get out before heading inside. Two women come forward as soon as I enter. The blonde is wearing just a thong and the other has pasties on over her nipples and a plaid skirt.

"Hello," the blonde says with a purr. I can instantly tell that she's a succubus, and she's trying to charm me with her aura.

"Hey, I'm here to see Aiden," I say.

"Aren't we all?" the other asks as she sets a hand on my chest and presses her breasts against my arm.

"Mine," Havoc says as he lifts up a spray bottle and squirts her right in the face.

She jerks back. "What the hell?" she asks as she looks at him startled.

"Where did you get the spray bottle?" I ask.

Havoc gives me a look filled with innocence. "Evan gave it to me to give to Badrick so he can spray that weed he's obsessed with. And once I heard we were going to Aiden's, I thought it would be perfect. I saw how they were all hanging on you the last time we were here. I'm just being precautious. Now if they want to hang onto me, they're free to do so. Come, ladies. Come to me." He holds his hands out as we walk into the next room. They look annoyed, especially with the spray bottle still in his hand.

Inside the living room are around fifteen half-naked women frolicking around. They have the TV on and are watching a movie on a screen nearly as big as the wall.

"You know… I would assume this would be your cup of tea," I say.

"It should be," he says. "But I've become a weak man."

I snort and keep walking as a pretty, dark-haired woman walks up and Havoc sprays her in the face. She jerks back startled.

"Stay away," he says.

"Havoc, stop," I snap as I set a hand on his chest.

He reaches up and takes my hand in his as he slides his fingers between mine and leads me into the room in the back where we can hear Aiden. I can't help but enjoy the touch of his fingers and squeeze them gently.

Aiden, Lanni, Evan, and Marco are waiting. Rehna is the only one absent, which is unusual since she's never late. I don't know if I've ever beaten her anywhere before.

Aiden is leaning back with a woman on each knee when we walk in. He smiles at me, and the women look over at me.

"Hmm… who are these two?" one with a bob cut says.

"You're with the demon now? How disgusting," Marco says.

"Marco! It's been two hundred years since I've seen you, and it definitely hasn't been long enough." I make sure I feign excitement as I look at him.

Marco is one of those men who know they're attractive to the point where they are obsessed with themselves. I have never gone anywhere with him when he didn't check his appearance in a mirror, in a puddle, or in the reflection of the sunglasses that were on the guy he just killed. In some instances, a person can be really ugly, but when you get to know them and realize they have a wonderful personality, you start to find them attractive. Marco is the opposite with his stupidly greased hair and perfectly manicured eyebrows. His face is blemish free, and his teeth are so white they will blind you. But his main selling points are the two beautiful white wings spread out behind him. Marco is a seraph, yet his angelic appearance doesn't reflect at all on his personality. Evan and

Lanni barely have any room on the couch because he has his wings out, and they take up most of the room.

A woman walks up to me with a soft smile. "Can I get your—"

Havoc sprays her right in the face, and she jerks back startled.

"Havoc!" I snap.

"Fine, take care of your own coat," the woman says as she glares at Havoc.

"Is that the water I gave you?" Evan asks as he yanks the bottle from Havoc's hand. "I put special water in there to help that tree grow!"

"Yes, and it's worked mightily well for keeping these beasts away from Miles."

I sigh and walk over to a chair and sit down. Of course, I'm across from Marco who is glowering at me.

"I thought you were dead," Marco says.

"Nope, I've been just fine."

"That's a pity," he says as he raises his wine glass to his mouth and takes a delicate sip. "I thought for sure that those chimeras would have torn you apart."

I narrow my eyes at the fiend. "And how did you know about that? I never told anyone."

He shrugs. "Oh… really? Huh… I have no idea." He licks a drop of wine off the edge of his glass as he watches me.

Havoc's attention turns to him as his eyes narrow.

"I never imagined you'd drop so low as to have relations with a demon," Marco says.

"I really hope you're the one behind this, so I can kick your ass," I say.

"What's going on between you two?" Evan asks.

Marco leans back and picks at a white feather. "Not a thing," he says.

The door opens and Rehna walks in. "I apologize that I'm late," she says as she walks in and sits down. "Let's begin."

"Okay… so you basically want me to ask everyone if they were involved in taking the book?" Aiden asks.

"Correct. Also ask if they were involved in moving the body," I say.

"Alright, let's begin," he says as he turns to Evan.

Incubi and succubae are interesting in that they can get almost everyone to answer to them. I feel like it might be their aura that persuades everyone to give answers for any questions they ask. They can make everyone feel lust towards them and persuade them to do almost anything. It's why Aiden becoming a boss was worrisome for the district, but Aiden isn't like that… anymore. He is a good man with a good head on his shoulders. All these women are here because they truly care for Aiden. They walk around half naked because they are happy with their bodies and just don't care, not because he asks them to. Hell, I've seen him trying to stuff sweaters on them because they "look cold."

Incubi and succubae automatically exude an aura of familiarity. Everyone enjoys being around them and would enjoy sex with them even more. But an incubus and succubus could also use their manipulation abilities to force people to only look at them. When it is directed at a person, it feels like a suppressing aura that causes one to only have desire toward the incubus or succubus. And when in that state, they will do anything for them. Just like giving them an answer for anything they ask.

Evan's expression changes as he looks at Aiden. His face softens as he smiles at Aiden like he's just stumbled upon the love of his life. Even though the aura is aimed at Evan, everyone in the room is feeling a bit of it, and all eyes are on Aiden.

The aura doesn't affect me at all with the barrier I have on my mind. Instead, I'm left fully functioning and fully aware.

"Did you have anything to do with the removal of the book that we are looking for?" Aiden asks.

"No, of course not. I would never want to bring that horrible man back to life," Evan says. "He killed my wife. He killed the only woman I ever loved. I needed him dead. I was going to do it one way or the other when Miles proposed the plan to me," Evan says.

"Do you know who removed the body?"

"No, I helped Miles bury it, and I pissed on that grave, but I don't know who removed it."

"Alright, thank you," Aiden says as he drops the persuasion before turning to Lanni.

Lanni is something none of us are quite sure of. She goes by the name Lanni, but that is the name of the body she found dead many years ago. She is able to invade the bodies of the recently deceased and take on their abilities. I am unsure whether Lanni has any abilities of her own outside of the whole body-swapping thing. She (or he) never speaks about any of it. And refuses to tell us beyond what we already know.

Right now, she is in the body of a twenty-year-old woman with frizzy blonde hair that looks good on her. She has bright blue eyes that are hidden behind thick-framed glasses. But the last time I saw Lanni, she was in the body of a middle-aged man. While she can heal the body from life-threatening things, the body continues to age, so it is not unusual for her to switch to a healthier or younger one. Whenever she leaves the current body she's in, the body "dies" again. We are all unsure if this would work on Lanni, but Aiden is oblivious to what she really is and tries it anyway.

She's instantly enamored as any human would be. She smiles broadly at Aiden and leans into him as he asks her the same questions. She has fairly similar answers to Evan's, so Aiden moves on to Marco.

"Yeah, I didn't even know about the book. This is the first I heard of it," Marco says.

"What about the body of Geoff?"

"I don't even know where they buried him, I was dealing with Rehna's wounds," Marco says.

Aiden nods. "Anything else you can think of?"

"I think Miles did it," he says.

"Why?"

"Because I want to blame Miles for something," Marco admits.

"Why?" Aiden asks.

"Because he wouldn't go out with me. He thinks that *thing* he hangs around with is better?"

"That was like two hundred years ago," I say. "You terrified me. And you never asked me to 'go out with you.' You told me I was a slave and once Geoff was dead, you were 'by all rights' my new owner."

"Well, I'm still annoyed," Marco says stubbornly. "I'm just so gorgeous, who wouldn't like me, you know? I mean, look at my face. Damn, I'm attractive. And my wings? Oh, they just make me even more gorgeous, you get me? Who would not want this body? But Miles' eyes have only ever been for Havoc and alright… maybe he's kind of hot, but come on, I have wings. And have you seen my penis—"

"Yeah, let's end this here," I say.

"Alright, that's all," Aiden says before looking away.

We all know that Marco is the most narcissistic person in the world, so none of his information fazes us. And definitely doesn't faze Marco either who continues to confidently sit there.

"It's huge," Marco says, even after the allure has left him. "HUGE."

"No one cares," I say.

"Huge" he mouths as he holds his hands in front of him with a good distance between them. A completely ridiculous distance. I've seen him naked before. It's definitely not that impressive.

"It's not the size that matters, it's what you can do with it," Havoc says. "And let me tell you what I've been doing with mine."

I turn my glare onto Havoc and he shuts up, but when I look back at Marco, he's still mouthing the word "huge" with his hands spread out even farther.

"So… Rehna, can you tell me about the book?" Aiden asks.

"I didn't even know about the book, but I heard about it from someone… I don't remember who though," she says.

"What about the body?"

"I'd been hurt, and I didn't go with them to bury the body. I didn't even know we succeeded until I woke up with a doctor leaning over me three days later," she says.

Aiden sighs. "Alright, thank you."

He turns to me as I try to figure out if I should fake the effect or let everyone know his charms won't affect me.

"I can't affect Miles, so what do you want me to do?" Aiden asks.

"Miles can drop his barrier," Rehna says.

"I did," I lie.

Aiden looks right at me, and I stare into his dark brown eyes. Even though I have the barrier in place, I can still feel something from the charm.

"It's not working," Aiden says, which tells me that even if I did fake it, he'd know.

"Miles, drop your barrier," Marco says. "What are you trying to hide?"

"I'm not hiding anything. My barrier is dropped. Must have something to do with the permanent barriers," I lie.

"This is ridiculous. Now you just look guilty," Rehna says.

"You can allure me," Havoc says. "I was with Miles the entire night."

Aiden looks over at Havoc, and Havoc is instantly attentive. "Were you with Miles the entire night?"

"I was. I never once let him out of my sight. He told me to ask for help for Rehna, but I couldn't leave him. I knew he was just sending me away because he thought Geoff was going to kill him and didn't want me to die as well."

"Miles helped bury the body?"

"Yes. And I know he would never dig it up. I am connected to Miles; I would know if he's lying. He didn't dig up the body. Miles was a slave to Geoff for years. Geoff kept him and his magic bound and beat and tortured him. He slowly started driving him crazy. There is no way Miles would bring him back. He gave up everything to kill Geoff. And was ready to give up his life that day. He had some spell planned to fall back on if it looked like we were losing. It would have consumed so much magic that it would have killed him, but it would have also killed Geoff. He was prepared to use it. Why would a man prepared to give everything up bring the man back? You can try to say that he could've done something when I wasn't around, which I suppose he could have, but these past few weeks, I haven't left him. He isn't involved."

"Did he ever do anything with the book? Move it? Tell anyone about it?"

"After he used the book to bring Valerie back, Miles tried burning the book. Geoff took to carrying it around because inside it were unspeakable acts he became obsessed with. He was carrying it the day he died as well. It's why everyone came to know about the book. But the spells were nearly impossible to perfect, and Geoff couldn't perfect them. The only reason he was able to do the spell to bring Valerie back was because he had access to Miles' magic. Geoff never would have completed it without Miles. Geoff was keeping Miles' magic hostage and was only feeding him bits so he could use the rest of his magic for his own spells. Miles had more magic than Geoff that day when we fought him, but he'd spent so long unable to use his magic that he didn't understand it."

For a moment, I feel weighed down by the information as I try to sort it out. "What? Geoff was… siphoning my magic?"

"Yes, with the markings he placed on your body," Havoc says.

"Why didn't you tell me?"

"I didn't want you upset. Because…" I can tell Havoc is fighting his words, but the allure is too much. "Can we stop?"

"Because why?" I ask, needing to know.

Havoc grits his teeth. "Because… I knew… at that age… if you… fuck… if you knew that your magic… was the cause for all his acts… you wouldn't have been… able to handle it. If Geoff had never found you, he wouldn't have had… the power to… destroy… fuck, make it stop."

Havoc grabs Aiden by the throat and lifts him up into the air as he stands. Aiden quickly drops the allure, and Havoc pulls back.

"It's my fault…" I realize. "All of those people who died? All the destruction? It was my fault? My magic did it?"

"You didn't have a choice," Rehna says softly. "He controlled you."

"Yes, but if I knew, I would have… done something! I would have…" What would I have done? Could I have done something?

"What would you have done? Kill yourself?" Havoc asks. "If you had, he'd have found someone else to use. You stopped him. You were strong enough to put an end to him."

All of it slams into me, and I feel like I can't breathe. What have I done? "Fuck… are we finished? I want to go home."

"Yeah… I think we are," Rehna says as she looks at me with an expression of pity.

I stand up and quickly head for the door as Havoc rushes after me.

"Miles, stop," he says as he grabs my arm and spins me around. "I'm sorry for not telling you."

I look down at his hand gently wrapped around my wrist. "I'm glad you didn't," I admit. "I'm not sure I could have handled it."

"You didn't have a choice," he promises as he wraps his arms around me. "He had control of your magic. What would you have done?"

I shake my head, wanting to get free of his comfort or pity or whatever it is. I feel like I don't deserve kind words. "Something. I would have done something."

"You did. You killed him. Everyone in there knows that if it wasn't for you, we wouldn't have even tried to mess with Geoff."

I pull away and he lets me. "I just want to go home. I can't believe you didn't tell me."

"Why? So you could beat yourself up about it?" he asks.

"I don't know," I admit. "Just… something."

He shakes his head. I know he wants to prove me wrong, but I won't let him.

"You can drive," I say as I thrust the keys at him.

I get into the passenger seat and put my seatbelt on. Havoc gets in, and silence fills the car as he drives. I stare out the window as I try to rethink my first twenty years of life and question where I could have done something different. But all I can see are the faces of those he killed. Their pleading looks. Their last words.

What have I done?

I can't breathe. The car feels suffocating. I grab for the door handle and find it locked.

"Pull over," I say as we pass by a clutch of trees.

"Why?" Havoc asks.

"Pull the car over!" I yell as I hit the unlock button.

He pulls over, and I yank the door open so I can jump out. The moment I'm free, I start running. I don't know where I'm running or why I'm running, but I need to get away. The air in that car was too thick. Unbreathable.

I race into the woods, not sure where I am going or how far I can go. I step over a fallen tree and my foot catches, making me fall onto my hands and knees. Quickly, I stand and look around myself, but it's still chasing me. That dread, that anger.

I scream, and the earth shakes as my magic rumbles, uncertain inside of me. I can see the tendrils of it snaking out around me, swirling around me. It's so comfortable. It's like my skin that fits me perfectly, but instead of the light hue, all I can see is a deep, dark red. The color of blood. The lighter hue of the magic is gone, instead turning from red to black with my thoughts, reminding me that it was responsible for thousands of deaths.

Havoc runs up and grabs me, causing my magic to constrict back into my body. "Stop this!" he yells.

"Let go of me!" I growl as I start beating my fists against his chest. "Let go of me!"

"Miles, this won't help! He would have killed people whether you were there or not." He refuses to pull away even as I fight against him. He holds me tightly, wrapping his arms securely around me.

"Yes, but with *my* magic, he was able to kill more. I watched him kill hundreds… no… *thousands* of people. I watched an entire city burn and was too fucking stupid to realize it was *my magic*."

He shakes his head. "How would you have known? You didn't even understand your magic when you came to him. You didn't know how to recognize your magic. He made sure you didn't! Miles, you are not at fault here. Do you know how many people I have killed? I've had so many masters who have controlled me to the point where I couldn't move without permission. They forced me to kill innocents and people I didn't want to kill, but I have, and there's nothing I can do about it. Nothing. And I know that. I know what it's like to feel controlled. And I also know it's *not* my fault."

I look over at him, startled, and realize that his entire life was like my first twenty years of life. Twenty years being controlled by others, but now I am free. He has lived his entire life being controlled.

"I'm sorry," I say, because in a way, he's still being controlled today. He might have agreed to this binding, but he isn't his own person.

He shakes his head as his fingers dig into me, like he's never going to let me go. "No, I didn't say that because I want you to be sorry for me. I said it because I wanted you to know that I understand that pain. It's horrible, and I don't blame you for feeling angry and upset."

"How have you managed years of it?" I ask.

"I had a lot of hatred and resentment aimed at others. At myself. But I haven't felt that way for years because you don't treat me that way," he says.

"How do you not see their faces all the time? They haunted me before I knew I was responsible. I can't imagine now. How do you handle it?"

"You find other things that make you happy and focus on them," he says as he kisses my forehead.

I grab onto him and press my face against his chest as I feel tears on my cheeks. The unshed tears for those who have died. For those never allowed to grieve again, I grieve for them.

Havoc gently wipes them away with his finger as he holds me against him. "It'll be okay." He runs his lips over my cheeks, kissing the tears away. "I promise."

I nod, but I can't get myself to commit to it. Even so, I know that I have Havoc here to help me get through it. He is my everything, and he'll help me through all of it. Desperately, I cling onto him, hoping that all these dark thoughts would just go away. In their place would only be thoughts of the man standing before me. So, I open myself up to him.

It's moments like this that make me realize how much he loves and cares about me. He has for many years, even when we butted heads. And it means so much to me to have his comfort, to have his arms wrapped around me.

"Thank you… for always being there for me," I whisper.

"I would never leave you, Miles."

Chapter Fourteen

When I get out of the shower, I notice Havoc's laptop is open. I sit down in front of it and pull open his recent documents. Of course, number one is a video, so I click on it and proceed to try and keep myself from murdering him as I watch the beginning of us having sex.

Seriously?

The next is the video from the other day, which again makes me want to murder him.

I open his documents and start going through his videos, curious about how many are of him screwing women.

"Whatcha doing?" Havoc asks as he comes out of the bathroom.

"Well, I thought since you can record me without permission, I can peruse your laptop without permission."

He shrugs while looking amused. "That's fair," he says as he leans against the arm of the chair. "That's a good one of us." He points at it.

"You have another one?" I ask.

"Oh yeah," he says as I right click it.

"Delete."

"That's alright, I have them backed up on like five different flash drives. I even took one back to the demon realm, so I know that you can't get to it," he says with a grin.

"How many videos of women are on here?" I ask as I open the trash bin, knowing he wouldn't think to clean that out too often.

"None," he says as I find nothing of interest there. "You seriously thought I kept videos of women all over my laptop? Miles, sometimes your ideas are so freaking weird."

"I just thought that maybe it was a fetish for you."

He gives me a fang-filled grin. "It's not, but I can share some of my other fetishes."

"I am… concerned, terrified, and slightly curious."

He snickers. "You better me." He leans in and kisses me, drawing me right into his touch as the door slams open.

Badrick sticks his head in through the door. "Can we go to my forest?" he asks.

I don't have the heart to tell him that it's definitely not big enough to be a forest anymore. "Sure," I say. "We're about ready."

"Well, it looks like you are playing on a laptop," he says, not at all impressed.

"I was waiting for Havoc," I say.

"I see… well, he is also playing on the laptop with you, so I believe you are both now ready," he says.

"Yes, Miles. We should be halfway there by now," Havoc says as he gets up and heads for the door. I follow them outside and into the truck. We drive to the woods and before the truck is completely stopped, Badrick leaps out.

He looks over at me as I get out. The impatience is clear on his face. "You are far too slow, human. Get on my back."

"Yuck, no. I really shouldn't," I say as if I wouldn't want to ride on the back of a sacred creature in the shape of a wolf.

"I insist," he says as he pushes me toward his back with his fluffy muzzle.

I jump onto his back, and Havoc shifts into a bird. I feel like I should never have to walk again. That I should be allowed to ride upon the back of this sacred beast like a king. Badrick jumps into a lope as Havoc flies just ahead of us.

When we reach the spot where the miasma has been cleared, Badrick stops and I slide off. Havoc shifts back and lands on his feet as his cloak flutters around him.

“So, Havoc… isn’t wearing that cloak slightly morbid in a way? I mean, it’d be like me wearing a cloak of human skin,” I say.

Havoc looks over at me. “What are you talking about? These are the feathers I plucked from my dead parents’ bodies which I then made a cloak out of.”

I look at him startled. “What?”

He grins. “It’s a joke. They’re actually aulmal feathers.”

“What the hell is that?”

“It was once a bird that was said to grant luck,” Badrick says. “To have a cloak made of that is quite astonishing, indeed.”

“Where’d you get it?” I ask.

“One of my previous masters made it for me. A woman that I cared about. Now what have you ever made for me of value?” Havoc asks.

“I don’t know… I made you an omelet this morning.”

“Yes, an omelet sounds so much better than a sacred cloak,” he says.

“It does?” Badrick asks in surprise. The sarcasm goes right over his head like usual. “That must have been one really good omelet. I request an omelet. And can you put coffee in it instead of cheese?”

“What? He’s being sarcastic,” I say.

“Hmm… he seems to speak in tongues,” Badrick says as he inspects the dirt.

I set to work with bringing water to two seedlings Evan managed to sprout on his last visit, and then continue clearing away the miasma, when my phone rings.

I see it's Sam and hope this means Iya hasn't done something horrible.

"Hello?"

"Miles, it's Sam… We received a call from another department, and I thought you would want to be one of the first to know that Aiden Blake was killed last night."

"What?" I ask, startled. Last night was when we'd seen him. When he'd asked each of us for the truth. And now he's dead? "Where at?"

"At his home…"

"Okay, I'll be there in forty minutes," I say as I hang up. "Badrick, I need you to run me to the truck."

"What's wrong?" Havoc asks.

"Aiden's dead," I whisper.

"What?" he asks startled.

I nod and climb onto Badrick's back so he can run us back to the truck.

"Are you alright?" Havoc asks.

I nod, not sure how I feel yet. "I guess. I get so sick of people dying around me."

He puts a hand on my leg and squeezes it tightly. "I know. I'm sorry you have to deal with it. Aiden was a nice guy."

When we reach the car, I leave Badrick there with the promise to pick him up later, and then drive to Aiden's as quickly as I can. There are police cars outside his residence when we pull up and park. I run to the front, but a woman steps up to block me.

"He's with us," Johnson says as he catches up to me.

"What happened?" I ask.

"I'm… hoping you can tell us that," he says.

Sam must have heard us because he and Iya are waiting in the doorway. "His heart has been removed which goes along with what you were discussing at the meeting the other day, but… how it happened is what we're confused about."

I step into the house and slow down as soon as I'm through the door. It feels like the fresh air has been pulled from me as the smell of blood hangs heavy in the air. I walk into the first room and stop, startled. It was the room where the majority of women had been watching a movie the night before. They are still there, but they are all lying dead upon the floor.

Bodies lie scattered everywhere. Furniture is broken and destroyed. I recognize the woman lying closest to me as the one who had greeted me at the door. She has a chair leg shoved through the side of her head. I kneel down and look at the wound in confusion.

Then I turn to the next woman who has bloody scratches all over her face. There is a neon pink, fake nail sticking out of her cheek, and her throat is torn.

"Those are likely teeth marks," Sam explains.

"Yes, but what kills with a bite that doesn't have fangs?" I ask as I find a woman lying half on her. Her pink nails are bloody. Skin hangs off the tips, and she's missing one nail on her right hand. Her face is concave, like someone hit her with something hard until her skull cracked.

"What the fuck…" Havoc says as he kneels next to me. "What is this?"

"I… don't know," I realize as I move to the next woman.

Each woman I look at has been brutally murdered one way or another, but they all seem to have been involved in the fighting. It doesn't look like they were fighting against just one of them, but instead they were fighting against each other.

"Where's Aiden?"

"This way," Sam says, and I stand up and follow him. We walk into the next room where Aiden is sitting on the couch alone. His eyes are open, but unlike the women, it doesn't look like he struggled. His shirt is torn open, revealing the wound in his chest.

I wasn't really close to Aiden, but I knew him enough that seeing him dead makes me upset. I've seen a lot of people I've cared about die over the years, whether it was from old age or murder or accident. It never makes it any easier. I feel like, in a way, this is my fault. I drew attention to Aiden by asking him to allure us, and by doing that, I involved him in this. Again, another death because of me.

"What was Aiden?" Johnson asks as we look down at the man.

"Incubus."

"Why would Geoff want the power of an incubus? Isn't that why you said he'd steal the heart? To gain their abilities?" Sam asks.

"The power of persuasion is very powerful," I say, as I reach toward Aiden's neck. I pick up the necklace that is around it and unlatch the gold chain. "I'm going to go upstairs where it's quieter and try to See something."

"Okay," Sam says.

"Havoc, Iya, can you guard me?" I ask.

"Of course," Havoc says.

"Will you be naked?" Iya asks. "I find that I can think better when I'm naked."

I glare at him, and he huffs out a laugh. With the two of them following, I head upstairs and into a bedroom. While Iya and Havoc clear away a spot on the floor, I draw the circle and then sit down. With Iya on one side and Havoc on the other, I kneel in the middle of the circle I've drawn and wrap my hand around the necklace.

I take a deep breath and close my eyes.

Aiden is walking through the room when his attention is pulled toward something. He looks around but doesn't see anything, so he starts walking again.

That's when everyone in the room stops moving. The women are all completely still as they stare forward, eyes vacant. I can't tell if whatever is affecting the women is affecting Aiden or if he's just confused about the reactions of the women.

But when his eyes snap up and I see the strange singing woman who'd been in the mansion, I know exactly what happened. I don't need to see anymore, but I don't leave yet. Her song has just begun.

Aiden is instantly drawn to her, walking straight toward her as the women in the room begin to tear each other apart. They're screaming and yelling as they hit and fight with anything in reach, tearing with their nails and teeth. Aiden isn't fazed by any of it as he walks into the other room and sits down on the couch. From here, he has a clear view of the women, but he doesn't seem to notice what they're doing to each other.

When only one is left alive, she stabs herself in the throat with a pen until she crumples to the ground. Then the far door opens as Aiden watches peacefully, and I see Geoff step in. He looks around himself, at the mess he has created but never slows. Things like this never fazed him.

He moves with a purpose as he reaches the back room where Aiden is still waiting. When he walks in, he extends a knife to Aiden who takes it without hesitation. And then Aiden stabs himself in the chest with it as Geoff watches like it is of no concern to him.

It's shockingly hard to see the man from my nightmares.

He hasn't changed. Even death didn't change him. He still appears to be in his forties with short brown hair and scruff on his face. He has narrow eyes which are black from the darkness of black magic consuming him. Slowly, he looks up and stares me right in the eyes, like he knows exactly where I would be in this vision.

"Time is growing closer, Milliant. Your death awaits. Your heart will be the final missing piece."

I jerk out of the memory so fast I'm disoriented. I jump to my feet, then trip and fall onto my hands and knees as Havoc rushes for me.

"You okay?" he asks.

"Yeah," I whisper.

"What did you see?" a voice behind me asks.

Everyone jumps as I turn around and look at Lanni who is sitting on the bed we'd pushed against the wall. She looks like a child as she balls herself up.

"Where did you come from?" Iya yells as he rushes at her.

"Iya, she's fine," I say, and he stops but not without snorting. "Lanni... we're fucked."

"Are we?" she asks.

"He has a woman who can control humans with her voice," I say.

She cocks her head. "Like a Siren?"

"I guess, but she's different. She's powerful, and she doesn't have to be in the ocean. I don't know what she is."

"Alright. So we have to kill her," she decides.

"Can we? Your human body will be weak to her. Havoc is the only one who wasn't affected by her," I say.

"Then I guess we find her and ask Havoc to kill her," she says.

"And hope we don't die in the process? Her song made all of them kill each other."

"I can help. If I die, you'll just need to find me a new body to inhabit," she says.

"We need to figure out who is involved in this," I say.

She lies down on her side as she stares at me. Then she begins tracing a circle on top of the sheet. "I may have an idea. I just need a body."

"What kind of body?"

"The body of a necromancer."

"How many days can it have been dead?" I ask.

"Five at the most."

"Then I have a body for you," I say. "What's your plan?"

"Well…" she says as she rolls onto her back, arms and legs sprawled out. "If none of us living know, then one of us dead might."

"Well, Harvor and Nicolas have been dead a very long time," I say.

"Perhaps… but they were there that day, and a strong enough necromancer could bring them back to life long enough to acquire information from them," she says.

"Wouldn't their mind be gone with their spirit?" I ask.

"They can force it back for a short period of time," she says as she watches me. She has her bare feet up in the air before flipping them back and rolling off the bed. She stands up, walks over to me, and kneels down in front of me so we're eye-to-eye. "Let us end this once and for all."

"Why do you trust me?" I ask.

She leans in really close so her lips are against my ear. "I don't trust anyone, but I need your magic." Then she stands up and looks down at me. "But I suppose I trust you more than the others. Where is the necromancer?"

"I would assume the morgue."

"Bring Harvor and Nicolas's body to me. I'll meet you there in two hours," she says before turning and leaving.

"Does she even know which morgue? Or where?" Havoc asks.

I really don't know, but I also never know with Lanni. "Just don't question her."

“Trust me, I won’t,” he says.

“Weird human,” Iya decides. “So… let’s go grave robbing!”

“Yeah… I suppose,” I say as I head down the stairs.

“Who was the lady who just walked downstairs?” Sam asks.

“I tried to stop her, but she just slid right past my arm without a word,” Johnson says. “Like I literally grabbed her arm, and next thing I know, she’s gone.”

“Lanni has a way of doing that. She’s going to help us. But I need your help first.”

Chapter Fifteen

Three hours later, I walk into the morgue with Nicolas's body in tow. No one quite knew where Harvor was buried, so I assume that if I don't know, no one else in the group does.

"So… this is just real friggin weird, you know?" Sam asks. "I've worked with nonhumans before all of this, I mean our boss is a vampire, but… we're bringing a guy back to life who died fifty years ago? Can he even talk?"

"Lanni tells me to do something, I do it," I say. "You don't question Lanni."

When I walk in, I find the medical examiner staring at us warily, and I find Lanni lying in one of the open trays.

The man rushes toward us, like we've come to save him. "I… have told her multiple times to get down… yet she refuses," he says pleadingly.

"*Yeah.* Sounds like Lanni," I admit as I walk over to her. "Hey, Lanni, that's where the dead people lie. And it's probably kind of gross that you're lying there. Especially if you plan on getting in my car later."

Lanni opens her eyes. "I asked him to close me up inside, but he refused. I would like to know how it feels to be dead."

She's so freaking weird. And Havoc thinks Nicco is strange? "Yeaaah… I don't think locking you up in a morgue will give you that answer, but I can lock you up if you want."

She stares at me for a moment. “That’s true. Now where is the necromancer?”

The medical examiner pulls open the drawer with the dead man inside. She walks over to him and touches his face. “He’ll do. Now… how would you like to kill me?”

I look at her in surprise. “*I* have to kill you?” I ask.

“Yes.”

Why do I have to do it? “Uh…”

She holds up a finger, and her eyes go wide like she’s come up with a brilliant idea. “Choke me to death. I’ve never been choked to death before,” she decides.

The medical examiner slowly backs away and heads over to where the two detectives are talking by the front door. I think he’s rethinking career choices at this point. I am too.

“Alright,” I say as I wrap my hands around her throat. “Like this?”

“Sure,” she says with a smile.

“Or should I put you in like a headlock?”

“What the hell is going on?” Johnson asks as he jogs up.

“I’ve figured out that you just don’t ask questions,” Sam says. “Iya does weird shit all the time, and I just turn around, put my headphones in, and bleach my eyes.”

“This is taking too long,” Lanni decides. “I like this body, so don’t mess with it.”

She grabs Johnson’s gun and shoots herself in the head as the detectives jump and the medical examiner yells something involving God.

Lanni’s body falls down, but before she hits the ground, the necromancer opens his eyes.

“Fits perfectly,” he says. It’s “he” now since Lanni has always asked that we follow the gender of the body he’s in since he has no true gender. A completely genderless being that takes on the persona of gender and identity. It's a good thing Lanni is a good person because he could become quite strong with the right body.

He sits up and stretches before stepping onto the floor. I hand him a blanket which he stares at and then wraps it around himself before walking over to the body bag that holds Nicolas.

We were all surprised when we had opened Nicolas's coffin and found, not bones, but a fully formed body of the man. He looks the same as the day he died.

"How intriguing," Lanni says as he stares down at it. "I guess the hard work has been done for us. He needed vocal cords to speak and a brain to think. This will be easier than I thought."

We get his body out and lay him on a table where Lanni starts to work on his spell. He has clearly been in a necromancer's body before because he seems to know exactly what he is doing with it.

When he's finished with the preparation for the spell, he turns to me. "Miles, may I use the bind that Geoff placed on you to siphon your magic?"

"What?" I ask startled. "I can help boost the spell."

"I need full access to your magic. I don't have time to become acquainted with this body and its magic," he says.

I hesitate and glance at Havoc, who doesn't seem to know the answer either. But I know that I have to trust Lanni some, or we'll get nowhere. "Fine," I say as I drop the barrier on my mind and let my markings show.

Lanni takes my hand as he leans over the body and presses his fingers to the man's face. It's so strange that Nicolas doesn't even smell like rot, as if his body can no longer decompose.

Lanni begins to whisper the beginnings of a spell I don't understand as I watch my magic flow straight into him. The lights in the room flicker, and the table Nicolas is on shakes as I see a twitch of his fingers. Slowly, his eyes open, and he looks around himself as we lean over him.

"H-Help… me," he whispers. His voice is rough and hoarse. It doesn't even sound like his own but instead like sandpaper grating against each other.

"What do you need help with?" Lanni asks. His words are slow and even, so the dead man can understand them.

"I… am… stuck… in this… body," he says.

"Who locked you in this body?" Lanni asks.

"I-I don't… know."

"Think. Was there anyone you recognized?"

Nicolas's eyes shift around like he can't remember how to control them. He's silent and unmoving but for a twitch in his fingers and his nails scratching against the metal.

"People… I… recognize?"

"Why did they bring you back?"

He considers the question for a long time. "Ask… about… book…"

"Did you tell them?"

"Yes." His eyes shift until they settle on me, and I see a flicker of something there. It's such a human emotion that looks strange on his stiff body. "The book… to bring back life… the book."

"Who needed it?"

"Rehna," he says. "Please… help me…"

"I will guide your soul back to heaven," Lanni promises.

"Thank you…" he says before closing his eyes.

Lanni begins to whisper something and the body quivers beneath his touch. Then his skin turns to ash and all that is left is bone.

"Rehna," Lanni says.

I'm still trying to figure out if I understood him correctly. "Rehna… but Rehna… she was alongside me the whole time. She nearly *died* in that fight," I say. "Why… but… *Rehna?*" That can't be true. Rehna couldn't possibly have anything to do with it.

"So what now?" Havoc asks.

"I guess we go speak to Rehna. Let me go back to my body," Lanni says as he lets go of my hand. He holds his hand out to Sam who just stares at it. "Gun."

Sam nervously looks at Johnson who doesn't seem to know much of what to say either. So, as Lanni takes the gun and wanders off to rid himself of this body, I fill in Sam and Johnson.

"How can we help?" Johnson asks when I'm finished.

"That's just it. You can't help until we remove the Siren or whatever that creature is," I say.

I kind of hope she is some kind of Siren because I know that Sirens can die. But can this creature die? I pray she can. She has already killed enough.

"I can go alone," Havoc says.

The thought of sending Havoc alone stills me. I couldn't handle sending him off to fight without me. "You aren't as powerful away from me as you are with me, I won't let you go alone," I say. Because what would I do if something happened to him? How could I continue on in this world alone?

"Are we headed over to Rehna's shrine?" Lanni asks as she walks up. My eyes are instantly drawn to the blood that is oozing from the bullet hole in her head.

Sam and Johnson stare at her, startled. "You… there's…"

"Your brains are leaking out," Iya says as he points.

"Oh… right!" she says, like she forgot about the whole ordeal.

We all watch in anticipation as she pulls open her purse and takes out a colorful little package. She opens it up and tosses the wrapping on the ground as she holds the yellow tampon plunger, sets it against the bullet hole in her head, and presses down on it. The tampon sticks to the blood and goo and hangs from the side of her head, the string dangling. "I don't have any pads on me, so that'll have to do. It'll clear up in a bit," she says. "Let's go, Miles."

"Sure…" I say uncertainly before turning to Sam and Johnson who both still seem to be confused and shocked. "Can you two go to my café? I'm going to take Iya with me since the Siren can't affect demons."

"But we can't just sit in a café when we have things to do regarding Aiden Blake," Johnson says.

"Hold on, hold on," Sam says as he waves his hands through the air. "Are we all just going to pretend we didn't see that happen?" He motions at Lanni who looks behind her like she thought he was talking about something else.

"Sam, just go with it," I warn him.

His eyes widen as he stares at me. "I'm trying, but… come *on!*"

"What's wrong?" Lanni innocently asks as she turns to look at me. "Did I do something wrong?"

"Sam was just impressed by your ingenuity," I say.

She smiles, and I notice there's blood between her teeth, but I just choose to ignore it. "Thanks!" Lanni will heal herself within a few minutes, and I can pretend that none of it happened.

"Of course. Now back to what I was saying. Sam and Johnson, I want you two to head back to my house, alright? Rehna knows who you are. The only place you are safe is at my house," I say. "Go now."

Johnson hesitates, but thankfully, he's willing to listen to me. "Alright."

I go out and get into the truck as Lanni, Iya, and Havoc get in with me.

"I can't believe Rehna would betray us," I say as I turn out of the parking lot.

"I can," Havoc says like he knew that from the beginning.

I eye him suspiciously. "No, you can't!"

"Maybe, but it makes sense now," he says as I pull out onto the road and head toward Badrick's "forest" so we can pick him up.

"Exactly what makes sense?" I ask.

"Just shut up, Miles. I'm trying to look smart because you think smart men are hot."

I can't help but grin. "Aw… well, I also think men who try hard are hot too."

He glares at me as I grin at him. There's something fulfilling about teasing him. It makes me remember just how much I care about him. How much I need him beside me.

I drive up to Badrick's woods and park the car. As I call Yoko, Havoc heads out to find him.

She picks up on the second ring. "Hello?"

"Hey, Yoko. I know it's your day off, but I need you and Baron to go to my house. I want you to stay inside and don't leave. I know you're not comfortable working with barriers, but I need you to modify my barrier at home and shut it down completely to anyone else. Only allow yourself, Baron, Sam, and Johnson to pass through the barrier."

"Miles, what's going on?" Yoko asks uncertainly.

"A long time ago, I learned that the easiest way to take down someone is through the people they love. I don't want that to happen to the people I care about, so please stay there and stay safe."

I can hear Baron in the background a moment before he takes the phone. "Miles, can my pack be of assistance?"

"Not right now. We are dealing with something that can affect the minds of humans. Even in your wolf form, I fear she can control you."

"But how can I help?" Baron asks.

"You help by keeping those three safe, alright? I'll need your help when it comes down to dealing with Geoff," I say as I see Badrick climb into the bed of the truck. The entire vehicle jumps about, making Lanni giggle as she presses her face against the back window.

Havoc gets in, and I start driving.

"Please, be safe," I say.

"Tell Baron that if he dies, I'll find Yoko a real husband," Havoc shouts.

"Why would I tell him that?" I ask.

Havoc shrugs. "Just so he can die peacefully, I guess."

"Baron, ignore Havoc," I say, but Baron just laughs. For some reason, the guy likes Havoc.

I hang up and turn down the road heading toward Rehna's shrine.

We aren't far from it, but I'm not sure what we're going to do when we get there. I don't know who is involved in this. I thought I knew Rehna. I thought of all people, she wouldn't have been involved in this. So can I trust the others? Are they in on it as well?

Havoc reaches over and takes my hand. I look down at it in surprise before glancing over at him.

"It'll be okay," he says reassuringly.

"We don't know that," I say.

He gives my hand a gentle squeeze. "You don't trust me?"

I trust him with my life, but I don't trust that we'll be safe. "I trust you so much, it's just…"

"Then listen to me. We will be okay, we always are. I will protect you with my life."

I bite my lip. "I'm not worried about my own life. I'm worried about losing someone close to me… especially you."

He shrugs. "Honestly, I think you might enjoy life more," he jokes.

"There's no way I can enjoy life more without you. Who would I blame things on? Who would I stare at in disbelief?"

He grins.

"Who would I share my life with?" I ask.

He lifts my hand up to his face and kisses my palm. "Don't even bother worrying about it. Worry about other things that are actually important. Like how handsome I am. Or worry about being good enough to be considered my mate."

I snort. "I'm real concerned."

I hear something faint as my eyes flicker to the radio, checking to make sure it's not on. When I look up, I see that someone has stepped out onto the road. Instantly, I make out Aiden's face. Aiden's eyes. Aiden's expression. He's standing there, judging me because I am the reason he is dead.

I yank the wheel of the truck without thinking, even though my mind is telling me that Aiden is dead and there's nothing there. Nothing but the sound of her voice singing softly in my ears. The truck plunges into the ditch, and I slam forward as the airbags explode. I hit the airbag hard as the truck rolls and comes to rest upside down.

For a moment, I'm disoriented as I look around. I reach for Havoc to make sure he's okay, but when I look around the truck, I realize I'm alone.

"Havoc?" I call in a panic as the music begins to invade my ears. I plug them with my fingers, but the noise is in my mind, tearing through my head.

I unbuckle the seatbelt that's keeping me dangling in the air, and I slam down onto my back. I roll over and look around as I reach into the backseat, but Iya and Lanni are gone as well. Did Badrick also get thrown out?

"Havoc?" I call, struggling to reach for our connection in my mind, but I can't feel it. All I can feel is an empty hole. The emptiness I would only feel when a demon working for me has died.

Panic consumes me as I grab for the door handle, but it won't open. Terror ripples through me as I struggle to grab onto my contract with Havoc. Even the magic that binds us is gone. It's empty. My mind is so empty. I'm alone. I'm completely alone, and Havoc is gone from me. He's gone forever, and I'll never see him again.

No! This is her doing. This is her song controlling me. Her song forcing me to believe he's gone. He can't be gone. I can't lose him.

The window is broken, so I kick it hard and the remaining glass breaks, showering down on me. I crawl through it as pieces of glass dig into my palms, but I can't stop. I need to find Havoc. I need to find him, now. I drop down, onto the ground and stand up.

"You killed me."

Startled, I turn around and see Aiden standing there watching me. He's standing next to the smoking truck, face full of terror and sadness as he condemns me.

"No… no I didn't! You were already a part of this when you became boss," I say, not wanting to face the fact that I pulled him in.

"I didn't want to help you. You told them I should do it. And look at me now. I'm dead now because of you."

I start backing up away from him as the song continues, soft and haunting in my head.

"No! No…" I whisper.

I turn and start running, but the trees around me are so thick, their trunks are pressed against each other. I can barely slide through them as they grow thicker and thicker around me. Every time I see an opening, their trunks swell, and I can't get through.

"Why did you do it?" she asks.

That voice. Not that voice.

I turn and look at Valerie as she stands there watching me with dead eyes.

"Why did you bring me back only to kill me again?" she asks. "I loved you more than anyone loved you. I cared for you. And you killed me."

No, no. Why is this happening? "You weren't you… you weren't right. You were killing people…" I say, trying to defend myself. "I had to!"

"You had to? You were killing people too. Think of all of the people who died by your magic!" she says, and her words are like a punch to my gut.

I hear a murmur of words and turn around as the trees press in tightly around me, turning into all the faces that haunt me. All of those who died by Geoff's hands and, in a way, my own.

"You killed us," a woman says.

"My child. She was just a child," a man says as he holds the lifeless body of his child in his arms. Her body hangs limply as I back away and bump into someone.

Quickly, I turn around and see all of the women who'd been with Aiden.

"Why do you get to keep on living and all of us have to die?" one asks.

"No! I didn't know!" I say.

One of them laughs, and I find his face in the crowd. "How could you not know? You watched us die, yet you cared too much about your own life to fight back," he says.

Their voices are deafening but still not as loud as the song as I stumble back. They begin to spin around me or maybe I'm turning, trying to find a way out. They're bumping into me, crowding into me, jostling me around as they grab for me.

"I'm sorry! I'm sorry!" I say. "It's my fault that all of you died. It's my fault."

"Your fault."

The voice is loud and clear, and everything stops spinning. The bodies wrapped around me begin to melt like they're made of wax. They sink to the ground, pooling at my feet until I'm standing in blood. It's thick, and when I try to take a step forward, I find it hard to walk.

"It's… your fault," the voice repeats, and my eyes snap up to the lone figure.

For a moment I'm confused as to who it is. I'm wavering between reality and a world the song has painted for me. Somewhere, buried deep, I know that none of this is real. That this song has found my secrets and nightmares and has made them a reality.

"It's… your fault," he says.

Geoff steps forward, walking toward me, through the blood like it is as thick as air. The blood never fazes him, never stops him.

"It's *your* fault, Geoff. It's all your fault! I didn't want to be like this! I didn't want to do what you made me do!" I yell as I pull my sword out.

His face twists into something inhuman as he laughs at me. Suddenly he's towering over me, as tall as the trees, and I am cowering at his feet like a coward.

"They're all dead," a voice echoes through my ears.

"His fault," another says.

"He blames others," another says.

"No! Can't you see? It's his fault!" I say as I aim my sword at him. "It's his fault!"

"Miles, listen to me," Geoff says.

“He’s delusional,” the voice says.

“He’s convinced he’s not at fault.”

“He killed them all.”

“It was his own magic. How could he not see it?”

“He could. He is just choosing not to see.”

“Listen to me,” Geoff growls.

I scream as I run at Geoff, the man who has ruined everything. Ruined my life and the lives of so many others. I scream as I near him, and he begins to shrink. He’s no longer towering over me as I grow closer to him and drive my blade right into his abdomen. He stumbles back but grabs me.

“Miles, it’s *not* your fault,” he says.

I look at him startled. Geoff doesn’t call me Miles.

“Shh… stop listening to her. She’s in your head. Get her out.”

“He’s going mad,” a voice says.

“He was always mad.”

I let go of the sword and clamp my hands over my ears as I turn around.

“Miles, listen to me. It is not your fault. As soon as you realize that, you can fight this. She’s holding you down because you believe her,” the voice says directly into my mind. “We can’t find her. It’s some illusion or something. We can’t find her. We need you.”

“Havoc?”

“Yes.”

“Havoc, where are you?”

“I’m right here,” he says. “Fight her. Can’t you feel my hand on your arm?”

I close my eyes and feel the warmth wrapping around my wrist. It’s almost burning hot, but it’s so welcoming in this world of cold. “Havoc, help me.”

"You need to help yourself. I can't get you to believe something you don't want to believe."

"Havoc, I can't do this."

"Yes, you can," he says. "Now fight it."

"You killed me," Aiden whispers into my ear. It's so real; I can feel his breath against my skin.

I killed him. If I hadn't suggested asking him to help us, he wouldn't be dead.

No… Aiden was the boss of a district that had been affected. He was at the meeting. They knew about him and his abilities before I asked him to help us.

"It's not my fault," I say.

"What about me? You think my death wasn't your fault?" Valerie asks.

My eyes snap open and I look into hers. "Valerie…"

"You slit my throat."

"And you thanked me as you died. You needed me to kill you. You couldn't live with yourself killing people. You cried every time you ate a heart. You wanted to die!" I say, and suddenly she's gone.

The song falters, and I feel a wisp of my magic. I search for the origin of the song as I turn and see her standing there. I whisper the name of fire, and it races along the ground and grabs onto her. She screams as it eats through her clothes. Her body goes up in flames, and suddenly she's gone.

Chapter Sixteen

I look around as the woods come to life around me. I see Iya and Lanni watching me from a distance. Quickly, I turn and see Havoc standing a few feet from me.

"Good job," he says with a warm smile. "We couldn't find her because we couldn't hear her song."

He wraps his arms around me, and I desperately grab onto him. I sink into his touch and memorize every inch of it. I had been so scared that I would never feel him again that I never want to pull away from him.

"Havoc… I thought you were gone. She was making me think you were gone. After the wreck, you weren't there and I couldn't feel your link." My stomach tightens at the thought of him being gone. Of me being alone again.

"Um… no, we were all there. We were… you know, kind of disoriented from the truck flipping and by the time I figured out which way was up, you'd broken the window, hopped out, and ran off."

Wait… what? "Seriously?"

"Yeah."

I squeeze onto him and just feel him there before me. I need to feel how real he feels and know that he's not gone. That he's still with me. He's not leaving me like everyone else has. He has promised to always stay with me.

“You okay? I didn’t even take a video this time since my phone was ruined,” he jokes.

And then something hits me. “Oh my god… I thought you were Geoff,” I realize. “I stabbed you!”

I pull back from him as I grab for his jacket so I can find the wound.

His hands still mine and hold me before him. “No, I’m fine, my lucky cloak stopped it,” he says with a smile.

Startled, I look up at his face. “It did?” I ask in surprise. And I had even made fun of that cloak!

“No, you totally stabbed me, but I’m fine,” he says with a grin. “I’ll just walk it off.”

“Havoc! I’m so sorry, let me see,” I say as I grab for him.

He catches me in a bear hug that locks my arms by my side. “I’m fine. I’m a demon. You could have stabbed me ten times and slit my throat, and I’d probably still live. I mean you already stabbed me once with your sword, if you get what I mean,” he says suggestively.

I turn my glare onto him in hopes he’ll understand the seriousness of this situation. “This isn’t funny, let me see!” I say as I try to push against him, but I’m scared I’ll hurt him. “Havoc, please.”

He kisses my forehead. “I’m fine.”

“No, you’re not. I stabbed you,” I say as I pull at his jacket. He holds it tightly as I stare at him desperately. “I need to wrap it. Havoc, please?”

“Do you trust me?” he asks as he looks down into my eyes.

“Yes…”

He smiles before kissing my forehead. “Then trust me when I say I’m fine.”

“Havoc…”

"Miles. Your concern makes me very happy. I *love* seeing you worried about me and caring for me, but I'm fine. I'm just happy you're alright."

I don't know why I was ever worried about my relationship between Havoc and me when it's clear that he has never wanted to leave my side. It just took us a while to see how much closer we could become.

I hear a noise behind us, and I turn quickly as I hold my hand up, ready to burn anything that steps into my path. But relief washes over me when I see that it is Badrick, and he has a band of people behind him.

"I brought the others," Badrick says.

I see that he has Yoko, Baron, Evan, Marco, Sam, and Johnson with him. Everyone is looking around curiously while Marco stands shirtless, chest puffed out, sweeping his hair back with one hand as his wings shine behind him. My entire attitude sours as soon as I see him. Too bad it wasn't him I stabbed.

"What are you doing? I told you guys to stay away," I say. "Especially Marco."

"Especially Marco," Havoc agrees.

"I waited until the singing lady was dead to bring them," Badrick says. "I heard her go 'araghagha,' so I'm assuming she's dead."

"That was just the sound Miles makes when he climaxes," Havoc says.

Badrick shakes his head as he stomps a paw down. "Oh no, it's not. I can hear you guys clearly from my room. It's much more 'Ah! Harder! Oh, Havoc! Ah!'"

"I'm going to burn both of you to death," I growl. The horrible part is Badrick isn't joking at all. He's dead serious about all of this because he doesn't understand that Havoc was being sarcastic.

Yoko scrunches her nose. "I'm going to pretend I didn't hear any of that. Miles, you can't just do all of this alone. We can help you."

“I was just told we would get some cool name like The Avengers,” Baron says. “That’s why I came.”

“The Penetrators,” Iya pipes in.

“Please don’t ever say that again,” Sam says.

“We should just call ourselves Marco because a name can’t get much better than that,” Marco says as he flexes his chest muscles.

I ignore him. “Yoko, Havoc’s hurt, can you help him?”

“Of course,” she says as she rushes over.

“Rehna knows we are here. We need to start moving in before she gathers more troops or runs,” Lanni says.

Havoc turns his back to me as Yoko starts to tend to him. I quickly move around so I can see how badly I hurt him. Yoko’s body is in the way, but I can see the blood, and suddenly that’s all I can fixate on. My body starts to feel hot, and I have the sudden need to sit down.

“Miles is having a panic attack,” Havoc alerts everyone because he couldn’t just keep it to himself.

“I’m not having a panic attack,” I mutter as I start fanning myself. I have seen some gruesome shit in my life, and none of it fazed me. I was used to it. But this? This fazed me. This fazed me real bad.

“He’s going to be fine,” Yoko says. “The cut isn’t super deep, and it’s in a good spot. Nothing vital,” Yoko says.

“I told you,” Havoc says.

“I stabbed him,” I admit.

“What?” Yoko asks surprised.

“I thought he was Geoff…”

“That lady was doing wacky stuff to your brain. It’s fine,” Havoc promises.

“Once, I ate this thing, and it did real wacky stuff to my brain as well,” Iya says. “Totally thought my head fell off. I couldn’t find it. So confusing. I thought I was married to a goat, and it was all so strange. I thought I had goat children."

"I am confused on how that helps this situation," Badrick says.

"I don't think it helps at all," Iya admits.

"So, what's your plan, guys?" Evan asks, trying to get us back on track.

Lanni, Havoc, Iya, and I look between each other.

"The plan you had when you decided to come over here," Evan says. "The Plan."

I look at Havoc who slowly looks away like the trees are more interesting.

"I'll leave this to you, Miles," Lanni says as she picks at the dried blood in her hair.

Evan stares at us in exasperation. "You don't have a plan. You just thought, 'Oh I'm going to go apprehend an ancient paladin without a single plan'?" Evan asks in disbelief. Honestly, at this point, he should just be proud that we've made it this far.

"Pretty much," I say as I continue to fan myself. "Anyone else think it's super hot?"

"We wanted to take her by surprise, and what is more surprising than a surprise that even we don't know about!" Iya says, like he's proud of himself for figuring that out.

"For once Iya is right," I say as I kneel down as the world threatens to collapse on me.

He grunts in approval.

Evan just nods slowly. "Alright, well then… here's my plan. We need to get Miles to Rehna. He's the most powerful of us, and it will take the most powerful to deal with her," Evan says.

"He looks real powerful," Marco says as he points to me where I'm lying on the ground in the fetal position while trying not to pass out.

"There's so much blood!" I say.

"There's barely any blood," Yoko says. "There. All wrapped up, good as new!"

"See?" Havoc says as he kneels down next to me. He gently sets his hand on my shoulder and squeezes it. "I'm fine. I've seen you cut a gryphon's head off and then tie his head to your saddle and ride with it for three days for a twenty-dollar bounty. Where is my strong, little snugglemuffin?"

"Gone," I moan. "Gone the moment I saw you wounded."

He laughs but reaches down and takes my hand before pulling me to my feet. "It makes me feel loved that you're so concerned about my wound."

He wraps me in his arms as I lay my head against his chest. "I'm sorry for stabbing you."

"I'm sure I deserved it," he says as he kisses my forehead.

"This is cute and all, but do you mind me continuing on with the plan?" Evan asks. "You know, since we are a little pressed for time."

"Just one more moment," Havoc says as he tips my chin up and kisses my lips softly. "Now you may continue."

Marco snorts. "Disgusting."

"Okay… So Badrick will get Miles to the front. The rest of us will deal with Rehna's guards," Evan says. "Sound good?"

"What am I doing?" Marco asks.

"Hopefully, being useful," Evan says.

He flutters his wings. "I'm always useful."

"Alright, everyone ready?" Evan asks.

"Do we have like… a countdown? Do we just take off? I've never been in a battle before, how does it work?" Baron asks.

"You just… kind of wait for one person to start moving," Lanni says.

"Why don't you wait in the truck?" I suggest to Havoc. "You're already hurt."

"Nope, not going to happen," he says as he gives my cheek a kiss. "I'm fine."

I nod slowly and walk over to Badrick. He kneels down, and I climb onto his back and rub his fur. "You ready?"

"Let's fuck shit up," Badrick says, and I stare at him as everyone glares at me.

Evan stops fumbling with some plant dangling from a string around his neck. "He's a sacred creature. What have you taught him to say?" Evan hisses.

"That has not come out of my mouth," I say.

"I heard Yoko say that before stepping in the kitchen. And everyone acted quite pleased when she was finished 'fucking shit up,'" Badrick explains.

"She definitely fucks shit up when in the kitchen." Havoc says with a grin as he shifts into a raven. "*Now, let's go*."

Baron shifts and steps in line next to Badrick.

"Ready?" I ask.

Sam looks over at me. "So… are we humans supposed to run? I feel like by the time we get there, the fight will be over. Or, I'll be so winded I couldn't fight. How do they do it in the movies?" Sam looks around, like he's expecting his own mount to ride into battle.

"I'm not a good runner," Johnson says. "I'm getting old."

"Let's all walk slowly toward the fight," I say as I raise my sword.

"Sounds good," Lanni says. "We are coming for you, Rehna!"

We start walking through the woods as I ride on Badrick's back, feeling like there's not a really good reason why I'm riding on his back at this point.

"*I can't fly this slow*," Havoc says as he lands on my shoulder.

"Nice weather," Sam says.

We look up at the sky and I nod. "Yes it is," I concur.

We keep walking as we zero in on the shrine.

"Anyone want to go for a steak after this?" Evan asks. "Assuming we win, of course."

"Of course we'll win, we're the Penetrators," Iya shouts.

"Who all would like to vote Iya out of our group?" Evan asks.

Everyone raises their hands. Even Badrick hobbles on three paws so he can raise one.

"Funny," Iya says. "I have been good. Miles, I did not penetrate the human, as you told me not to, even though he asked me to."

Sam's face turns bright red. I could probably fry an egg on it, it's so red.

"I told you that you could if he asked you to," I say.

If a bull's face could show horror, Iya's is showing it right now. "Seriously? Oh heavens and hell… I have made great mistakes," Iya cries. "Sam! He says it's okay to penetrate you!"

"I'm going to run ahead and hope I get killed," Sam says as he takes off jogging.

Suddenly, the ground begins to shake, and Badrick leaps back.

"Let's move out," Evan says.

Badrick jumps into a run as Havoc flies above me to lead the way.

"*Follow me, I'll weave you around the guards and get you to the shrine*," Havoc says, so I tell Badrick since he can't hear him.

Suddenly, a woman steps before us and raises her hand as she begins to chant. The ground beneath our feet begins to shake and Badrick stumbles. Marco swoops down from the air, holding his spear high as he drives it down at the woman. She falls back as another woman, identical to the first, steps forward, but Badrick avoids her before I can see what tricks she has up her sleeve.

I can see Baron fighting a werepanther as Evan lifts up his bow. The shrine is just in front of us, when I hear a flutter of wings. Badrick pulls up quickly as Rehna's two gryphons hit the ground.

"Go, I can handle them," Badrick says.

I leap off his back and hit the ground as he runs toward them. They rush in with claws and beaks, ready to tear into him. Badrick slams a paw into one, driving it to the ground as the other leaps into the air and dives at him. I slide past them as I rush through the door and step into the front room.

"Miles," Rehna says from where she's kneeling at the altar.

She rises and turns to me, wearing her full suit of armor, lance at the ready.

"Havoc, find the celestial being. Rehna will just continue to heal if the being isn't stopped," I say.

The celestial being is the woman who looked into our minds when I first brought the detectives here. I only realize now how dangerous that had been. It was a good thing that I hadn't completely opened my mind to her. The celestial being has kept Rehna young and alive for many years. She never ages, and I know from experience that every hit Rehna takes, unless it is a direct kill, will heal within minutes as long as the being is near her.

"I'm on it," Havoc says.

"Be safe, she'll be guarded."

"You'll never touch her," Rehna says as she smiles at me.

All I can see from beyond her helmet is her smile and her cold eyes. She pulls the face protector down as she turns to me. The armor is white with a peculiar glow to it. It's clearly meant for her, and it allows its wearer full movement because it fits her perfectly.

"Of all people, Rehna, how could you do this?" I ask.

She chuckles. "You don't know me as well as you think, Miles."

"Obviously," I say as I pull my sword free and face her.

She lets out a battle cry and runs straight toward me. I raise my hand and call for fire as it races along the ground. She brings her hand up, and a barrier comes with it, blocking my fire and letting it die. She spins around and brings her lance down hard as I leap back to avoid its pointed end. The issue with fighting with a sword against a lance is that she has three times as much reach as I have, so I'm stuck spending more time dodging than swinging.

She drives it down hard, aiming it toward my legs as I step back to avoid it and then move in. I swing my sword as I invade her space and bring the blade down across the seam of her armor, but it bounces right off. The jar of it radiates up my hand as I hold onto the hilt tightly. That's when she hits me with her lance, forcing me to move back.

"Nice armor there," I say.

"It's made from dragon skin," she says.

I raise an eyebrow. "What? Dragons aren't real."

"They used to be," she says confidently.

"Someone made that up just to make you pay a fancy price for their suit," I say.

She glares at me. "It's dragon skin."

"It looks like metal to me," I say.

"Dragon. Skin."

"Sure, sure," I say as I assess the situation, but Rehna doesn't give me time.

She stabs at me as I move back, so I swing my sword, knocking her lance away. I call upon the name of fire and drive it at her as she gloats. She doesn't even block it this time. She just stands with arms outstretched like she's calling upon the gods to shoot me down. When the fire hits the *metal* (not dragon skin), it doesn't even damage it.

She laughs as she walks toward me. "Not so powerful now, are you? I had this dragon skin armor designed specifically to deter your magic."

"*My* magic? You've been thinking about my death for a while?" I ask in surprise.

"I knew you were too smart, you'd figure it out," she says.

"Actually, Lanni did," I say. "I was kind of just put at the forefront of this operation because I have more power than the rest of them."

I pull a marker out of my pocket and start to draw on my hand.

"No, you don't," she says as she rushes straight at me. I do manage to dodge the blow to my head, but in the process, smear the symbol on my hand.

I grab for the air and bring it down as it swirls around her. She growls something at me as the wind magic flings her back, off her feet, and she slams into the wall. She rises to her feet as I try to fix the smudge on my hand. But now I have to draw it on my other hand, and I am not ambidextrous. A blind three-year-old could have drawn a better symbol on my right hand.

She rushes at me, so I realize that it'll have to be good enough. I meet her in the middle of the room, and knock her lance away, but she's too far for me to reach. She steps to the side as I push away from her lance, and she pulls a knife out as she lunges at me.

I, admittedly, am not expecting it, and she catches my arm with the knife. I fall to the side to avoid a more fatal blow before rushing in. I clap my hands together as I call upon the earth to aid me. I press my hand against her armor, so my palm is flat against it, and the magic explodes between us. She's flung away from me, hitting the ground on her back as I drive my sword down. The moment it hits her armor, the metal of my sword shatters and I fall forward.

"That was my favorite sword!" I cry as I hold up my broken sword. It's about half the length now, and her lance is still full length.

As she stands, I see a crack in her armor where I touched it. So the spell did work. I just have to keep working. Keep moving. Keep alive.

She swings hard before swooping up. You'd think being in a small room like this, she would choose to use a sword instead of such a long instrument of death, but she is phenomenal with it. It's apparent by how she's driving me away from her.

I back up into a corner, hoping it will block some of her swings, but they just become tighter, forcing me into a smaller area. I shove fire at her again, but she doesn't even blink as she moves toward me. So I pat my pockets down, looking for something to aid me. All I have is my wallet, so I chuck it at her. It smacks her helmet and she jerks back, startled. I rush in and set my hand against the same spot on her armor and push my magic into it. The tendrils snake through my fingers and wrap into a ball that explodes, throwing her back. It sounds like a small bomb when it goes off, making my ears ring.

Even as she stumbles back, she moves her lance, catching me in the side. I turn and rush in for her as she swings her knife at me. This time, when she turns to face me, I see that the metal is blackened and cracked. There's a gap where the metal has begun to separate, and I rush for her. She's expecting it and swings her lance, catching me hard with the handle as I'm thrown back against the altar. I fall into it as the stone cuts into my back, and she charges at me with a battle cry.

I scramble back, rolling over the altar and hiding behind it as I light the entire room on fire. With enough smoke and flames, she might not be able to see where I'm at. I keep the fire burning even though the shrine has wards to keep anything from catching on fire. I slide around the altar and see that the flames are making it hard for her to see me crouched so low to the ground. So I move toward her, crawling on my hands and knees (yes, you can still look badass while crawling) and leap forward as she turns toward me. I drive my broken sword through the crack in her armor and keep pushing as it sinks into her skin.

She cries out as she stumbles back. I pull the sword free as I press my hand against another weakened spot in her armor and tear another break into it. I slam my sword through it and she falls back.

"Havoc, please tell me you've stopped the celestial being!"

"*Working on it,*" he says in my mind.

"We can't have her heal," I say.

"*Working on it means I'm working on it!*"

"Work on it a little faster."

"*Maybe if I hadn't been stabbed, I would be working on it harder?*"

I quickly shut up and focus on keeping Rehna down. "Why did you do it?"

She laughs as she looks at me. There's blood running down her lip, but I know if Havoc doesn't stop the healing soon, she'll be back to normal in minutes. "All of it was Geoff's idea. He saw how powerful Valerie was becoming by feasting on the hearts of those with magic. He knew you were stronger than him. He knew it was only a matter of time before you overthrew him, so we planned it all. He knew it all. I told him of your plan to attack him, and he agreed to fight. He knew he wouldn't win, but he knew that if he died, he could come back as something greater. Something bigger than all of us. A god."

"He's not a god," I say.

"But he will be. So during the fight, he hurt me on purpose so no one would suspect me, and I could stay close to you. Harvor and I were going to bring him back to life after he'd died. But then Harvor was killed, and without the mage, I had no way of finding anyone powerful enough to resurrect Geoff. So, I took his body and had the celestial being, which Geoff gave me, keep his body from decaying. I also forced her to keep me alive so that when I found someone strong enough, we could bring him back. I did about six months ago and was finally able to bring Geoff back to life. He becomes stronger every day. And soon, he'll be stronger than all of us," she says with a grin as she sits up. She must have started healing, but I don't do anything yet.

"Where is he?"

She just laughs. "I won't tell you that."

"*I have stopped them*," Havoc says.

"Perfect," I say as I set a hand against her chest. The armor shatters, and I press my sword against her throat. "I told you it wasn't dragon skin."

She glowers at me, but she knows not to move. Havoc returns with the celestial being behind him. She must have been forced into aiding Rehna, or I doubt Havoc would have let her live.

"You okay?" Havoc asks.

"I'm good. What about you?"

"I have a stab wound… oh wait, that was from you. Nope, I'm fine," he says, and I glare at him.

"You're going to have another one if you don't drop it. Now go get Sam or Johnson. They can take her to prison and see if they can get any information out of her," I say, and Havoc leaves to find them.

"I'll never speak," Rehna says.

After a moment, Sam and Johnson return with Havoc.

"Do they need help outside?" I ask.

"No, the fighting seemed to have stopped with Rehna's fall," he says.

Sam fastens the handcuffs embedded with runes on Rehna which won't allow her to use her magic. Knowing they'll be safe, I leave her to them. Then I step outside to where everyone else is waiting.

"Everyone okay?" I ask.

"For the most part," Evan says. "You realize you're now boss of this district?"

"What?" I ask as I look at him, startled. "Nope. Not gonna happen. Evan, you can be boss."

"I'm already boss of a district."

"What about Marco?" I say as I look over at Marco as he stares at his hand in horror. I notice there's a very small splotch of blood on it.

"My *face!*" he screams as he touches his face again. "My *FACE* has been cut!"

"Never mind," I say.

"My beautiful face is ruined," he says as he looks around with wide eyes. He literally has a scratch the size of a fingernail on his cheek.

Lanni looks at him. "I think I'd be more worried about the chunk of flesh hanging off your leg," she says as she pokes it.

I look down and realize that someone has flayed open his leg and a piece of it is dangling.

"Women are drawn to scars on the body, but my face cannot be blemished!" he says.

"It looks pretty bad," she says as she pushes down his pants and looks at the cut. "Maybe a bit of glue will fix that right up?" Then, as we all watch, she pulls his boxer briefs down. "Your penis is really not that huge. You had me believing it was really big."

"Somehow, I think you're most fit to be the boss," Evan says as he turns to me.

"That is depressing," I say.

"I agree because you're not very fit, but somehow you're the most fit."

"Evan?" I ask.

He plays with his little plant necklace. "Hm?"

"You have daisies braided into your beard and you think I'm not as fit as you are?" I ask.

Epilogue

We head into Rehna's shrine where the state council has agreed to meet. There are a few of Rehna's affairs that need to be situated, so we thought it would be best to do it there. When we arrive, the only people already here are Evan and Willow. It looks like Evan has Willow cornered while telling her the significance of a willow tree, and Willow is trying to assure him that her mother wasn't even thinking about a Willow tree while naming her.

So Havoc and I sneak past them and head into the shrine.

"Finally, you are to become boss. And when you do, I want a statue erected in my honor," Havoc says. "Nude statue."

"With a tiny little leaf over your genitals," I decide.

"Are you saying my genitals can be covered by a tiny leaf?"

"Wee tiny," I say as I hold up my fingers to show how tiny it needs to be.

"Erect me a statue," he growls.

"Yeah… that's probably not going to happen. And as soon as I find someone adequate to run this place, I'm dumping it off on them," I say.

"Have you ever wondered why your mother sold you for a bag of potatoes?"

"Well, seeing as she actually didn't even think I was worth that much and just left me on the street, no, can't say I have ever wondered," I say.

"Huh… Well, anyway, the moral of my story is that you're an idiot for not staying as the boss."

"That's not a moral," I say. "And I will stay as the boss for a short period of time."

He grumbles but stops when he notices me running my finger over something in my hand. "What's that?"

"You were complaining that I never got you a gift while your favorite owner made you a cloak," I say.

He gives me a devilish grin. "Ooh, you got me something. Better be expensive."

"Uh… yeah sure," I say as I hold up the ring between my index and middle finger. There's a green hue about the metal that makes the words written on it appear to almost shine white.

"Are you asking me to marry you?" he asks.

"No!" I say as I look at him in shock.

"Good because I'm already married to like three people, and a fourth would be a bit too much."

I glare at him as he laughs. "I'm joking! I've only ever gotten married once, and I didn't know at the time that we were getting married. She spoke another language, and it was a confusing time, but she's been dead for like four hundred years, so you have nothing to worry about. I didn't even get to sleep with her!"

"You know what? On second thought, I'm tossing it."

"No! Let me see it." He holds his hand out, and I stare at his fingers for a moment before dropping the ring into his hand.

"I made it out of the metal from Rehna's armor so it will never bend or break," I say.

His eyes go wide. "So this is made of dragon skin?"

"For heaven's sake, dragons aren't real!" I say.

He laughs as he runs his fingers over the markings I drew onto it. Even though it was done with just ink, the magic keeps the words burnt into the metal.

"Aren't you going to put it on?" I ask.

He twirls the ring around between his fingers and looks up at me. "I don't know… I can feel your magic in it, and I don't recognize the spell, so I'm a bit wary. I mean, for all I know, this could force me to be your sex slave for eternity."

"As if you would complain," I say.

He nods slowly. "You're right!" he says as he slides the ring onto his finger. As soon as it's in place, the spell glows, and I'm pleased it actually worked. "There's a lot of magic in this little thing. What is it?"

"It's a spell that will allow a demon to never have a master again. The demon can roam the earth of its own free will and never have to abide by any mage's command. Besides my own of course. I don't want you to get too cocky, but if I were to die, you would never be used by another mage."

Havoc is staring at me, expression unreadable.

I shift, oddly nervous. "So… do you like it? I mean I can make you another one that forces you to be a sex slave if that's what you prefer? I can wrap it in Komodo dragon skin if you want so you can tell people that it's dragon skin."

"Miles…" He reaches out and catches my hand as I watch him. "I… this is… I don't have the words to tell you how much this means to me. I just… can't explain what this means to me. Thank you so much."

His words make me unbelievably happy, that I almost feel embarrassed. "Yeah, it's no problem. It took me like an hour," I say as I try to brush off his words. I've never seen Havoc at a loss for words when trying to be kind.

He cocks his head as he stares at me. "*What*? My *freedom* has been at your fingertips, and it only took you an hour?"

"Yeah… maybe… but if I would have done it sooner, you wouldn't have had this cool metal," I say with a smile. "And I had to find the spell and everything!"

He laughs and shakes his head. "Even to this day, you still impress me." He leans in and kisses me softly on the lips, so I press up against him.

"Ew, gross."

I pull back and look at Lanni who just smiles at me before walking into the meeting room. People are beginning to file into the shrine, so I step away from Havoc.

"Are we headed to the meeting room?" Evan asks.

"Yeah, let's go," I say, but as we walk, I grab Havoc's hand and tug him back. "I have one more secret for you." I look up at him as he looks at me in interest. Havoc has always loved a good secret even though he can rarely keep it.

"What's that?" he asks, blue eyes locked onto mine.

I press up against him until my lips are just against his ear. We are right outside the meeting room door where everyone is talking about something. "I'm naked."

He quickly looks me over, clearly seeing me clothed, and raises an eyebrow.

"What?"

"It's an illusion that I have clothes on. I came naked just for you," I say.

"Oh my gods," Havoc says as he reaches out and touches my chest. Even though his eyes are fooled, his hand isn't, and he grins. "You're going to sit through a council meeting butt ass naked? Your *first* council meeting where they decide if you're worthy to be the district boss?"

I grin mischievously at him. "Yep."

"I love you," he says, and the words make me smile. It's not as if I didn't already know he did, but it's nice hearing them.

I can't wait to see where life takes us now that we're together. I just wish Geoff wasn't involved. "I love you too. Now let's go," I say as I walk into the meeting room and take a seat in Rehna's chair. She's probably rolling in her grave knowing my naked balls are smooshed into it. Willow, Jacob, Evan, and Pepper all turn to me. The only other person there who isn't of the council is Lanni, whom I invited.

"Alright, let's first go over a few things," Evan says and turns the floor over to me.

I talk to the other council members about what happened with Rehna as well as what happened following her arrest. Rehna knew her end was near and made sure to prove it by giving us no information. Even when they brought in a succubus, she was able to avoid giving any information that would help us. Without the celestial being, her body began to age rapidly, and within three days, she passed away.

We tried getting more information out of her, like where Geoff is or who was controlling the Siren, but either she didn't know or she was taking it to her grave.

"So, Geoff is still out there growing more and more powerful?" Willow asks.

"Yes, but we will stop him," I say. "We will do everything we can to stop him. We *have* to do everything to stop him."

"So that brings us to our next topic. We need to decide if we would like to vote in Miles to take Rehna's place. All in favor say 'aye.'"

Everyone says "aye" without hesitation.

"Well, that was simple," Evan says. "Alright, Miles, you have your second in mind?"

A second is the person who helps run the district but is also there to take care of it if the boss is gone. I can't have Havoc as my second since if I leave, he generally goes with me. I'd asked Yoko, but she told me she couldn't even run her own life, let alone a district.

"I would like to suggest Lanni," I say as I motion to her.

"Understood."

"I have one question first," Lanni says with a sweet smile.

"Of course," Evan says, giving her the floor.

"Do I have to be naked as well?" she asks.

Everyone looks around in confusion as I stare at Lanni the Traitor. Dammit. It must be why she said "ew gross" when she walked in.

"Why would you think that?" Evan asks.

She sets a hand against her chest dramatically. "Oh! Miles has an illusion on! Forgive me! I've always been able to see through his illusions," she says with a sweet smile still on her traitorous face.

Everyone turns to look at me. Willow's face scrunches up, and Havoc is trying his hardest not to laugh.

"Are you…" Evan stops to compose himself. "Are you naked right now?"

I look at him like he's an idiot. "What? No! Of course not! Why would you think that?"

"I'd like to suggest the removal of Miles Shavold as district boss. All in favor, say 'aye,'" Evan says.

Everyone says "aye."

AUTHOR'S NOTE

If you want to be the first to know about what's next for Miles and Havoc, and to be the first to know about the release of book two, join my reader group, Alice Winters' Wonderland here! I frequently put up teasers, short stories, and giveaways! (There's currently a few Hitman, Villain, Within the Mind, and Hidden in Darkness short stories that can only be accessed there!)

You can also sign up for my newsletter where I do giveaways before each release! If interested, sign up for my newsletter at: https://www.alicewintersauthor.com/

If you'd like another action/comedy, check out The Hitman's Guide to Making Friends and Finding Love!

Thank you so much for taking the time to read my book! I really hope you enjoyed! And last but not least, if you enjoyed, please consider leaving a review! Reviews help others find books and my books find new readers!

Made in the USA
Columbia, SC
18 December 2024

49015358R00152